BURN

The **PRETENDERS** Series

Drive
Crash
Burn

TAMARA LUSH

BURN

The **PRETENDERS** Series

 by wattpad books

CHAPTER ONE

LILY

Procrastibaking is the art of delicious distraction. Since I lost my job a month ago, I've become an expert.

I've used baking—something I was never much into before—as an avoidance tactic. A way to deflect from the fact I was fired. A vehicle to avoid looking for a new job. A break from real life.

And today, the afternoon of the Florida Grand Prix race, my newfound baking habit is serving as a stress release of sorts. I'm channeling my inner Martha Stewart and making double chocolate chunk cookies.

I tune the small TV monitor in the kitchen to the race and line up my ingredients. Flour, sugar, butter, eggs. I'd even found some gourmet fair trade chocolate chips at a health food store. Like there's anything healthy about these things.

I shouldn't be watching this race. But a mixture of habit, curiosity, and a touch of self-torture win out. As the television blares with pre-race interviews, I plop the stick of butter in a bowl and dump a cup of sugar on top.

Papa's at the race, probably pacing in the garage. Ready to give his team a rousing, inspiring, and legendarily gruff yet loving pep talk. There's no way he'll mingle with the crowd, so there's little chance I'll see him chatting with the Sky Sports announcer, who's roaming the track for his infamous interviews with celebs on live TV.

Grid Walk with Gordon, the segment's called. It's been on for years. Viewers love it, and watching it makes me grin, thinking how my father has always loathed the cheesiness of Gordon's questions.

"Oh, there's Savannah Jenkins, the owner of Jenkins-Annunziata Racing. Savvy? Savvy?"

I look up, straightening the glasses on my nose so I can better focus. Her team is one of my father's main competitors.

"How are you feeling about today's race? It's the first Formula World in Miami, so it's quite historic. Your hair looks marvelous, by the way."

Of course Gordon would comment on her flowing red mane. "Do you compliment all the team owners' hair?" Savannah says in a flat tone.

I bark a laugh. Savannah's a friend. We're both about the same age but took vastly different life paths. She embraced the Formula World life, married a driver, became a team owner. I was once my father's intern in hopes of following him into the family business, but then I ran from the sport and pursued a safer path: business school and a job at an auto racing game developer.

It all worked out so perfectly, until it didn't. Maybe real-life racing would've been a more secure path, ironically. A more personally fulfilling one. But I doubt it, given the position I'd been in all those years ago.

I know Savannah well enough to detect she's worried about today's race. That little furrow in her brow tells me everything and I am sure she's also annoyed with Gordon and his sexist questions. Plus, it's June, which means it's hotter than hades in Florida today. Savannah's face has bypassed dewy and is well on its way to a full-blown sweat.

One more reason I'm glad I'm in my cool, air-conditioned kitchen, baking.

"We've worked out any issues with our cars that we had back in Toronto." Savannah smiles tightly and tries to edge away from the reporter.

"Any driver you're particularly worried about? Anyone you think could beat your guys?"

Savannah inhales sharply. "Every team should be worried about Max Becker on the Onassis team. He's the most experienced on the track, and as we all know, is ruthless when he's behind the wheel."

"You'd certainly know, Savannah, since your husband and Max were rivals and then teammates . . ."

I dip my head and focus on the bowl of butter and sugar. Initially, I'd planned to use the mixer, but instead I take a fork and attack the butter, mashing it together with the sugar with harsh, almost violent, strokes.

At the track I'd be drinking champagne, hobnobbing with the celebrities in the garage. I'd see friends there, maybe have a few laughs about the old days when I was younger and wilder and took risks.

Papa would've been so thrilled if I'd been at his side, and that fact makes me feel guilty as hell. The track is only about twenty miles from my condo in downtown Miami. But I couldn't. Couldn't face the world after my career recently ended in a spectacular flameout. Couldn't face the press asking about every detail of my life, once again.

And most of all, I couldn't face Max Becker, my father's star driver.

The reporter drifts away from Savannah and drones on for several minutes, interviewing an actor who obviously knows nothing about the sport.

"Aaaaaaaand there's a man here I always like to talk to. It's the driver of the hour, the man with everything to win and the most to lose. Max Becker, three-time world champion and odds-on favorite to take home a fourth driver's trophy this season. Max? Care to say a few words about your latest race with Team Onassis? Well done on that pole position during qualifying."

My head snaps to attention and I lean closer to the TV screen that hangs under a cabinet. A pair of bright blue eyes and rumpled dirty-blond hair fills the screen. It's a face used to winning; the arrogant expression of a man used to getting everything he wants because of his incredible, ridiculous, all-consuming talent.

"It's going to be a tough race. Sensitive circuit. None of us knows the track. All I need to do is stay away from the walls and I'll win. You know that." His smooth, slightly German-accented voice still makes my heart flutter, even after all these years.

The reporter chuckles. "There's that legendary Max Becker confidence."

A self-assured smirk spreads on Max's pouty lips.

"Could you flatter him any harder? Jeez, Gordon, give him a big, wet kiss," I say aloud to the TV.

"This is half the battle. The mental part." Max taps his temple.

"How do you think your recent breakup with pop singer Ella will affect your driving?" the reporter asks.

I snort. Like Max cares about anything but the sport right now. When I broke up with him he was able to walk away from me and never look back.

Max shoots him a withering stare. The smirk is gone. "Ella and I were never a couple. We're friends. Nothing, especially not women, affects my driving. You know that."

"I sure as hell do," I reply. That was the one thing that kept me from total despair after I left him—that he'd thrive. And he has.

Max claps the reporter on the shoulder and melts into the crowd on the track. I turn back to the butter and sugar mix, then give up and set the bowl on the stand mixer. It's only then that I realize my heart's racing faster than the RPMs on those cars.

There are times when I wonder what life would've been like had I stayed with Max, and this moment is one of those times. Would I have eventually gotten used to the "WAG life"—the glitzy, fast-paced world of wives and girlfriends of professional athletes? Would my father have eventually accepted our relationship? Would my father have hired the man I was dating?

It's the same, ruminating thought spiral I've had for years, and the answers are clear. I'd have never gotten used to the lifestyle, and Papa would've been bent out of shape for years had I continued dating a driver. And since I'd seen what the sport had done to my own parents, I knew I'd made the right choice.

With a sigh, I pause for a glass of water while the mixer does its job. For the next twenty minutes, I preheat the oven and throw the rest of the ingredients into the mixing bowl. The cookie dough is ready when the drivers are in their cars and on the grid, and instead of scooping the dough onto the sheet in perfect round balls, I swipe a spoonful of raw dough.

"It's three o'clock here in Miami and the cars are pulling away for their formation lap for the inaugural Florida Grand Prix," the announcer says.

You're not supposed to eat raw dough, but whatever. I slide the spoon into my mouth and stare at the screen while leaning against the island counter.

"As the cars make their way around the track, this is the lineup: Max Becker from Team Onassis on pole position, Hsuki Morishita from Force Japan beside him in the front row, Esteban Alba from Team Onassis, and João Olivera from Mercedes in the third and fourth places."

I tune out the rest of the grid position announcement while I shovel more uncooked dough into my face. Max once told me that the moments before a race were the second most exciting thing he'd ever experienced, a rush like no other.

Seven years ago I'd asked him what the first most exciting thing was. I was twenty-four at the time, he was twenty-two.

"You," he'd replied.

Stupidly, I'd believed him. Maybe he'd believed it himself. He'd been a virgin. New to the world of professional racing and to the money, glamour, and girls that came along with it. This was before he became a tabloid sensation; before he turned into the superstar athlete he is today.

Back then, those blue eyes were wide and trusting. His hair was blonder and his smile more genuine. His face was less angular then, padded with a little plump of fat. I adored everything about him, and even now, my heart aches when I see him on TV.

There are deep, dark parts of me that are still raw about how our relationship unfolded. How my fear of commitment ruined it all. Which is the main reason why I didn't go to the race today. That and the fact that I didn't want the press to ask me about my recent, well-publicized layoff.

It was my father's day, not mine. I preferred to be out of the spotlight at all costs.

"The cars are making their way around the final corners to start this Grand Prix during a sweltering Florida afternoon."

I set down the spoon and open the second package of chocolate chips, shoveling a handful into my mouth. The formation lap is a casual drive around the circuit to warm up the tires. Soon the cars will be back in place on the grid, pausing for a few seconds before the race formally begins.

"Becker is about to start on pole position, and he leads this new season in the championship by twenty points. Adrian Onassis watching in the garage . . ."

The camera cuts from the track to my father, who stands in the garage with his arms folded, staring at a monitor. His white hair is rumpled, and face looks uncharacteristically beet red. Perspiration runs down his cheeks, and I grimace at the sight.

"Goodness, Papa. Get into the air conditioning. Drink some water," I murmur to the TV. Why he insists on being in the garage when he could be in one of the team's air-conditioned trailers with all the TV monitors is beyond me. He knows the Miami heat is brutal.

The camera flashes to a different scene. "And look, there's actor Jack Foxx, who starred in that Formula World miniseries, and his wife, singer Misha. I see a few others, too, a few A-listers watching in the Force Japan garage. All eyes are on the pole position because Max Becker barely squeaked out that first spot over Hsuki Morishita. Can Morishita fight Becker back? Has Max Becker finally loosened up and allowed himself to have some fun on the track?"

Another announcer comes on and discusses Max's well-known, and very calculated, risk taking while driving. I've heard this discussion a thousand times from announcers over the years. Categorize, analyze, and opine.

But Max Becker always surprises everyone.

Sure surprised me a time or two.

"The Florida Grand Prix, about to get underway before a hundred and fifty thousand fans in Miami. The lights go out and the race begins!"

I hold my breath as the cars pull away. This is always the best part of a race, seeing who will emerge from that first cluster of cars.

Sometimes there are wrecks this early, serving to weed out the unlucky and unprepared drivers. Sure enough, a couple of cars collide and skid into the gravel.

Max pulls ahead of the competition with ease, as I suspected he would.

"Becker's got the best start . . ." The announcer chatters on about how Max is looking strong and the car's handling well. Good. Papa will be thrilled. But neither he nor Max will relax for the next fifty-seven laps, not until that checkered flag flies. I probably won't either. It's a dangerous sport, yet another reason why I'd broken up with Max. Seeing a person I loved that close to death almost every weekend was too nerve-racking for my soul.

Don't get me wrong; I love the sport. But being with a man driving a car is a different story entirely.

I exhale and turn back to the cookies, spooning them onto the sheet while listening to the race. I slide them into the oven and set the timer for twelve minutes.

As the smell of vanilla and sugar fills the air, I can't get an image of Papa out of my mind. His eyes took on a certain sadness when I told him I couldn't attend this year, but, mercifully, he didn't ask why. Maybe he knew. Or perhaps he figured I wasn't up to such a crowded event only a month after a very public dismissal from my job as the human resources manager—excuse me, "chief people officer"—for a new and wildly popular tech company.

There was another reason too. I didn't want to face Max. Oh sure, I'd run into him at races over the years, but he'd always been on another team, so it was easy to avoid any lengthy conversations. Now that he's my father's driver, well, that's a bit more difficult.

We'd end up at the bar making awkward conversation or at some buffet in the cafeteria, asking each other questions over plates of chicken. Worse, I'd have to pose next to him for the team photographer, and the idea of being that close to him makes my entire body break out in a sweat.

The first batch of cookies finish, and I slide them onto a rack and bake another sheet. I keep one ear on the race as I clean up, and when the second batch is finished, I lose myself in organizing my fridge.

I can only imagine what an announcer would say if they were narrating my life right now.

The disgraced executive of a popular auto racing video game company leads an exciting life, arranging her fridge on a hot Sunday afternoon. Most women like her would be having brunch at a posh New York hot spot or vacationing in the Alps. Not Lily Onassis. She's a lone wolf, preferring cookies to Coach bags and sneakers to Saint Laurent. And look at her outfit. She can't even be bothered to change out of yoga pants and a coffee-stained T-shirt. So much money, privilege, and potential, and she chooses a plain-Jane existence. She's notoriously private, has been for years since she was rumored to have been a relationship with Formula World superstar Max Becker. At the time, he was a driver for a rival team . . .

An hour passes, and in between scrubbing the scuzz leftover from a rotting peach in the produce drawer and tossing a Styrofoam container of takeout that's a couple of weeks old, I check the race. Max is still in first place, and it appears as though he'll win. Papa's excellent instinct for luring drivers from competing teams has paid off again.

The chirp of my cell jolts me away from the television. I pad into the living room, where the phone sits on the coffee table.

Adam McLean, the screen says.

Weird. It's my father's assistant. Surely he's at the race with my father.

"Hey, Adam. What's up?" I ask in a brisk tone.

"Lily, don't panic. I have some unfortunate news. We're sending a driver for you."

"What? Why? What's going on?" I press my free hand to my throat, as if to hold in my heart, which feels like it's lodged there instead of in my chest. Whenever someone tells you not to panic, that's literally the only thing you can do.

"It's your father. He passed out in the garage during the race and is on his way to the hospital now. We need you there as soon as possible."

CHAPTER TWO

LILY

A little over an hour later, I'm running into an enormous hospital in downtown Miami. I'd had the presence of mind to wash my face, sweep my hair into a messy bun, and change out of my dirty clothes and into a blue tank dress and sneakers, but hadn't showered.

A doctor in a white coat meets me in the lobby. He has kind eyes and a gentle smile, but his brow is furrowed with concern. I can see the sweat on his forehead, beading in the fluorescent light. I try to explain who I am and why I'm there, but my words come out in a jumble.

"What happened? Papa! How is he?" I'm breathless with worry and fear. Nothing like this has ever happened to my father. Quite the opposite; even at sixty-three he seems strong and strapping, invincible even.

"I'm Dr. Mihir Patel, and it's nice to meet you, Ms. Onassis. I'm so sorry to meet you like this, but your father had a heart attack while at the race."

"What? No!" I press the heels of my hands to my forehead.

"He's stable now. We've given him medicine to thin his blood and nitroglycerin to help improve blood flow and ease the work the heart needs to do. We're also giving him thrombolytic medications, what we call clot busters. We want to begin the angioplasty procedure, but he insisted on seeing you prior to that surgery. We've also been in contact with your mother."

"Surgery?" I seem to only be capable of yelling one-word responses.

"Angioplasty is a common procedure. It allows us to see inside the arteries and look for the blockage. Once that's found, we'll insert a stent . . ."

Dr. Patel talks for a few minutes while I steady myself against a wall. My father had a heart attack? But he runs and stretches and Mumsy even convinced him to drink kale smoothies once a week. Where is my mom? I can't keep track of her. Hell, Papa barely can, and he's been married to her for more than three decades.

"I need to see him," I blurt.

"Absolutely, we've got him stabilized." Dr. Patel indicates I should follow him, and I'm silent as we ride an elevator and then walk down a long, sterile hallway that's lit in a bright, menacing fluorescent glow. He pauses before opening a door. "We'd like to get him into the operating room as soon as possible."

I push past the doctor. There, in a bed, is my wide-shouldered, strong father. Only he doesn't look so robust right now. His skin is a disturbing shade of gray, and his eyes are shut.

"Papa," I cry, rushing to his bedside. I take his hand in mine, feeling the cold, clammy skin. His chest rises and falls with labored breaths. Discomfort is etched on his face. The tube in his nose is taped to his cheeks and the wires are attached to his arms and the machines are beeping. I can hear the the entire system monitoring his vital signs and the steady drip of the IV. His breathing is slow and shallow.

I can also hear my own heart, pounding in my chest. He opens his eyes.

"*Kamari mou,*" he murmurs. That's what he always calls me. It's a Greek phrase for "my pride," and the words have never made me sob as much as right now.

He says something in a long string of Greek, words I don't understand. Even though he's lived all over the world—and spent years married to my American mother—he always falls back on his native tongue when stressed or upset. He never thought to teach me the language, always insisting that I study Mandarin and Spanish instead during my years at boarding school in New England.

I gently sit on the side of his bed and take his large hand into my two smaller ones. "What happened? How do you feel?"

"Better with this damn oxygen, I guess. I was in the garage watching the tenth lap and then I blacked out. Next thing I knew I was in an ambulance. Apparently, Jack found me on the floor. I don't remember much, only that I came to on the ride here to the hospital."

Jack is the team's engineer. Who else saw my father at his worst? I press my forehead to my father's hand and tears leak from my eyes.

"Lily, don't cry, love. I'm going to be fine. They're going to *roto-rooter* my arteries and I'll be good as new. I'm glad you're here now, though."

I lift my head and am at least a little reassured to see the twinkle in my father's deep-brown eyes, probably because he thinks he's clever remembering the American phrase roto-rooter. "I'm not leaving your side or this hospital until you do. But you need to get into surgery right away. Dr. Patel said—"

"I know what he said, he wants me to go under the knife and I'm okay with it. I managed to hold him off until you got here."

"I'm here now, so let's not wait. Let's get you fixed up and back up north." Where we can hire the best specialists, where he'll be comfortable in his own home, and where I can keep an eye on him. "I also need to get in touch with Mum. She's—"

"Adam and the doctor have already called her, no need to worry. I have to ask you something before I go into surgery, kamari mou. Something important. You must do something for me right now. It's critical, especially in case I don't pull through."

"Don't think like that!" It's impossible to hide the crying now.

"We must prepare for the worst. That's why I need to ask you this favor."

His unruly gray hair is sticking to his moist forehead. Probably he's going to tell me to take care of his little dog, Athena, who lives at his home in Connecticut. "Yes, Papa. Anything."

"You have to go talk to the team. Today. After the race." There's a tightness in his voice that he can't hide, and surely he must know the race is almost over.

"What?" I frown.

"The team. I want them to hear about me and my condition from you. Today. As soon as possible."

"Okay, I can do that." Don't really want to, but I understand why he'd ask me to speak to the guys. I'm his only child, and many of his longtime employees are like family. I grew up with them and worked with them back when I was an intern. A thick lump forms in my throat.

"And there's something else." He coughs and I rub his arm.

"Do you want me to get the doctor?" I'm wide eyed as he barks out a few coughs.

He takes a few deep breaths after the fit subsides, holding up his finger and wagging it back and forth. "I'm okay."

"You're not okay!" I squeeze his fingers, trying to will some of my strength—and common sense—into him.

"Hush. It's a little tickle in my throat from this oxygen."

"Do you think we should try to get you to New York for this surgery?" My thoughts race ahead, thinking how he'd be closer to the family home in Connecticut.

He shakes his head. "The docs say there's no time. They barely allowed me to wait for you to get here. This is a great hospital and I trust Dr. Patel. He went to Harvard, you know."

I heave a sigh. This heart attack is the result of long days on the track, the pressure to win Formula World, that entire nomadic, wild lifestyle. It's fine for a man half his age, but not for him. We're going to have a serious talk about his health, but now isn't the time. I stare at him for a beat. "What else were you going to ask me?"

"Since your obligations to your old company have ended—" He begins coughing again.

That's a polite way of putting it. Technically, my obligations ended when I was so fed up with the sexual harassment situation at my company that I tweeted a photo of one of my fellow executives who'd said filthy things to me. I figured that the harasser would get fired, but no. I took the brunt of the punishment because I'd "put the company's business on social media." Never mind that I'd tried to get the ear of the CEOs for months. But those are merely details that are now firmly in the past and irrelevant right now.

"I'd like you to take over running the team until I'm well enough. Dr. Patel said I might be out of commission for a few races at least."

"No, no, no. I'm not qualified to run the *entire* team. And I'm going to stay here and wait for you to get out of surgery. You'll probably be out for more than a few races. This isn't some minor procedure."

"Honey, I'm either going to live or die in this damn surgery, and you being here will have no bearing on it. You worked for a racing game company that most of the drivers use for off-season training. You have a great mind for business and know the sport in and out.

You've been on Formula World tracks since you could walk."

"But that doesn't mean—"

He interrupts me, steamrolling over any possible objection. "Keep an eye on the financials and boost the team's morale. You're my eyes and ears. A figurehead. The team runs itself. Give some interviews, make some inspirational speeches. I don't want there to be a perceived power vacuum on the team, and the press needs to know that our family is still in charge."

He thinks I can do all that, while I'm worried about him? Surely the heart attack has affected his brain too. I look around helplessly for the doctor, but he's deep in a conversation with the nurse, looking at my father's chart.

"Papa, there's way more to the job than that. Can't you get Uncle Christos to fill in? Or Jack, or—"

"Christos is in worse physical shape than I am. You know I've always wanted you to—"

"Work with you on the team. I know. But it's not my skillset. I'm an HR manager."

"You're a lot more than that. You know how to manage people. I'm asking you to make it your skillset, at least temporarily. A few races, starting with Austin next week. The ones here in America, and perhaps in South America after that. Keep morale high. Those drivers need direction and coddling. Especially Max. Esteban, too, but in a different way. You'll figure it out. You're a smart woman."

He wants me to *coddle* Max Becker? The man whose nickname in the press is "the Iceman"? It's almost ironically hilarious because Papa didn't want me around Max seven years ago.

But things have changed. Max is a champion, the top driver on my father's team.

I clear my throat and pull my hand away from my father's so I can retie my hair. Prior to the start of the season, I'd given my father an earful about why Max wasn't the best hire for the team. He'd disagreed. Naturally, he was right; Max was an amazing hire. I didn't want him so close for personal reasons, but Papa operated like he always did.

The past is like your ass, he always said. Behind you.

"I don't know if Max takes direction well, Papa."

"Like any driver, he wants to win. That's all. You know him better than most."

The weight of his words hangs in the antiseptic-scented air of the hospital. "Um," I whisper, my eyes darting around the room.

"I know it will be difficult, given your history with Max. But that's all in the past now. And Lily?"

"Yeah?" I try to swallow but my mouth is too dry.

"Try to keep your relationship with Max aboveboard. I don't care what the two of you do in private, but in public keep it on the up and up. I know the two of you had, er, a powerful connection, and maybe I was wrong back then—"

I interrupt him, not wanting to hear any more. It's so weird that he claims not to care now, when he was so angry back then. "Please. Stop. I'm not having any relationship with him, ever. This isn't the time to discuss all that. You need to relax."

The last thing I want my father to think of before he goes into surgery is how angry he was when he found out his daughter was screwing a younger, rival driver.

"Okay. I have faith in you, Lily. You will inspire the entire team. Please? Tell me you'll do this. I'll feel so much better going into this surgery. Let the team know I'm doing okay and that I'll be back as soon as I'm physically able. They need to hear the news from you, my only daughter."

The idea of spending weeks—possibly months—being Max's boss seems like the worst idea I've heard in a while. But it's near impossible to argue with Papa when he's lying in a hospital bed. And it's not like I've got anything else going on, being unemployed and all.

"But, Lily, one thing. One more thing?"

I'm unsure if I want to hear any new requests. "Yeah?"

"No twitting."

I scrunch up my face, not sure what he's talking about. "Wha—"

"Tweeting," he interrupts, waving his hand slowly in the air. "Don't tweet about the team. Or post, or whatever it is you do on that damn social media. Don't get in a situation like you did at the game company." He's one of the few people left on earth who doesn't need to worry about social media, because he's hired a crack team to handle it. To say that I'm envious would be an understatement.

"Papa, definitely not. Never." I'd deleted all my social accounts after the game company debacle, and I'm in no hurry to reclaim them, much less tweet about Formula World. Just the idea of interacting with guys who live in their moms' basements and think they know the sport better than I do sends a shiver of disgust through me. "Seriously. Don't worry. I'm finished with social media."

Papa nods, relieved. Dr. Patel loudly clears his throat, and I jump a little. I'd forgotten the doctor and nurse were in the room, I'd been so blindsided by my father's request.

"How are we doing? Ready for surgery?" the doctor says.

I look at him, then at my father, and finally remind myself to shut my mouth.

Papa reaches for my hand. "Please say yes, kamari mou."

"Okay." I nod slowly. "Yes. Only until you're better."

He smiles weakly then starts coughing again. A fresh well of tears fills my eyes, and I fold myself on top of my father, giving him a soft hug. "I love you," I murmur. "You're going to be okay."

He has to be. What would I do without him?

"Love you, too, Lily."

Dr. Patel and the nurses come closer to the bed, which is my cue to stand and clear the way for them to take my father out of the room. I do, while wiping away tears.

"Now get to the track," Papa says, mustering a little grin.

The doctor and one of the nurses wheel him out of the room. Another nurse materializes, an older lady with jet-black hair.

"He's in great hands," she says.

"Thank you. How long will the surgery take?"

"Two, three hours. We'll call you when it's done and tell you when you can visit. I wouldn't plan on being able to see him tonight, since he'll likely head to the ICU once the procedure is finished. Tomorrow morning, most likely."

The fact that I can't see my father until tomorrow—and maybe not ever if surgery doesn't go well—steals the breath from my lungs. The nurse says I can stay in the room to gather my thoughts.

"Would you like a hug, dear? You look like you could use one," the nurse says.

"No," I blurt, then immediately feel terrible, like I always do. There are very few people in this world I like to touch, and strangers aren't among them. My old therapist claimed I suffered from social anxiety, and the effects of a mother who wasn't physically affectionate. Or it could be due to how I'd felt self-conscious about my looks as a teen, growing up plain in a world full of rich, cliquish girls who liked to be effusive in their affection. Even though I'm well over those issues, I still don't like touches from strangers.

"Sorry. Please don't take offense. I appreciate the gesture, but I'm not a hugger."

She smiles and backs out of the room, leaving me alone.

I slump into a chair, head in my hands. My knee bounces up and down, jiggling like it always does when I'm nervous. Everything's happening way too fast for my liking—I'm more of a methodical planner, one who hates surprises and likes to have lots of advance notice. If I had my way, I'd camp out here at the hospital until I could see Papa, then hold a meeting with the factory racing team at his corporate offices in New York.

I pick up the phone and text my mom. She and my father keep separate residences because their relationship is, in her words, "complicated," but she'll surely be concerned. The doctor said he contacted her.

She's a "pro-aging social media influencer," whatever that means. All I know is that she has almost as many Instagram followers as my father's racing team, and that she loves to pose in gauzy outfits that garner hundreds of thousands of likes and would make Stevie Nicks envious.

When she doesn't message back immediately, I haul myself to my feet. There's no time to wait for her response. I have to get the track now to fulfill the promise I made to Papa. Even if it's going to suck.

CHAPTER THREE

MAX

"Easy, Max. Easy. You've got room on the inside but it'll be tight." Jack's voice in my earpiece is the only thing in my brain. It's as if my body and mind know exactly what to do: win.

At the beginning of turn four, I maneuver my car to the right of Morishita's. He's my top competitor, an excellent driver, but unfortunately for him, he's left enough room to allow me to pass on the curve.

"You're doing it, Max, you're doing it!" Jack's voice hums with excitement.

"Payback," I growl. Morishita had overtaken me right after the first pit stop and had been in the lead despite my starting the race on pole position. Now I'm snatching victory from the jaws of defeat, and I pull ahead of my competition on the straightaway.

"One more lap. You've got this, Max." Jack's tone is still filled with tension, but with a definite jubilant tone.

Out of the corner of my eye I see Morishita drive slightly off the track and cut the chicane, allowing me a wider lead. Even over the roar of the car's engine I can hear the cheering in the stands. There's nothing like the approval of the fans, and that's one of the things keeping me in the sport.

"Two car lead now, twenty meters. Bring it home, Becker."

I can feel the familiar tingling in my balls, the sensation that tells me I'm going to win the race. I accelerate a little harder for good measure, and then comes a loud *pop*.

"What's going on?" I yell into my earpiece.

The car slows from 200 miles per hour to 180. I press the accelerator all the way down but the car doesn't respond. Jack's going nuts in my ear. 160. 150. 120.

"What the hell?" I yell.

"Pull aside! Pull aside! It's the engine. We can see." Jack and the team have visuals on all the inner workings of my car from the garage, and the guys groan and shout as Morishita passes me.

"No, I'm going to try to bring it in."

"Max, pull over. I repeat, pull over! It's dangerous!"

Dammit, no. If I can somehow glide to the finish line, it'll count as a full race. I might even eke out a point or two. If I pull over, it's a DNF.

There's another pop, and wisp of smoke. *Scheisse. Shit. Merda.* There aren't enough languages to swear in. I'm only half a track away from the finish line, and there's no way I'm going to make it. Car after car zooms around me, and I slap my hand on the steering wheel while I guide the car onto the gravel.

The crowd's going even wilder now, but not for the right reasons. Like me, they're upset that I—the number one driver and the top contender for the championship—have a big, fat DNF for the important Miami race.

I lift myself out of the car as my competition hurtles past me some fifty yards away while going a hundred and fifty miles per hour.

I grip the edge of the car, my fingers digging into the fiberglass. I heave myself up and out, searching for traction on the ground with my feet. The soles of my shoes make a crunching sound on the gravel. I stand back to look at the car. The front end is engulfed in smoke, and probably soon flames.

The smell of burning plastic and metal fills the air, and I want to spit on the car.

Du Hurensohn. You son of a bitch.

Other drivers would have a big, dramatic display of disappointment right now, but not me. I don't even take off my helmet as I make the walk of shame back to the garage.

In my mind, however, I'm losing my shit.

When I reach the pit, I pull off my helmet. The words "forced to retire after a certain victory" waft from the announcer on the loudspeaker. I want to punch something but keep that emotion bottled inside me. Instead, I grit my teeth so hard that I can feel pain in my sinuses.

It's so hot that the air barely registers on my sweat-drenched face. I don't acknowledge the rest of the team or the few VIPs in the garage as I stalk up to Jack and pull him aside. "What the fuck?"

The lanky Australian engineer shakes his head. "I know. I know. The engine crapped the bed, mate. It's the worst luck. We're going to get to the bottom of this."

"Did Esteban have any problems with his car?" My younger teammate—a guy who is affable, kind, and above all, scandal-free—has been doing incredibly well for his first year in Formula World.

Jack shakes his head. "Only your car. The engineers are looking into it. I'm really sorry, Max."

He's known me long enough to understand that I don't want a barrage of questions. We've worked together on and off for seven years now, both as competitors and on the same teams. This is our second team together, and the first year he's my engineer.

I lean against the wall and run a hand through my hair, which is damp with perspiration. I feel like punching something but would never debase myself with such a public show of emotion.

"Have you seen Lucas?" I ask Jack.

"I'll find him." Jack walks off, and he yells to the team over the roar of the crowd. "Anyone seen Silva?"

As I'm gulping down what feels like a gallon of water, my assistant, Lucas, runs up.

"Holy shit," he says. "You okay?"

"Fuck, I dunno." I shake my head.

"C'mon. Let's go talk." He puts his hand on my shoulder as we walk into a private back room. Already I'm calmer.

Unlike other drivers' assistants, who mostly carry water and helmets, Lucas is my everything. He started as my physiotherapist when I was a rookie driver, and soon morphed into my right-hand man. He has a degree and a background in physiotherapy and health science, and before he came to Formula World he worked with the Brazilian Olympic track team. Above all, he makes sure I'm in top shape both mentally and physically.

He's also my best friend.

Lucas is responsible for everything from my daily routine to my diet to my travel arrangements. Hell, we even have matching tattoos of the word *Loyalty* written in our native languages on our right biceps. Some tabloids have speculated we're gay. We're not—we're more like twin brothers, even though he's Brazilian and five years older than me.

We slump onto two hard, plastic chairs.

"It was like the engine ran out of steam. I don't understand," I tell him.

He grunts, and I explain what happened on the track. That's what

Lucas is best at: listening. He asks a few questions about the engine, then says, "Your shoulder. How did that hold up?"

"It was fine. No issues there." I pause, then let out a string of German swear words.

Lucas raises an eyebrow. "Wow. I've never seen you this emotional after a DNF."

I scowl at him. "That's not true."

"Something else might be going on here."

I'm gulping water so hard that a trickle runs down my chin. After I wipe my face, I sigh. "I'm not prepared for a therapy session now, man."

"I'm just saying, it seems like you're taking this hard. I know you want to win but something tells me you're upset for different reasons."

Lucas knows me too well.

"This doesn't have anything to do with the fact that we're in Miami and that's where—"

"Absolutely not." I shake my head. "I'm going to hit the shower. I'll see you in a few, in the debrief room."

I can tell he doesn't believe my answer. Nothing gets past him. Aside from my parents, he's the person I'm closest to in this world.

"I'll get a recovery drink ready," he says, hauling himself to his feet.

"Thanks, appreciate it."

We fist bump. The only silver lining is that I can take a shower without the hassle of the post-race press conference. It'll be necessary to do a few interviews after my spectacular failure of a last lap, but at least I'll be clean.

We slip out the back door of the garage and stalk to Team Onassis's Recharge Station, a massive mobile home made with sustainable Austrian timber. On the way I'm ambushed by a reporter, someone from a German newspaper.

"Max, what happened out there on the track?"

Although I want to yell at her, I've never been violent or hostile with the press. It's not my style, not even when I was a younger driver and in my truly out-of-control days, back when I was on a team with Dante Annunziata—a wild man in his own right, before he got married.

Lucas and I stop and stare at the reporter, a middle-aged woman who knows her racing. She's been on the Formula World beat for years. "I was headed for a win and something went wrong," I reply in German. "I lost power, and the team lost points. It's as simple as that."

"Thank you for the questions," Lucas says smoothly. "I'm sorry, but we have to go now." It's his role to eliminate all distractions on race weekends, including nosy reporters.

Even though she's asking a barrage of questions, I clam up and we stalk into the mobile structure, where press isn't allowed. That's where Lucas and I part. Him to the kitchen, me to my driver's room. There, I can shower and seethe in peace.

I wave at the woman behind the front counter—it's where the team can also get snacks, drinks, and much-needed espresso—and she buzzes me through a triple-locked door and into the back. My room is on the second floor of the behemoth building, which the team constructs and deconstructs for every American race. There's a second one in Europe for the races there; Onassis has spared no expense with his old family money.

Esteban's room looks like a playroom, with video games, a mini-foosball table, and a beanbag.

Compared to his, my room is sterile. A massage table is the only thing that looks out of place, with its crisp white sheets and small pillow. The armoire is functional and white, housing my necessities. The desk and chair are small and tan, matching the sofa. The only splash of color comes from the framed photographs of my hometown of Tübingen, Germany, on the walls.

I want no distractions in my moment of failure. No media. No fans. No frills. The only one allowed in here is Lucas unless I say otherwise.

I strip off my suit and hang it on the rack, feeling my muscles tense as the cool air hits my skin. During some races I lose up to ten pounds in water weight from sweating alone, which is why I have a case of water in the corner. I reach for one and inhale the liquid, then pad into the shower and turn it on cold, gasping as the full blast hits me. I slap my hand on the wall, half expecting the entire building to come crashing down around me. I'm that angry.

Winning today was crucial, and not only for the points. Oh, sure, I want to win the championship. It's been two long years since I've had a truly excellent finish, since I won my last championship. Last year was a bust with my old team, and now I'm with Onassis. This year we have the best car in the league, or so I thought. Now I'm having my doubts, given the way the engine blew up today.

On the last fucking lap.

This hadn't happened to Esteban's car, and I automatically wonder if I have an inferior machine. Rationally I know I don't, but doubts creep in after something like this. Maybe this is my sign to finally leave the sport after years of injuries and neck pain—and after getting a call from the head of a startup electric race-car circuit in Germany. They want me to be a consultant, which would require me to retire as a driver. I haven't told anyone this, not even Lucas. It'll take time for me to process this offer.

I douse myself in soap, a knot of failure tightening in my gut. There was another reason I wanted to win here at Silverstone, a reason far less rational than winning another championship. One that Lucas alluded to; one that I didn't want to admit aloud.

I lather my hair, practically scratching my scalp raw as I scrub.

Lily Onassis. I'd wanted to win for her. The boss's daughter. The woman I'd lost my virginity to when I was twenty-two. She'd been an intern for her father's team one season. I was driving for a different team back then, and sleeping with a rival team's intern was taboo, so we spent eight months sneaking around, slipping into each other's hotel rooms all across the globe.

When that season ended, she broke my heart.

She lives in Miami, and since this is the first year that the city's held a race, I figured she'd be here today. Or at the after-party. I wanted her to see me win on her home turf. Before every race, I like to have a personal goal for winning. Sometimes it's as simple as "Mama's watching on TV and I want to make her proud" or "I'm doing this for that little kid with cancer because he's my number one fan."

Today it was "I want Lily to see that I'm a champion."

"Fucking stupid," I mutter as I rinse off. This is idiotic; she knows I've won the Formula World championship two times since we ended our relationship. I don't need any more external validation, championship cups, or money. Hell, I'm not even sure how much longer I want to be in this sport.

But it would feel good to see Lily Onassis admit she was wrong when she broke up with me. She's the only woman who's ever rejected me.

Maybe I'll skip the after-parties entirely and fly to Germany to see my family instead. Seeing Mama, Dad, and my younger brother always helps me focus. I'll avoid all the post-race hoopla and get on the private jet. Or maybe Lucas and I will take a weekend trip to surf in Costa Rica. But he's a newlywed, and probably wants to see his wife, a model who lives in New York. Maybe I'll just fuck right off to Costa Rica alone.

I've gotta get out of Miami, preferably before tonight's parties.

Because the last thing I want is for Lily to look at me and think I'm a loser.

CHAPTER FOUR

LILY

Adam and Tanya, the team's public relations head, greet me at a side gate of the Miami track in a chauffeured electric golf cart. I climb in and we whiz away, slowing only for the security at various checkpoints.

The aftermath of the race is all around us: sanitation crews picking up trash, teams packing up giant tractor trailers, a few fans lingering in the VIP area hoping for autographs.

"We've asked the entire team to meet us in the garage," Adam says, his long face pinched with worry.

"Perfect. Anything else I need to know before I talk?" I'm back in corporate crisis mode, something I'd thrived at in my last job. At least until the crisis involved me.

I've known Tanya for years. She was head of PR for Team Eagle, the racing outfit that Max went to after we broke up. Tanya is almost forty and has seen a lot in Formula World—so much that she seems entirely unfazed at the moment, while Adam and I are both drenched in sweat and have faces pinched with worry.

I've always admired Tanya's tough-as-nails demeanor. We're not exactly friends, more like friendly acquaintances. I suspect this is going to change. It could go either way—we're either going to be besties at the end of this situation or we're going to hate each other.

"Max is in a bit of a state because his engine blew up on the last lap, and he was leading the race," Adam says.

A bit of a state in Adam's dry, polite UK English probably means Max is irate and possibly even had a tantrum on the track. Most drivers would, from what I've seen and experienced in my years observing Formula World.

"Max controlled himself well, as he always does. But I could tell he was pissed." Tanya's voice is matter of fact.

"Ouch. How did Esteban finish?" Since everyone knows of my history with Max, I'd prefer to deflect any conversation about him, at least for right now.

"Tenth," Adam says, and Tanya groans.

"It's been a shitty day," she says.

Yeesh. "So the team's already in a foul mood." I can't tell if the dismal race results are going to make it harder or easier for me to give this announcement.

"Pretty much," Adam says.

"Does anyone know about my father? Any rumors leak? Anyone see him taken away?"

Tanya shakes her head, her shoulder-length brown bob flipping in the wind. How does she avoid frizz in this humidity? "I don't think so. He was in the back of the garage, and one of the guys in the garage dragged him into the back room with the air conditioner and called for help. The paramedics took him out the side door, which isn't accessible to the press or public. People probably assumed the ambulance was there for someone who had heatstroke."

My poor father. I'm about to ask if them if they'd noticed any signs of illness but we're at the garage. The golf cart stops and we all climb out. Next to the garage is one of the team's cars, a sleek black and orange open wheeled Formula World car. My father's passion and purpose. As if on cue, the side door opens.

Jack, one of our two team engineers, fills the doorway with his large frame. He's tall and blond, his skin tanned and rough, as if he spends all his time outdoors. He looks like a man who's spent a lifetime surfing, sailing, racing . . . and winning races. His expression is grim but brightens when he spots me.

"Lily!" Just when I think he's going to extend his hand to me, he folds me into a giant hug.

"Blrb," I mumble into his armpit. It's one of the many reasons I hate hugs. I'm short and always end up mashed into someone's underarm or boob area and am forced to inhale their body odor.

I wriggle out of his grip, feeling my skin crawl. It's nothing against Jack, he's a lovely man—I'd had dinner with him and my father when he was first hired to the team a year ago. But I simply hate hugs. They feel weird and fake and uncomfortable to me.

And after races, there's the sweat factor. All these folks are covered in buckets of perspiration, and now I'm immensely squicked out, right when I need to focus.

"How's Adrian?" Jack asks, oblivious to the fact that I'm practically itching from the cold, clammy odor that lingers on my skin.

"He's in surgery now. Before he went in he made me promise to say a few words to the team."

A burble of voices comes from inside the garage, various accents mingling into one low buzz. Jack gestures to me. "Anything you want to discuss quickly before you go in?"

"Yeah." I softly shut the door and motion for Tanya, Jack, and Adam to join me in a huddle. The two men are so tall that I must straighten to my full height of five feet two inches tall and crane my neck to make eye contact. Normally I'd wear heels to a meeting so important, but I hadn't anticipated any of this when I hurriedly threw on my sneakers back at my condo.

Tanya's gaze lingers on Jack. I'd heard rumors years ago that they were sleeping together, but never asked anyone to confirm because it was none of my business. And at this point, I don't care about anyone's past flings. I simply need to break the bad news and we can all hope Papa recovers so I can go back to my stress baking. Moping. Sleeping. God, has it been a month already?

"I'm taking notes," Tanya chirps, whipping a phone out of a waist pack.

"My father asked me to be in charge of the team for the next few races."

Men's egos in this sport can be fragile, so I say this without a hint of emotion. If Adam and Jack are shocked, they don't show it. Tanya's thumbs fly across the phone screen and after a flash, she looks up.

"When do you want to send out the news release? How many interviews do you want to do? Or should we call a news conference? We could hand pick a few reporters—"

I hold up my hand as if I'm in total control, when I'm anything but. The idea of speaking to the press sends an unpleasant shiver through me. "News release only. I'm in no shape to talk to the press today, or tonight. We'll deal with it tomorrow."

"People are going to want to hear from you," she says firmly.

"I don't care. They'll get a news release. Then we'll send a second when Papa's out of surgery and then, *maybe*, I'll talk to a few selected journalists." I stare her down and she finally bobs her head in affirmation.

Whew. Won that battle.

"Adrian's always wanted you to join the team," Adam says softly.

"He has his wish, temporarily. But this is the last thing I want to be doing right now."

"I guess he figures you have the time," Jack says.

Was that a jab? My firing from the racing game company one month ago was national news. Although harassment of women in tech had long been an issue by the time I was fired, the way I publicly brought it to light was . . . unusual. And, looking back on it, I'd probably been a tiny bit nasty in tweeting my complaints and the photo of a guy who said I'd be a "good lay" during a very public conference. But I'd had enough, and I'd snapped. I'm used to odd looks and pointed verbal barbs, so I merely look Jack squarely in the eye.

"I have nothing but time. Let's get this announcement over with."

The four of us march in. Jack first, then Adam, and finally Tanya and me. The thick, humid smell of sweat mixed with rubber tires hits my nostrils, and I flatten my back against the far wall, behind Adam. I can see the tiny beads of sweat dotting people's foreheads and upper lips. Shirts sticking to his skin. The room is small and stuffy and I can't breathe. I want to run but I promised Papa that I'd do this for him.

A few of the guys in the garage, longtime employees of my father's, wave and smile in my direction. A chorus of murmurs ripple through the crowd, things like *Why's the boss's daughter here* and *Where's Onassis* on nearly everyone's lips. Conversation sizzles like grease in a pan, spitting and popping on the barbecue. I can't help but think of Papa. This is where he got his start, way before I was born. This is where he found the success and family that he cherished.

That makes what I'm about to do a little easier. This is a friendly group of people, all of whom care deeply for my father.

I peek around Adrian's shoulder, looking for one man in particular: Max.

The last time I saw him was four months ago at a party at the team's headquarters in New York before the season started. I'd made an appearance for Papa, said a polite hello to Max—who was chatting up one of the grid girls who holds the umbrella over drivers before the race—and promptly left. It was during a time when I was going through a particularly rough patch at my job, when the executives refused to take me seriously about the climate of harassment. I hadn't wanted to torture myself by watching Max flirt his way around the party.

Jack stands at the front of the room, holding his arms out and pushing the air toward the sides of the empty garage. "Make a circle, everyone, make a circle. That's it. Like we're in grade school. Spread out so we can see everyone. We've got a team announcement. Lily Onassis, Adrian's daughter, is here. Lily?"

He sweeps his arm wide, as if welcoming me into their space.

I step around Adam, nervous as all hell. My heart pounds with the same intensity as a revving engine on the starting grid. I scan one side of the makeshift circle, but don't spot Max's familiar face.

"Hi, everyone. I'm sorry to have to tell you this, but my father wanted you to hear it from me. He collapsed during the race and had to be taken to hospital. He had a heart attack, and he's fine, but he's in surgery now."

Gasps and murmurs fill the room, giving me the time to survey the other side of the circle. My gaze locks on Max's assistant, Lucas, which means my ex isn't far, since they're virtually inseparable.

There. There's Max.

Standing with his back against the wall, arms folded, coolly appraising me as if he's going to critique my performance. Max Becker, golden boy with the faded tawny hair. He's aged a little since I first met him seven years ago, but he's no less gorgeous. An angel and a demon all in one body, the press used to say, and I couldn't agree more.

We lock eyes for a second, and it's as if the noise, the odor, and the heat evaporate. Our entire eight-month relationship comes rushing into my mind—all the late-night conversations about our hopes and dreams, the laughter, the fierce, desperate kisses.

I shake my head and hold up a hand, tearing my eyes from Max's beautiful face.

"Please don't worry. My father doesn't want you to be concerned. We're getting him the best care and he'll be back on his feet in no time. He also wanted me to tell you something else." I pause to lick my lips, knowing this will be the bigger shock for the team. "He asked me, well, made me promise, you know how Adrian is—" I pause to allow the guys some much-needed laughter.

"He wants me to take over for him during the next few races."

A hush descends into the room. My gaze goes to Max, like he's a magnet for my eyes. But instead of him returning my attention, he stares at the floor. Lucas leans into him and whispers something in his ear, and Max moves his head up and down.

He stares right at me. His expression is cold.

What had Lucas said? I'd always liked him, probably because he was the only person who knew of our relationship and approved all those years ago. But perhaps he's changed his mind about me in the ensuing years. Which is fine. I don't care if he hates me, but now that I'm in charge, we'll be forced to work together so Max can win.

A pang of anger and hurt shoot through me. He really despises me that much. I turn toward Jack, who by now is clapping. The others join in. Even Max, after a second.

Jack rests his hand on my shoulder and I tense up, worried that a very public hug is on the horizon. "Lily and I and the rest of the executive team will get all the details ironed out over the next few days. For the rest of you, carry on as usual. We've got a race in Austin next Sunday, and that needs to be our priority. We're going to win for Adrian."

"That's right, stay the course. Prepare for the race, and send prayers to Papa. Thank you all," I call out. "I'll be sure to give him your regards when I see him tomorrow."

Jack and I step back and the men in the room—it's almost all men, like almost every Formula World team—break apart from the circle and talk in small groups. Some shuffle outside, probably to discuss the team's future now that I'm in charge. This, I can handle.

Max's obvious disappointment? It's a little tougher to swallow.

"That went as well as could be expected," I say to Jack.

"Absolutely." Jack's normally cheery voice is a little flat, or perhaps I'm imagining it. "Ah, I believe someone wants to chat with you."

He points over my shoulder. Please don't be someone wanting to give me a hug. With a pasted-on smile, I turn.

My breath hitches. Max is standing there with a grim expression on his face. Oh crap.

CHAPTER FIVE

LILY

Max is disconcertingly close, with only a flimsy plastic chair between us. I grip the back to steady myself, because his unyielding ice-blue eyes are laser focused on my face. It's as if he's scrutinizing every feature and pore. Dammit, I hadn't put on makeup, and that somehow makes me feel naked and vulnerable. I'm still in my glasses, the black-rimmed ones that make me look like an owl.

I never could read him, and not knowing what he's thinking is somehow even more unnerving now that we're older. His face is angular, but not severe—more model-like than harsh. His hair is a little longer now, still messy and wet, probably from his post-race shower.

"Oh. Hey, Max." My voice is soft, but my mind's in the gutter with the thought of him naked and wet.

We stand there, awkwardly, sizing each other up. Most people would extend a hug in this situation, but not Max. He knows better and shoves his hands into his jeans.

"Lily." The sound of my name on his lips sends an electric charge through my body. It ignites every nerve ending and sets my skin on fire. It's a physical reaction that I can't control, and it used to happen every time he said my name when we were together.

Back then I loved it. Now? It's more than a bit disconcerting. I've *got* to get a handle on myself. Part of me also feels an uncomfortable amount of guilt, because I was the one who ended things. It was my fear of commitment, my hatred of the lifestyle, my certainty that it wouldn't work, that led us to this point of awkwardness.

"Hey," I repeat, in a dumb, breathy voice.

His tanned face is tense, probably because he's worried about Papa, and a muscle in his jaw pulses, betraying the gravity of the situation. A black T-shirt clings to his shoulders, chest, and stomach, showing off his hard-earned physique. Unlike most Formula World drivers, he's on the taller side, a fact that the press loves to discuss and dissect.

Another member of the team, a Chilean guy named Rodrigo I've known for years, approaches. His arms are open wide, and I step back. Dammit, I need to tell Jack to informally let everyone on the team know that I don't want to be touched or hugged. Where is Jack, anyway? He seems to have evaporated into thin air.

Max, who knows my dislike of hugs, blocks Rodrigo by physically moving closer to me and shooting him a steely glance.

"Ooh, sorry to interrupt. We'll catch up later, Lily," Rodrigo says. I give a weak wave as he wanders off.

I press my hand to my forehead. "Thanks for that," I mutter to Max.

"I saw the look in your eyes. Like a cornered cat."

We're entirely too close now, but I can't go anywhere because I'm wedged between a wall, a chair, and Max—and it doesn't look like he's moving. Maybe he thinks he's trying to shield me from further unwanted hugs. I guess this is a plus.

"I'm sorry about your father." His voice is quiet and has taken on a low tenor, one that drifts effortlessly into my ears. It's as if he doesn't want anyone to hear us talking. As if everyone in this room knows we used to sleep together, and he's trying to hide the evidence.

Just like old times.

"Thank you," I reply, a little too loud.

Max presses those full lips of his together. His eyes meet mine and for once, he looks like he doesn't know what he wants to say. The confidence I'd seen hours ago during those track interviews has evaporated. Truthfully, he seems a bit shaken. I guess it's understandable since he's always looked up to my father as a pioneer in the sport. And Papa is his boss, the man who is paying him millions of dollars to perform and drive flawlessly.

His bottom lip trembles slightly, and he seems to be having trouble finding the right words. I can see the conflict in his blue eyes, a battle between what he wants to say and what he thinks he should say.

"Where are you . . . ah, how long will your father be in hospital?"

"I don't know. He's in surgery now, or should be. The doctor said they'd call once he was out, and that I could see him tomorrow morning. I'm sure he'll be in rehab for a while. I don't know how it all works, but I'm hoping to sort it all out by tomorrow, then get to Austin."

Some of this plan hinges on talking with Mum, who'd sent me a text saying she was catching a flight to Florida soon. I wave my hand around the conference room, at the people in small groups, speaking in hushed tones. The team. My team, for the time being.

"Where are you staying?" His tone is devoid of any context and the question catches me by surprise. Why does he care? Doesn't he know I live in Miami? Seemingly the entire world does, if the doxing after my firing is any indication.

"My condo. I live here now. In downtown Miami."

A little, rueful smile dances on his lips. "Oh right. For a minute, I forgot."

"I should gather my father's stuff from his hotel room, or ask Adam to do it. Papa thought about bunking with me but felt it best to be near the team." So many details to keep track of already.

I don't mention the hotel name, nor does Max. Probably because it was where we first hooked up, seven years ago. This was before Miami even had a race. The teams had been here on a layover, doing some promotional event in tandem with NASCAR.

I reach for my water, distracting myself from ogling Max's high cheekbones. I'd always loved that part of his face, and recall how I'd trace the sharp planes with my finger while we lay in bed. A memory, of us in a hotel—always a hotel—rushes to mind. We were in Spain, and the way the light illuminated his face is forever burned in my mind.

An angel.

Max puts his hands on his hips and looks around, as if he's in the garage, assessing which tires his crew should use for a race. "I was planning to go to Costa Rica to surf for a few days."

He always enjoyed risk-taking adventure trips on his days off. Truthfully, I'm a bit relieved that he's going to leave immediately. It will make my life easier for a few days, give me space to get used to this situation.

"I'll catch up with you in Austin."

"No." Max shakes his head. "I'll stay here and skip the surf trip. I can do that any time."

He says this right as I take a sip, and I'm so shocked that I nearly spray water all over his chest. Instead, I swallow-cough, and Max leans in. "You okay?"

"Definitely. Yes. Very okay," I stammer between coughs. He's so close that I can smell his cologne now. The scent is exactly the same as when we were together, an airy and crisp smell, like ozone in the air after a lightning strike mixed with freshly cut grass with a hint of masculine musk.

I hold up my hand as I take a half step back, needing distance from his touch. From him. "You don't have to stay here. You should go to Costa Rica."

"I wouldn't feel right." He shakes his head. "I need to be here for Adrian when he comes out of surgery. I'm the senior driver on this team and would like to see him. If that's okay with you."

The plastic crackles under the grasp of my fingers. "Let's see how he does in surgery today."

"If you're going to be in charge, we need to talk about the next few races. You need my impressions of the team and of the upcoming race. We have a lot to discuss."

Like us? Are we going to finally discuss how we ended? I don't ask this, but the question hangs in the air as we stare into each other's eyes. The air between us is charged with a jumble of emotions, at least on my end. Regret, desire, fear—they're all racing through my veins, causing my heart to thrash wildly in my chest.

And he's probably feeling absolutely nothing.

There's a reason the press calls him the Iceman.

Naturally, Max breaks eye contact first, to check his Rolex. I remember when he first was sponsored by the company and how excited he'd been when he'd gotten his first free timepiece. He'd slipped it on my wrist and then proceeded to take off my clothes, saying he wanted to admire two beautiful things at once.

He'd always made me feel like I was the most gorgeous woman in the world. Even though I knew the truth; that I was plain, regular, basic. Max never bought into my insecurities.

I fan my face with my hand. He's still entirely too handsome, with his rumpled, golden curls, that mouth with the perfect Cupid's bow upper lip, that straight, aquiline nose.

I can't help but remember the way it felt when his lips brushed against mine, soft and gentle at first, then harder, insistent. The way his mouth tasted unexpectedly of wintergreen. The way his hands felt on my skin, rough and calloused from working on cars but somehow gentle too.

What would it be like to feel those hands on me again?

"Talk?" My face contorts into a grimace. Maybe I didn't hear him correctly. It is loud in here.

"Yes. Talk. We need to talk." His glance is edging into glare territory, and I'm not fully sure why. "Let's say nine at the Setai hotel bar, the one by the pool?"

It's been seven years since I've been to the Setai bar. It's where Max and I had our first real conversation. We'd spent hours talking in a cabana next to the pool one night after a long day of promotion. One thing led to another, and after two mojitos, I followed him to his room. Because of that evening, I've always associated mojitos, cabanas, and palm trees with heady, unbridled lust.

I simply cannot allow those memories to interfere with the issues at hand. I try to compose myself, but I can feel the heat rising in my cheeks. *Crap*. He probably wants to ask me about the game company scandal. I press my lips together to form a smile.

"That's great. Nine. Papa should be out of surgery by then." At least I hope he is.

Max doesn't say anything, just bobs his head up and down. Then he turns without saying good-bye, leaving me breathless and puzzled and feeling way off kilter.

This leaves me four hours to not only worry about my father but ruminate over what Max wants to discuss during a private meeting at a swanky South Beach bar.

CHAPTER SIX

LILY

"Crap, crap, crap."

I shove my feet into the pair of sneakers near the door of the suite. I'm never late for appointments or meetings, but tonight I'm a mess. It's already ten minutes after nine, and I just hung up with Papa's doctor. I've decided to stay at my father's suite instead of home, since I'll likely want to collapse after this meeting with Max, and can't bear another round of bumper-to-bumper Miami traffic. Plus, the hotel is closer to the hospital.

After snatching my purse off the bed I race out of the room, down the hall to the elevator, and walk outdoors to the pool bar. The crowd is beautiful and sleek, quintessentially Miami, and I'm painfully aware that I look like hell, a manatee in a sea filled with models.

No one recognizes me, and I like that. It's my superpower, being able to seamlessly blend in anywhere. I used to think it was a curse being plain, but now I know otherwise. I'm stealthy and effective this way.

The pool area is low lit, but I can make out Max sitting in the back corner at the edge of a cabana, looking like a rich tourist instead of a man who drove around a track for three hours at two hundred miles per hour only hours earlier. Tall palms sway with the warm breeze, and a hint of pool chlorine and coconut oil hangs in the air.

Pop music that I don't entirely recognize hums in the background, and a few people are deep in conversation over expensive cocktails. There are a couple of people from the team in the hotel; I know this because Adam informed me that they're packing up the garage and temporary buildings on the track and leaving for the next race in Texas. But these are race fans, rich ones, who are wringing out one more night of partying.

Max lifts his hand and waves me over, but there's no smile on his face. For the hundredth time, I wonder why he's asked me here.

As I walk to his cabana, I stare at my feet. The last thing I want is for him to think I'm eager to impress him, although one look at me and he'll know I'm not trying to make an impression on anyone.

My hair looks like a ferret's nest and my face is ashen and worn. He probably thinks I've crawled out of a garbage pile. Meanwhile, every other person in this place looks like they walked off the cover of a magazine.

When I reach the cabana, he holds the curtain open for me. The interior is illuminated by two faux candles, making everything seem insistently sensuous. There are two chairs and a loveseat clustered around a low wooden table. I choose the chair. "I'm so sorry. I've been waiting for the hospital to call with an update about Papa."

"How is he?" Max sprawls on the loveseat, his eyes full of intensity. My face flashes hot, because I feel that old spark between us.

I take a deep breath. "He's okay. As well as can be expected. The surgery went a little longer than the doctors anticipated—four hours—but it turned out well. They're observing him in the ICU and I should be able to see him tomorrow. He had a near-total blockage in one artery and they said it could've been . . ."

It's impossible to say the word *fatal* because it's too frightening, and for the first time in a few hours, tears claw their way into my eyes. I swallow, hard.

"Sorry. Sorry." I try to stop the tears but they spill over my lids. When I reach for a bar napkin on the table, Max is already holding it.

"It's okay. This is all scary and unexpected. It's going to be difficult for you." His tone is low and growly, with a touch of annoyance, and I take the napkin from him to wipe my face. Most men would try to hug me, come around to my chair and put their arms around my shoulders.

Not Max. The sweet Max I used to know would've done that, but this man, older and hardened, doesn't bother. He thinks that little of me. Or he's embarrassed by my very public display of grief. Probably that's it, because Max almost never shows emotion around other people, and definitely not in a hotel cabana while others are drinking and partying.

I gulp in a few breaths, settling my quivering insides. "I'm fine. This whole thing took me by surprise since he seems, seemed, so healthy."

"Took me by surprise too. It was shock to everyone on the team."

"You didn't notice anything out of place this morning at the team meeting or in the garage?"

Max studies me for a beat and I wave my hand dismissively. "No, that's a silly question on my part. You wouldn't spot anything, you were focused on the race."

"Actually, I noticed that he was sweating a little more than usual, but I thought it was because he was hot." Max sips from a glass of water.

"It was a brutal day today." I lean back into my seat and look around for the server.

"Brutal is a good way of putting it." He runs a hand through his hair and sighs.

"I'm sorry about the engine. Saw the highlights on TV. It was the first thing Papa asked the nurse when he came out of anesthesia. Race results." A sad little laugh escapes my lips.

"Did the nurse tell him?"

"They claimed not to know anything—I'd given them strict instructions to not say a word. He was too out of it to know it was a lie."

The muscles in Max's chiseled jaw tense for a brief second, then relax. That's about all the indication I'm going to get that he's angry or annoyed. His eyes are seemingly boring into mine, and I shift uncomfortably. Good lord, he's somehow even more magnetic, more alluring now than when I first met him. Before he was an eager, brash guy, and now he's all man, silent and broody.

"Where's the server anyway, I need a dr—"

I'm almost immediately interrupted by a waiter balancing two plates of food on one arm, and tray with drinks.

"Here we go," the server says in the most upbeat tone I've heard in hours. "Sashimi and a mojito, and a vegan burger for the champion."

My jaw drops. Max had gone ahead and ordered for me. He'd remembered the exact thing I'd ordered all those years ago that night we first hooked up in a room on the tenth floor of this very hotel. Max flashes a smile, displaying straight, white teeth, and murmurs a thank you, but I'm sure inside he's cringing at the word *champion*, considering how he flamed out on the track today.

"Will you need anything else?"

Max leans back and extracts his wallet, taking out a hundred-dollar bill. "If you could keep any press and autograph seekers away, that would be perfect, bro."

The server takes the money and does a little bow. "Yes, sir. My pleasure." He thanks Max profusely as he backs away.

I'm still stunned about the sashimi and stare at Max. "What's this?"

By now, Max has already picked up his burger and is lifting it to his mouth. "Sashimi. It's your favorite."

The fact that he remembered this, then went ahead and ordered for me, is such a shock that I fumble with the chopsticks. They clatter to the table and I scoop them up.

"Is that okay? Would you like something else?" he says between bites, ignoring my clumsiness.

"Yes, it's fine." I move some wasabi from the plate to a small vessel, eager to change the subject. He got lucky, or is being polite, that's all.

"When did you become a vegetarian?" I eye his plate suspiciously. The Max I used to know loved meat in all forms.

He lifts a shoulder. "Lucas is still my trainer, and he suggested it at the beginning of the season. I agreed to try a no meat, no alcohol diet, and I think it's working well. It's not much fun, but whatever it takes, right?"

"You do look amazing." Dammit, I didn't mean to blurt that out loud. But he does. The lean, sinewy muscles of his forearms and the rock-solid biceps make it difficult to stop staring.

He grins, the first real smile I've seen him express. "Thanks. You're looking—"

"No." I wag my finger and pick up my mojito. "I look like hell. Feel like it too."

He swipes a French fry off his plate and pops it between his lips. He chews while studying me, swallows, then finally says, "Nah. You're still beautiful."

I almost choke on my drink but swallow a mouthful in time and cough softly. Did a compliment just leak from his mouth? Even when we'd been together, his compliments were reserved for intimate moments only, under the cover of darkness and usually whispered in my ear.

Obviously, he's only being polite. He's a European man, after all, and has an almost uncanny instinct of how to flatter women of all ages.

"Now it's my turn to apologize." He grins lasciviously. "I probably shouldn't say that to my new boss."

"Oh, please, Max . . ." My voice trails off, because I'm not sure what to say. There's a little part of me that wants to soak in the compliment and flirt mercilessly with him, the way we used to. But I know better, partially because I am, technically, the person running this team.

And because I'm certain he's said those words to dozens of women over the years. I might have been the first woman he slept with, but I definitely wasn't the last, if the tabloids over the last several years are even a little correct.

The last thing I want is to be treated like all the others. As it stands, I was first. First in a long line of women, but still number one.

And I absolutely hate to come in second, to anyone.

"What?" He sips his water, seemingly unbothered by my protest. "I can't tell you that you look good?"

"I don't . . . it's not . . . we shouldn't fall back on . . ." Flustered, I take another gulp of my drink, which is cool and strong. We can't do this. "Max, why did you ask me to dinner, anyway? Did you want to ask about what happened at my former job?"

He takes a bite of his burger and I eat a couple of pieces of raw salmon while he chews and swallows.

"No, that wasn't why I wanted to have dinner with you. But tell me about the racing game company." He dips a fry into a little tub of mayonnaise.

"You didn't hear why I was fired from my last job?"

He shakes his head. "Not really. I try not to read much of the news when I'm racing. I get too worked up."

I hate responses like that, and I stab a chopstick into the blob of wasabi, then lick a little off the tip. Maybe the intense clearing of my sinus cavities from the spice will help me answer this question. "A guy I worked with loudly told people at a conference that I'd be a good lay."

Max stops chewing, swallows, and glares at me. "What?"

"That kind of talk is common in tech. I'd been telling the executives in the company about how the few women at the office were treated. They ignored me. I endured a lot of that kind of behavior. So did the other women. Little things, like comments about my body, or photos on my desk, or drunken propositions at conferences. I ignored it the best I could for years, but it became too much. When that incident at the conference happened, I snapped. I tweeted it, along with the guy's photo. I let anger get the best of me, which wasn't cool. It snowballed from there, exploded all over social media and Reddit, and I was raked over the coals by tech bros. My address in San Jose was leaked, my car was egged, I received death threats. You know. The usual."

I try to say all of this in an easy, breezy way, like my entire life wasn't upended, like I hadn't lived for weeks in fear. Max's expression is a mixture of horror and disgust, and I don't bother with explaining further about the online harassment that ensued. Max knows the price of fame.

"You had to put up with all of that? Even though you weren't in the wrong?"

"I was a bit in the wrong by taking my company's issues public. But in fairness, it was only after I'd tried to tell HR and the executives about what was happening to me and the other women."

"I had no idea."

"Why would you? Most people outside the tech sphere don't know what women go through in that industry."

"You won't be treated that way in Formula World, you know."

I jiggle my knee, wishing I was anywhere but here. I wasn't so sure of Max's statement, because in my experience, whenever a woman works in a man's world, she's subject to all kinds of abuse, both subtle and overt. But perhaps he's right, or maybe I'll be shielded from such behavior because I'm the team owner's daughter. "I hope not. We'll see."

"I'm sorry, Lily." His expression softens, as does his tone.

"No need to apologize. You're far from the poster child for toxic masculinity. Anyway, tell me why you wanted to have dinner and chat." Both knees are jiggling now, *up down up down*, and I force myself to stop by pressing my heels into the ground.

"Yeah, ah, I wanted to bring you up to speed about the quality of my car. Since you're running the team. This is a conversation I would've had with your father after today's race. I have a lot of concerns, and someone needs to fix things, otherwise both me and the team will lose. I'm sure you and your father don't want that. We need to win."

His suddenly cold demeanor makes my hunger evaporate and my stomach plummet with disappointment. He doesn't want to catch up, doesn't want to talk to me at all—he only wants to discuss business.

I set down my chopsticks, no longer hungry, and reach for the pen and small notebook I always keep in my purse. This is exactly the position I didn't want to be in: steeling myself for another heartbreak from Max.

"Certainly. Please tell me all about the car."

CHAPTER SEVEN

MAX

Normally, around women I'm a simple man, and I make my needs and wants well known.

No strings, just fun, sex only. A few laughs, some drinks, a night in a hotel room, and we both move on.

But Lily . . . she's different. Always has been since the minute I ran into her in the days before my first race in Monaco all those years ago. I can't help but think about that day when I stare into her beautiful face right now, as she takes a sip of her drink and fiddles with her chopsticks.

We were all at a club, multiple teams. It was days before the race, so we were all letting off steam and having a few hours of fun. I was with Lucas and a few other drivers. We were all young back then, excited to be the toast of Monaco, surrounded by wealth and beauty.

Being guys barely out of our teens, we laser focused on a group of grid girls, the women who hold umbrellas over the drivers before the races. They were all impossibly tall and gorgeous, like human versions of gazelles. But there was one who was short. Disheveled, with long, dark hair flying everywhere. Wearing glasses and a simple black tank dress.

"Who's that?" I asked the driver standing next to me. I nodded in the direction of the women. "The brunet."

He thought I was referring to a tall girl with long, black hair who was standing next to her, but I was talking about the other woman, the one the tall girl was laughing and chatting with. They started to dance, and while the tall girl swayed like a ballerina, the shorter one danced with absolutely no rhythm at all. She laughed the entire time, her face illuminated with something I rarely saw in this world: authenticity.

I grinned. "No, the other one. The one who's dancing like a robot."

"Dude," Lucas chimed in. Back then his Brazilian accent was thicker. "That's Onassis's daughter."

"The team owner?" I asked, confused. Why hadn't I seen her before?

"She's interning for him this year. Apparently, she recently graduated. She hangs out with the grid girls."

I hadn't believed in love at first sight until that moment. Lily had always thought of herself as plain, and I never understood why. I was instantly captivated by her curves, her hair, her humor. The fact that she allowed herself to be silly in a club with the world's most gorgeous models and wealthy people told me more about her character than any expensive outfit.

That night I hadn't had the courage to approach her. But I did later, in Miami, at the very place we're sitting in now.

Her beauty is still disarming, even now that I'm older and way more experienced. I know this because of the way I'm blathering on about my car and what happened on the track today.

I simply don't know what else to talk about. Hell, there's a lot I want to say, but something's stopping me. Pride, probably. And anger. I never fully got over her leaving me. It's not that I want to punish her or make her pay for what she did. I understand why she decided to end things, and it even made sense to a degree. But I feel raw and wounded in her presence, like I did when we broke up, and I'd rather set all those old feelings aside.

I'm also shocked at her story about her firing. I never go on social media—I have people for that—and I've long learned that reading comments about anything is a waste of time and mental peace. I'd read about her firing in the *Wall Street Journal*, but that story had been a sanitized version of what had really happened. Some guys on the team had whispered about it, but the people closest to me knew enough to not utter a word about Lily. Lucas made sure of that.

The fact that any man would disrespect her like that makes me want to punch someone. But she doesn't want to hear that, I'm sure. Just like she wouldn't want to listen to me dissect our failed relationship. And now with her father's health crisis and her temporary takeover of the team, she doesn't need me complicating her life even more.

So, I'm going to be a good boy and muster the one quality I'm not known for: patience.

I'll be Lily's friend, her team confidante. I'm not going to seduce her, not going to flirt, and I'm definitely not going to apologize or bring up our past. There's no point in dredging up those feelings.

"You were driving and lost acceleration all of a sudden? No other warnings?" She looks up from her notebook and tilts her head. Good god, she's stunning. I've always thought she looked like the women in those Greek frescoes, with flowing curly dark hair and a dreamy expression in those hazel eyes. Age has made her look more delicate and vulnerable somehow, or maybe that's what life has done to her.

The glasses are different, more angular and modern than she used to wear, and they give her a sexy, serious look. I'd love to see her completely without clothes, wearing only those black-rimmed glasses. A vision of us on a bed, naked, with her wearing her old glasses flits into my mind.

My pants feel uncomfortably tight, and I shift in my seat. "None. I was coming down the straightaway, bringing it in for a win, and it was like the entire engine shut off. I slammed my foot on the gas, and nothing."

She purses her plump, glossy lips and a dissatisfied sigh leaks out of her. "I'm sure you've talked with Jack and the other engineers, right?"

"Not yet. Everyone was too upset about your father. We have a debrief call tomorrow. From the diagnostics I was able to look at on the computer, it looks like a component in the power unit."

She takes notes, all business. Clearly she's not remotely interested in me, not the way she once was. That's evident by the way she's taking notes, talking in a clipped tone—and by the way she rebuffed my lame attempt at flirtation when I told her she looked beautiful.

"We've got a week until Austin. My plan is to visit my father as soon as I possibly can tomorrow, arrange his care in New York, and land in Texas by the afternoon. When I get back to the hotel room tonight, I'll get an email chain going with everyone, because we need to figure out if this engine issue was a one-off or could affect both cars going forward. I also want to be on the debrief call."

"Esteban's car performed well. He told me that it seemed to even get stronger as the race went on." I wonder if she knows that fact about Esteban's car cuts to my core.

"We'll get it sorted out. Tell me, how's Esteban as a teammate? I don't know him well."

"He's young, he's talented, he's a good kid. You know this new crop of drivers. They're—"

"I don't, actually. They're what?" She waits for me to respond.

"They're all, I don't know. Good. They don't party, they're serious, kind of mercenary."

For the first time tonight, Lily laughs. Hard. Oh Christ, I missed that laugh, and it makes me grin. "What?"

"That's what everyone said about you when you first started."

I let out a snort. "Hell, no."

"Yeah, they did, when you were with your first team. Remember? They called you all business, no fun."

"I quickly disabused the press of that." I smirk, and her face falls. Now I feel bad for acting arrogantly, but I'm sure she knows that I worked out my feelings about our breakup in the beds of other women.

"You certainly did."

"What?" I lean in, curious to know why she's suddenly somber.

"Your reputation in the tabloids. It's virtually impossible to go anywhere on this planet without seeing your exploits."

"Don't believe everything you read. You should know that *Mausbär*." Maybe calling her by an old nickname will get us out of this conversation.

She rolls her eyes. "Please. I know you well enough to understand that a lot of it's true."

"What do you mean by that?" I demand.

She takes a deep breath, almost like she's steeling herself for what she's about to say. "Look, let's get it all out on the table. This is awkward, us working together."

"Not for me. Not at all." I lie. Like a rug.

Her eyes narrow, obviously not believing me. "You don't have any problem working for me after we . . . since we . . ."

"After we, what, Lily?" I want her to say it. I need her to acknowledge what happened between us, since we'd been too immature to have a detailed conversation about our breakup back then.

"Since we slept together," she hisses.

I pause to clear my throat. That's what she thinks? It was only sex between us? Because I remember something quite different. I sit up a little straighter. "Yes, that. And no, I'm an adult. I can work with you despite our past. The question is, can you?"

"Obviously," she snaps, pushing her plate away. "Listen, I'm sorry. It's been a long and emotional day, and I apologize for bringing any of this up. I'm going upstairs to call the hospital and crash. I appreciate you ordering food for me, I was famished. And, like I said, we'll get to the bottom of what happened with the car, I promise."

She slides out of her seat and parts the cabana curtain.

"Lily—" I jump up to follow her. "Wait, I'll walk with you."

"You don't have to." She gives a little dismissive shake of her head, but I'm not going to let her stroll out of here alone. Not when there might be reporters, zealous fans, or worse. You never know.

By the time she's finished her sentence, I'm already dropping a couple hundred dollars on the table and standing up. "C'mon."

The voices in the poolside lounge melt into an indistinct murmur. Everyone is watching us. I'm obviously the most recognized driver in the sport, and by now, word about Lily's father has probably spread over the news and racing blogs.

Out of sheer protective instinct, I put my hand on the small of her back as we walk past the pool, past the DJ, past the palm trees. Her gaze slides to me for a millisecond, but she doesn't pull away or say anything. She knows not to make a scene, as do I.

The fronds of the palm trees sway in the slight breeze, a perfect scene for a perfect Miami evening. The pale blue lights from the pool reflect off the tiles, and quiet laughter spills from the cabanas. I try and focus on all those things instead of how warm her back is under my hand. How the only thing separating my hand from her bare skin is a thin piece of fabric.

I open the door for her and we walk into the lobby, where we're ambushed by three men with cameras. "How's your father, Lily?" a reporter shouts.

Oh fuck.

We keep moving, toward the elevator. I know not to even look into the paparazzi's eyes, but Lily shoots them a glare as they shout questions.

"Dammit, I should've gone to my condo," she mutters to me.

"There's still time. I can call you a car."

She shakes her head and tries to march to the elevator, but the reporters are relentless.

"Ms. Onassis, can you talk about your father? How's he doing?" A skinny guy shoves a phone in her face.

"Is it true that you're going to be in charge of the team now?" Multiple flashes from a camera ignite, almost blinding me.

"Are you trying to make a statement about women in Formula World?"

She mutters to me, "How did they get in here, anyway? Doesn't this hotel have security?"

"Good question," I shoot back. Usually hotels keep the press away from us. Then again, I wouldn't put it past someone on a competing team who was here having cocktails spotting us and sneaking in a reporter or two to try to make Team Onassis look bad. Shenanigans like that happen all the time.

Another reporter steps into my path. "Will you tweet about every incident of sexual harassment that you encounter?"

Lily's eyes turn hard and glassy. I need to get her out of this situation immediately, because she hates this. I do as well, but media attention always seemed to wound her. It was one of the reasons she gave when she broke up with me. That she didn't want to live under a microscope.

"What's it like having your former lover as your employee?"

At that question, she turns and glares. I haven't been around Lily much in the past seven years, but I know her well enough to understand when she's had enough.

"No comment," she says in a loud, clipped tone.

The press goes wild, snapping photos and shouting even more questions. I wrap my hand around her upper arm and tug her toward the elevators. By now, hotel security has materialized, attempting to get between us and the reporters.

This only results in a crush of bodies, as these things often do. I wrap my arm around Lily and fold her into my body as we make our way through the throng. One of the security guards presses the button for the elevator and another clears the way as the doors slide open. We hustle in.

"Penthouse," she says in a curt tone, and I jab the button. It's the same floor that I'm on, where all the suites are located.

The press gets a real treat for a few seconds before the door closes. Lily swears under her breath and as I turn my head I get a whiff of her vanilla-scented shampoo.

"It's okay," I murmur. "Stay calm."

My arm's around Lily's shoulders, and she's tight and intimate next to my body. I won't lie; it feels incredible to have her nearby.

She feels right, in a way no other woman has.

"You know I hate it when people tell me to stay calm." Her voice is the vocal equivalent of the word *sneer*.

The minute the doors slide shut she wriggles out of my embrace and slumps against the elevator wall, pressing her palm to her forehead.

"Holy hell, I'd forgotten what that was like. It's one of the reasons I've tried to stay away all these years," she says with a sigh. "I don't know how you've handled it for so long."

I can only guess the other reasons. "I'm sorry. We should've anticipated that. The news of your father and you is going to make racing headlines for weeks."

She squints. "Don't you have bodyguards these days?"

"Normally, I do, but I gave them the night off. Thought I could handle eating dinner in the hotel with you then go to my room. Apparently not."

The elevator stops and the doors slide open. She bursts out, not waiting for me, and I walk fast to keep up with her.

"We should look into a security detail for you," I say as we stop at a door at the far end of the hall.

She's holding her key card in midair, her face drawn and pale. The encounter with the paps really shook her. It's something I take for granted, but it's only at times like this that I realize how utterly absurd and nerve rattling it really is.

"Yeah. It's one of the many things on my to-do list." Her voice quakes a little.

It's only then that I realize her hands are shaking, almost too much to insert the key card. I gently take the card from her and insert it into the slot, pushing the door open. More than anything, I want to wrap my arms around her and tell her it's all going to be okay.

But I know that's exactly what she doesn't want, and what would ruin me. She dislikes hugs, and even more than that, hates when people question her competence. If I try to calm her down she'll assume I don't have confidence that she can handle this situation—or run the team.

And truthfully, she'd be right. I'm not sure she's capable of either. Not because she's not smart enough or competent enough. It's because

Formula World is largely an old boys club, and the pressure from the media is relentless.

Her hazel eyes flash to me and she steps inside. "Okay, we'll talk more about the engine in a day or two. Let me send some emails. I need to sort through things in here. This was my father's room, and his assistant is supposed to have sent me a bunch of information that I need to read through tonight. I have a mountain of stuff to look into, and hopefully by tomorrow I'll be up to speed."

She's rambling, like she always does when she's nervous. God, if I could only fix all this for her. But I can't. Not now, and maybe not ever. I can't get emotionally involved with her again, because it might break me. I don't trust her fully after what happened between us. Don't trust her with my heart.

After giving her back the key, I run my fingers through my hair and glance down the hall, hoping that the hotel won't let any press up here. "Listen, this news about you and your dad is going to hit the papers and be wild this week. Maybe for a couple of weeks. You haven't been around the sport, so you don't know how bad it's gotten with paparazzi and bloggers and amateur videographers. And don't even get me started with the TikTok creators."

"I'll deal with it. I can handle anything. It can't be worse than what I experienced at my last job." Her jaw is set in a rigid line.

"If you need any help, I'm always here. Tonight, I'm right down the hall. You can call or knock for anything. You know that, right?"

She shoots me an appreciative little smile. "Thanks."

By now I'm filling the entire doorway, resting my forearm against the frame. "And maybe at some point we should discuss us."

"Max, absolutely not. I'm in no shape for that tonight, or tomorrow, or ever. What happened between us is in the past. We were kids. Let's leave it at that. We've got some serious adult shit going on here and I've got a team to run. Your job is to win. That's all. Win for the team. For my father."

Our eyes meet, and I swear, the temperature in the air notches up about ten degrees. The desire to take her in my arms, the desire to kiss her, is too powerful. I wish I could tell her that all these years, I've won races for her.

A memory of the first time I saw her flashes in my brain. It was at a club. Hours after we met, we kissed and kissed in a hallway, risking everything. When she looked at me, it was as if she could read my mind and see what I was thinking. We had so much in common. I'd like to know if we still do, and there's only one way to find out.

"Lily," I whisper.

We're only about a foot apart, and it would be easy for me to step forward and claim her mouth. Like I used to. But this is such a delicate, messed up situation that I don't dare.

If she wants me, she can kiss me. Fuck, I hope she kisses me, trust be damned.

"Max." My name on her lips makes my heart soften like it hasn't in years. I used to love when she whispered it in my ear when we were in bed together. It made me feel virile and invincible.

The tension between us crackles and sparks. The moment I've wanted for so long is finally here. I lick my lips, anticipating the taste of her.

Everything about Lily's appearance is different from the last time I saw her. Her hair is darker and shorter, her eyes are red and tired, her clothes are new and trendy. And then there's the sadness in her eyes, which I've never seen before. But the one thing that hasn't changed is how fucking gorgeous she is to me.

The downcast look on Lily's face makes me want to fix everything for her, Make it all okay. Her expression is all because of her father, and the ensuing crush of media. Her jaw still hasn't unclenched. Her hands are at her sides, balled into fists.

A kiss would relax her. I lean in a few inches, ready, waiting for her to make the next move. Normally my swagger with women is undisputable, but Lily always did—and still does—make me feel like a bumbling teenager.

"Good night, Max." She slowly closes the door, and I have to step away to avoid getting smacked in the face. *Shit*. She shut me down. I can't blame her, not after the day she's had. But it reopens an old wound, one that's barely healed.

CHAPTER EIGHT

LILY

"I can do this." As I speak aloud, I clutch a string of *komboloi*, or Greek worry beads. Papa bought the strand for me years ago when I was having a difficult time with exams in college, a little trinket he'd picked up during a trip.

Over the years, I'd nearly loved them to death, the azure blue of the beads shiny and familiar in my fingers.

"I am stronger than I think."

I take a deep breath and stare into my hazel eyes in the mirror. The dark circles underneath are barely hidden by the tube of concealer I found in my purse. I tuck the beads into my purse and swipe on some lip balm. *Gah*. I look haggard.

"I am worthy just as I am."

I release the breath into a long sigh as my phone lets out a shrill ring in the other room. Back when I worked at the video game development company, I'd said these mantras to myself every morning before I went into the office, in hopes they'd change something, anything, about the terrible working conditions and the harassment that I and other women were constantly subjected to.

They hadn't, but I'd continued to repeat my mantras until the day I was fired. Since then, I'd gotten out of the habit, assuming they were merely rubbish. Now that I'm faced with getting my father back to health and running his Formula World team, I need all the help I can get. So it's mantras and worry beads every morning from here on in.

I can do this.

In the living room portion of the palatial suite, I scoop up my cell. It rings while it's in my hand. Since five this morning the phone's been blowing up with texts, calls, and emails. Almost all are from reporters wanting to know what's going on with my father, with me, the team.

It's the part of this whole situation that I want to hide from but can't. Eventually I'll have to give a news conference, but I'd rather do it after talking with Papa and his doctor this morning. Knowing his prognosis will give me the strength to tackle everything else. I'll also need to get the team's PR department on board. Dammit, I probably should've done that last night.

Everything happened so quickly, though. Even now, it feels like a long, bad nightmare.

This call is different, though, because I know the number and the person on the other end. I answer after the fourth ring.

"Anh," I cry.

"Sweetie, are you okay? I'm so sorry, I was on an all-night flight. How is Adrian?"

The lilting accent of my longtime friend is a balm to my ears. I'd met Anh de Havilland when I was an intern for Papa's team and she was a grid girl, holding umbrellas over drivers and stunning the world with her Vietnamese-French beauty. Now she's in charge of hiring the grid girls—they're both men and women now, and called promotional models—for all the races, employed by the company that owns the rights to Formula World.

"He's okay. I'm going to visit him. Where are you? I was going to come find you yesterday, but time got away from me."

"*Mais oui.* I was with Bryce in Italy, but now I'm in Austin."

Bryce is her longtime boyfriend, a top motocross racer from Oklahoma. He's the American boy next door, complete with a cowboy hat, and he and Anh make a dazzling, if not startlingly different, couple. "I had to fly here early because two models are out and I need replacements. I have a long day of tryouts and interviews. Are you coming? I heard the news that you're in charge of your father's team."

"Yeah, I'm flying out today after I visit the hospital. Will you be around for drinks tonight? Coffee? I know you're busy." Unlike me, Anh is an extreme extrovert. She's always got a packed schedule, which is one reason why we've drifted apart since I left Formula World.

But she's the kind of lifelong friend that you can see after many years and it's like no time at all has passed.

"I can't wait to see you." I sigh. "I've got a lot to tell you."

"I'm sure you do." Her words are pregnant with meaning, probably because she's one of the only people on this planet who knows the actual, full history of me and Max, not just the rumors online and in the paddocks. "Text me immediately when you get to Austin."

"Will do. Can't wait to see you, it's been too long."

She bids me good-bye in French, and I hang up.

There's a knock at the door, and I look up, alarmed. My god, I've been up for an hour and it's been nonstop.

It's probably Adam or the bellhop coming to collect everything, including my father's luggage. Staying in this suite was a terrible idea, and not only because of last night's paparazzi swarm. The bed was too hard, and the pillow was oddly large. I should've gone home. That way I could've binged on cookies and made my favorite coffee.

Instead, I'm running to see who is pounding at the door. "Who is it?" I yell.

"Lily, honey?" comes a woman's voice. "Yooo-hooo."

When I fling it open, I find my mother, looking characteristically gorgeous. Effortless. Her style is best described as coastal grandma, with flowy linens, soft cottons, chunky jewelry, and a vaguely bohemian vibe. She's in a cream-colored ivory jumpsuit with a turquoise stone the size of a golf ball around her neck. In her polished hands is a cup of coffee. She doesn't say anything or hug me as she sweeps inside.

"Mumsy. Good morning." There's a touch of sarcasm in my voice because my mother is a wild card. I never know what she's going to do or where she's going to show up. Today it's my hotel suite. Tomorrow, who knows. For all of her faults, I love her with all of my soul. Still, she can be annoying.

"Hello, dearie. Your hair looks so much better that shade of brunet, you know. Vibrant. Like polished mahogany."

"I haven't washed it for two days."

She stops to appraise me up and down. It's as if it's been three minutes, and not three weeks, since we last saw each other.

"Hmph," she finally says.

I extend my hand. "Thanks for the coffee."

"That's not for you." She takes a sip and I let out an exasperated groan.

"Come on," I whine.

"Fine. But you could've ordered room service."

If I'd done that, I'd have risked more paparazzi. She hands it to me. "Ew. What is this?"

"It's my chaga mushroom coffee. Can you believe they sell it in the lobby here? How progressive."

I hand it back, only slightly disgusted, because Mum's always trying something new. "You could've called. Texted. Let me know that you were showing up. I was about to leave to see Papa and then I have to get to Texas."

She waves a hand dismissively. "I was only in North Carolina. It was no trouble to cut my yoga retreat short and hop a quick flight here."

"How did you know where I was?"

She lifts a shoulder into a shrug. "I knew your father was staying in this hotel, and Adam told me you'd spent the night here. I tried calling but you didn't pick up."

"How did you know Papa was staying at this particular hotel?"

Mumsy yawns. "I visited him earlier in the week. He called and was lonely. So I spent the night."

She peers into the bedroom. "I'm sure housekeeping changed the sheets."

I don't hold back a grimace when I see her coy little smile. Their relationship is . . . odd. Has been my entire life, which is probably why I've been reticent to get too deeply involved with any man. Emulating my parents' eccentric, weirdly open marriage isn't what I want out of life. I know that Mum had an affair or two, and Papa probably has too. Some parents are secretive. Mine are anything but. They also bicker a lot. But somehow they end up coming back together after every speed bump, and often act like newlyweds. It's chaotic and I can't imagine being in a marriage like that. My father's obsessive involvement with racing doesn't help the situation either.

"I'll come with to see your father this morning. In fact, I was thinking I could stay here in Miami and care for him at your place. It will be much more homey than a rental. I've already talked on the phone with Adam at length, and we've worked out the details."

Now I'm gaping at her in open-mouthed horror. Mum and Papa have lived apart off and on for a while, claiming they love each other but have a hard time living under the same roof. Yet they do things like hookup in hotel rooms, apparently.

"Do you think that's such a great plan?"

Mumsy looks at me as if I've sprouted a third arm as she sits on a brocade loveseat. "Lily, he is my husband. He needs me to care for him. Who else would do that job?"

"Whatever you say," I mutter, leaning against the door. I'm wondering if Mum will stress him out even more, but I don't say that aloud.

"I also came because of you. Your texts last night gave off a very"—she waggles her fingers in my direction—"unsettled vibe."

"Naturally I was unsettled." I snort. "I'm still unsettled. Papa had a major coronary event and he's asked me to take over the team. It *is* deeply unsettling."

"And that's why I'm here. Someone needs to care for Adrian while you run the team. What?" Mumsy blinks her giant blue eyes, which are framed with fluffy fake lashes. "Don't make that face."

She's one of those people who can somehow drink a cup of brown liquid while wearing light-colored clothing and not spill a drop. Unlike me, who has a fresh blob of green toothpaste on my dress. Which I wore yesterday.

Should've gone home last night. Should've never had dinner with Max. Maybe if I'd listened to my instincts, I could've slept in my own bed and not tossed and turned last night, thinking about Papa—and Max. I also spent a long hour or two beating myself up about how I snapped at the photographers too. Can't wait to see that play out on Page Six in the *New York Post*.

Ugh, Max. A memory of his intense gaze staring into my soul last night comes to mind, and a pleasurable shiver goes through me. I clear my throat nervously.

"I'm worried about Papa. And I don't know if I'm the best person for the team."

"Oh, *pfft*. How hard can it be? The guys know what to do. You need to show up at some races, give some interviews, stand around with headphones on, and stare at monitors. You're overqualified, in my opinion." Mum's always been dismissive of the sport, probably because it was the one thing that robbed Papa's attention from her.

I don't respond because I'm absorbed in my thoughts. It hits me anew that I almost kissed Max last night in my discombobulated, emotional state.

"Lily? What is it? Why do you look like someone took away your Christmas? Don't worry about your father. He's going to be fine. We'll talk with the doctor. And don't start with the imposter syndrome about running the team. You know that half those male fools on the team would gladly trade places with you, and they don't have the experience or knowledge you do."

"Yeah," I mutter.

"Then what's the problem . . . oh. Oh. I know what your issue is." Mum's concerned expression morphs into a smirk.

I give her a side-eye. "I have no issue. Let's get to the hospital."

"Max Becker."

It's difficult not to react, but I manage. "This has nothing to do with Max."

"You're fibbing. You're worried about working with him."

Mum was the only other person besides Anh I'd told about Max seven years ago. Of course, Mum had heard the rumors, but only she and Anh knew the truth of how I felt. She swore she wouldn't tell Papa the gory details, because he was already angry enough at the little he did know. To my knowledge, she never said a word. She knows everything, from how we started to why we broke up. And since we're close, almost more like sisters than mother and daughter, she can read me like a book.

"Mum." My voice comes out in a strangled groan. "We had dinner last night. It was torture. Tor. Ture."

She clicks her tongue against the roof of her mouth. "That's not going to be simple. The team will be, but Max won't."

"No. It's not easy. Especially since he's being nice and kind and I don't know. Decent. Plus, he's still really hot." I sniffle a little for emphasis. "Last night we had dinner and were ambushed by photographers in the lobby. I almost melted down. I can only imagine what's in the tabloids today."

"Oh, I've already seen. Basically a lot of speculation about you and Max."

"What? You saw that? Why didn't you tell me? What did the papers say? I couldn't even look online this morning."

"Yeah, it's the usual. There's also some gossip about your father being on death's door. And you allegedly 'lashed out.'"

"*Pfft*. There's no allegedly. I did lash out. You know how I hate those sudden press scrums."

"This is one of those situations where you're going to have to put your feelings aside, Lily. Block out all the noise and static and focus on being your incredible self."

I stare at her with one squinted eye. She seems to think that an uplifting Instagram meme sentiment will somehow save me from the emotional hell I'm stepping into.

"I seem to always put my feelings aside. That's the trouble. I'm finding it harder and harder to do."

"Such is the way of life for women in our world."

"Well, not you," I say, almost in an accusing tone.

"Not me, not now. Now that I'm sixty, I have, as the kids say, zero fucks to give. That's why I started my late-in-life career as an influencer. I stopped caring about what other people think. But trust me, when I was your age, I shoved all those emotions down. For my job, then for your father, and for you."

I sense that Mum's ramping up for a philosophical lecture, which is the last thing I need this morning. Anyway, I know all this about her and my father. Which is probably one of the top reasons why I was reluctant to build a life with Max—because racing would always get in the way. "Let's table this discussion until we can do it over drinks. We've got to get to the hospital."

"Okay, okay. But I want you to calm down and breathe. Center yourself." She shuts her eyes and pinches her thumb and forefinger together.

"Mum, I'll breathe later. Chop chop."

She opens her eyes and shoots me a reproachful glance. We both stand and I grab what little stuff I have and shove it in my oversized purse.

"Adam will come get Papa's stuff. Don't worry," Mum says.

She opens the door as I'm checking my face in the mirror. On a good day, I look cute but plain. Today I look basic and exhausted.

"Well, hello there," she says in an exaggerated, throaty tone.

What now?

I whirl around to find Max standing in the doorway. I hadn't heard him knock.

"What are you doing here?" I demand.

His hands are stuffed in his pockets, like they were when we said good-bye last night. His face is pinched with worry. Standing a respectful distance behind him are two beefy-looking guys who are obviously his bodyguards.

"I thought I'd come by and see how your dad's doing. Have you talked to him?" He glances from my mother to me. Our eyes lock for a moment, and once again my face flushes hot in his presence. This has got to stop.

Mum clears her throat and turns back to Max.

"We're on our way to see him," she trills. "Why don't you join us?"

I squeeze Mum's elbow, propelling her out the door and past Max, who smells freshly showered and yummy. He's wearing jeans and a Team Onassis polo shirt that shows off his taut, muscular chest.

"I'm sure Max has better things to do, Mumsy."

"No, I'd like see Adrian." Max's tone is even, so emotionless it's disarming.

"And I'm sure he'd love to see you too," Mum says firmly.

What I want isn't a priority here, and I can't argue with Mum's logic. Max is my father's star driver, and I'm sure he would appreciate a visit from him.

"I've got a car downstairs." Mum pulls away from me and threads her arm through Max's. "Let's go."

I bite back a sigh and follow them out of the hotel. One of the bodyguards leads the way, while the other follows behind our little group. Max is a perfect gentleman, gallantly escorting Mum through the lobby door like they're going to a ball. People stop to stare at them and take photos. I skulk behind, hoping I'm hidden behind the beefy bodyguard.

Outside the hotel there's a small gaggle of press clustered near a bench across the street. Like he did last night, Max puts a protective hand on the small of my back as we all speed up toward Mum's car as the paparazzi barrel toward us, shouting questions. My gut tightens at the sight of the cameras but today, I control myself.

I barely have time to wonder why Max's touch sends little electric sparks through my body because we all hurriedly slide into Mum's chauffeured car, barely managing to avoid the reporters. It's a Mercedes, with a massive backseat. Somehow I'm in the middle, mashed between Mum and Max.

One of his bodyguards is in the passenger seat, while the other is apparently following behind in an SUV. This is how it's going to be for the next several weeks, months even, if I take over the team.

As we drive off, a photographer shoves his camera almost against the tinted window of the car, in hopes of getting a photo of me and Max.

"They never stop, do they?" Mum asks in a cheery tone. She's always been amused by the media attention that came with Papa owning a team. Now with her new career, she kind of thrives on that spotlight. Mercifully, she knows how uncomfortable I am with being in the public eye, so she doesn't encourage the spotlight when we're together.

Already I feel suffocated. We ride in silence for several long, awkward minutes.

I glance at Mum and she's fiddling with her phone. "Did I tell you that Ralph Lauren asked me to do a campaign on Instagram? They want vibrant older ladies." Her laugh is like the audio equivalent of champagne, bubbly and light.

"Mmm, no, you didn't," I grunt. How I ended up her daughter is beyond me. Mum's ethereal and positive and I'm plain and grumpy.

My eyes slide to my right and Max's leg. His hand is resting on his thigh, and I study it for a second. This only serves to remind me of how he used to run those exact fingers over my body, through my hair, across my lips . . .

I screw my eyes shut. This cannot be happening. I can't have lusty thoughts about Max. I'm his boss. Ugh, that even feels weird to think. And even if I wasn't, I'd only be making a fool of myself. Max almost certainly doesn't feel like he used to about me.

"Max, how are your parents, anyway? Are they still in Germany? Such lovely people. And your brother? How is he?" Mum turns and peers around me.

"They're doing well, thank you for asking, Mrs. Onassis. They're still in Tübingen. I'll tell them you say hello."

God, his manners are impeccable.

"I wondered whether to take a couple of days to visit them between races, before Austin, but I decided not to because of the situation with Adrian. They're planning on being at a few of the races in Europe. They'd wanted to come over for the American races, but my brother had a health issue so they're home now while he recovers."

"What happened to Hans?" I blurt, suddenly alarmed. Six years younger than Max, his brother was born with Down syndrome.

"He's fine. He had a minor stomach issue but it was corrected with surgery. We flew him to a great hospital in Berlin and he was out within a week. He's almost fully recovered, but my parents didn't want to stress him out by bringing him to America."

Max's words are smooth and collected, but I see a flicker of anguish in his blue eyes.

"Were you able to be with him in the hospital?"

Max shakes his head. "I was in Sochi at the time."

Hans is probably Max's favorite person on the planet, aside from Lucas, and I know it must have affected him deeply to have to race while his brother was undergoing surgery. But that's the way of Formula World—it's not like a driver can take a sick day, because every missed race means lost opportunities for points. For a driver to miss a race, it must be a life and death situation. And even then, most drivers choose to race; Papa once had a driver whose mother died on a Saturday and he raced the next day. And won.

"I'm sorry."

"Hans is tough. He made it through and is doing well."

"That's good to hear. Where's Lucas?" The two are inseparable during the race season, have been for Max's entire career. It was one of the things I adored about Max, that he could have a close friendship with a man without shame or apologies.

"He went home to see his wife in New York for the night. He's meeting me in Austin later tomorrow."

I open my mouth, stunned. "I hadn't realized he'd gotten married."

"They eloped only a few months ago at a small ceremony in Brazil. She's a model."

Lucas always had a taste for stunning women. I imagine that his model wife has model friends, and they were also at the wedding, thrilled to flirt with a famous racing star.

"It was a gorgeous private ceremony on the beach," he murmurs, and turns his head to look out the window at the Miami traffic. I focus again on his hand, which is still resting on his thigh but is now curled into a fist. There's a part of me that wants to take his hand, unfurl his fingers, and press my palm against his. Squeeze his hand and tell him it's all going to be okay—and hear it back from him.

That's what we would've done seven years ago, in private. But a lot has changed since then. Everything has, really.

And that's the crux of the problem facing me right now: that by virtue of being the team owner I'm confronted every minute with the fact that I broke up with Max. It was possibly the worst decision I've ever made, and now I need to relive it over and over.

CHAPTER NINE

MAX

"Thank goodness there's no media in here. They'd never fit," I say in a semi-joking tone as the seven of us pack into a too-small elevator at the hospital. It's me, Lily, Mrs. Onassis, a doctor, a nurse, and two of my bodyguards. Everyone but Lily laughs at my attempt at hospital humor.

This is a place where people are too focused on the immediate, the crucial, the tragic, to recognize us, and the hospital's diligent about keeping reporters away. The doctor mentions that it's not protocol to let so many people into an ICU room, but they're making an exception for us because of who we are.

The familiar and omnipresent smell of antiseptic soap permeates everything. It reminds me of being a teen and visiting Hans in the hospital when he was small. Hospital scents have always made me feel anxious and uneasy. My stomach tightens as those old fears surface, but then I remember that everything's okay for the moment. That Hans is safe and that Adrian is getting the best care.

Being a Formula World driver is an exercise in zen. It's all about living in the moment. That's a simple philosophy on the track, far harder in real life. Everything is okay, for now.

Lily's eyes meet mine and she shoots me a little smile, one I can't interpret.

I used to know exactly what she was thinking, how she was feeling. I've never experienced that with any other woman, and now that I can't with her, it's frustrating. A little disappointing too. I also can't shake my anger toward her. With the desire that swirls in my body, it's an uncomfortable mix.

We troop down the hall to Adrian's room in silence. The doctor opens the door. Adrian's in a private room in a private wing, and the decor here is more like a hotel than a hospital. But the hospital smell remains.

"Mr. Onassis, you have some visitors," the doctor announces cheerfully.

"Papa!" Lily cries, rushing into the room first. "You look so much better today. Your color's almost back."

She goes to his bedside and kisses his cheek. Her father chuckles, but instead of his usual robust laugh, it's a weary sound. It's a sound that speaks of pain and the newfound knowledge that he's mortal—something I'm not sure the gregarious Adrian ever considered before this week. I stand back with my bodyguards, and watch as Lily and Mrs. Onassis fawn over Adrian. Lily strokes her father's brow and Mrs. Onassis brings him a cup of water.

"Papa, look who wanted to come see you. I hope that's okay." Lily rubs her father's arm and glances at me.

Adrian's eyes crinkle at the corners as he shifts in my direction. To the side of his bed, monitors beep softly.

"Hello, sir." I smile at him and move toward Lily. She stands to allow me to move closer, and in the process, she squeezes my upper arm. I get a jolt of adrenaline from her touch and sit at the edge of the bed. Adrian's eyes notice Lily's touch. Nothing gets past him, and suddenly I'm a rookie driver again, sneaking around behind the powerful man's back.

I clear my throat. "How are you feeling?"

Adrian smiles. "A little rough around the edges, but I'm going to be back in action soon. My wife's here and she's going to whip me into shape."

He winks, which makes me laugh. Adrian is truly one of the men I admire most in Formula World, and working for him is everything I thought it would be. I'm going to miss his presence on the track.

"I heard about the race. Finally got an orderly to tell me the results. They wouldn't even let me watch the damn recaps on television." Adrian shakes his head.

"They weren't supposed to tell you about the race," Lily says, scowling.

"Maybe it's best if you don't focus on that right now," I say. "We'll work out the issue with the engine."

"That's what the doc over there says, that I need to let it go, but it's difficult not to think about it while I'm lying here. What happened with the car?"

"You don't need to worry about the cars now." Lily's voice soars across the room.

Her father slowly lifts a hand and moves it through the air in a dismissive motion. "Tell me what happened."

I explain, making sure to keep any disappointment or anger out of my voice. "We're going to discuss it in a call today with the engineers, sir."

Adrian inhales deep, then coughs once. "You're still doing well in championship points. I'm confident we can come out on top this season. But what the hell happened to Esteban?"

"Father." Lily's voice is sharper, a warning. She turns to the doctor, her hair flying everywhere. "He shouldn't be stressing himself like this, should he?"

The doctor pulls her into the hall to say something in private. When she's gone, Adrian tugs on my arm again, demanding my attention.

"Now, Max, I need to tell you something. Come a little closer." Adrian coughs a bit but beckons me with a hand that's attached to a tube.

I scoot a little nearer so he doesn't have to strain.

Lily and the doctor are huddling together right outside the door. For a second I'm mesmerized at the sight, of her mere presence so close to me. I never thought I'd feel this again, it's been so long. Even the harsh florescent light can't hide the spark in her face. Her profile is refined and soft, like an antique cameo. Her lips, so pink and perfect, stick out in a slight pout, her nose scrunched, her eyebrows furrowed as she focuses on Dr. Patel.

The tabloids used to call her plain, unglamorous, even ugly. Nothing could be further from the truth. To me, she's the most beautiful woman I've ever seen, and now that her face is pinched with worry, I'm concerned about what all this stress will do to her.

She's wearing the same dress as yesterday, and it skims her figure without being too sexy. Probably to others it's a plain dress, but to me it's tight enough to make me remember the curves of her body. This drives me wild, to be honest. But right now she doesn't need my lust—she needs my friendship. If she doesn't want that, the least I can do is provide a listening ear and a shoulder to lean on. She deserves to feel valued and loved. I know this even though I'm still haunted by how we ended.

Adrian jolts my attention away from his daughter when he reaches for my arm and clasps it, and that's when I realize that he's more physically weak than I expected. He did have major heart surgery yesterday. Still, it's a shock because he's usually so filled with exuberance.

Perhaps he's not going to recover as quickly as we all anticipate, and this realization sends a pang of fear through me, in part because I want the man to live a long life, and I don't want Lily to hurt in any way.

I also don't want to be part of a team in chaos. This is a crucial year for me, racing-wise. I shove the thought back into the recesses of my brain as quickly as it comes, as selfish as it is.

"It was my decision to have Lily take over the team. Only for a couple of months until I recover. I need you to be professional, which means none of that nonsense, you hear me?"

"I understand, sir. She's an excellent choice." It's not like I can express my real feelings, that having her as my superior is disastrous for both my concentration and my heart. That working for someone I'm attracted to *and* angry at could erode my focus.

"You need to step up and be even more of a leader."

"In what way?"

"Some of the team might not want a woman at the top. You're the star. You have to set an example. Make sure everyone treats her with respect and follows her orders. She went through hell at that game company. You know I loathe those racing video games."

His gruff words make me grin. This is the Adrian Onassis I know: totally old school about racing. Although lots of us drivers use video games and simulators to practice, Adrian thinks drivers are too reliant on tech these days and don't spend enough time in actual race cars.

"Lily's a bit stubborn. Like her father. She might not want your help at first."

That's an understatement. "Okay," I hedge.

"She's going to need someone to bounce ideas off, and I want that person to be you. You're the senior driver, you've been with three other teams, and your instincts are impeccable. I want you two to work well together, you hear? No shenanigans, no controversy. You got it?"

His eyes narrow, and I shift in my seat. Busted.

My voice dips an octave. "Absolutely. I'll help her in any way I can."

What am I supposed to say? No, sir, I won't try to screw your daughter?

Lily walks back into the room, a model of efficiency with a fake, bright smile pasted on her face. Somehow she's procured a clipboard and a pen. "Okay, we need a family meeting with the doctor. Max, could you step into the hall for a few minutes? Mum and I need to discuss a few things in private."

I jump to my feet. "Sure, sure."

"Max can stay, he's like family," Adrian protests.

"Papa," Lily says, her tone a warning.

"See what I mean?" He looks at me. "Stubborn girl."

Lily tilts her head to the door.

"How about I go down to the Starbucks and get you some coffee? Anyone else want anything?" I offer.

Her mother chortles. "Good god, you've got him trained already, Lily."

"See? This is why she'll be excellent for the team," Adrian says.

"Mum. Papa. Please. We need to focus on Dr. Patel's plan." Lily's voice is sharp, and she scowls in my direction. "Coffee would be amazing. Thank you. Please ignore my parents."

I grin and walk out, humored by her words. If only Mr. and Mrs. Onassis knew what I'd be willing to do for their daughter—and if only she would let me.

CHAPTER TEN

LILY

The meeting with Dr. Patel goes better than expected. Because Papa's surgery was a resounding success everyone at the hospital agrees that he should be discharged in about a week. He'll need to rest for at least four to six weeks, and might be cleared to return to the race circuit at that point.

"We'll have to evaluate, though. You'll need physical therapy," says the doctor.

"I'll make sure he follows orders," Mum chimes in, patting Papa's foot. In response, he playfully scowls.

I do the math in my mind. Six weeks means four races, almost back-to-back: Austin, Las Vegas, and Montreal, one weekend after another. Then there's a weeklong break and Mexico City. After that is Brazil. I know the schedule by heart. That's not too bad, I guess.

No major global travel to contend with. I inhale and catch a whiff of Max's cologne that still hangs in the air.

No, the schedule is terrible. Superbad.

Dr. Patel finishes talking and says he'll give us some time alone. When he leaves, it's the three of us: me, Mum, and Papa. I wish I'd given in to my father and allowed Max to stay. His presence would be oddly comforting, since I anticipate this conversation to be tense. My father can be as unyielding as a boulder.

Mum and I sit on the bed, on either side of Papa.

"We have a ton of logistics to work out," I say brightly. "Like where you're both going to stay while he recovers, whether you're going to New York—"

"We're staying at your condo when he gets out of here, then we'll decide on New York," Mum says firmly. "You have to get to Austin, dear."

Papa nods in agreement. As if they're both on the same page, which is unusual. His stubbornness and Mumsy's lack of filter has caused some pretty spicy arguments over the years. Usually this happens during times of tension, like when Papa's team is losing, or when Mum went through perimenopause.

"Are you sure you don't want me to stick around for a few days?" I ask.

"No," they say in tandem.

"Gosh, way to make your only child feel wanted."

"Kamari mou, you know we'd rather have you here with us. But the team takes priority."

"Always the team," Mum groans.

"Not now, Eileen." Papa warns her.

"Enough, you two. No arguing. Please don't antagonize him, Mum. We need to go over what Dr. Patel said."

"Yes, don't antagonize me, Eileen." Papa reaches for Mum's nose in a playful gesture, and she kisses his hand.

"Don't egg her on." I warn him. "Fine. I'll go to Austin today."

I spend the next three minutes talking about Dr. Patel's plan, and my father raises a finger. "Yeah?" I ask.

"You and Max go on our jet together," Papa says.

Mum winks, and I shoot her a simpering glare. Had either of them heard anything I said about the medical plan? "Fine. We're going to have to come up with a statement to the press, you know. They've been begging for details for hours. I haven't even looked at what's in the papers, I'm sure all sorts of lies have already made it into print."

"You should've already met with Tanya. Where's the phone? Let's call her." Papa tries to twist to his bedside table with a grunt. Mum stops him.

"I'll call her from the car. You relax and focus on getting better. Mum, you're staying here?"

She waves me off and I stand. "Go, go. We'll be in constant contact. Find Max and get out of here. I've got this under control."

I'm not entirely convinced but bend down to kiss my father's forehead anyway. "Dr. Patel says you're out of the danger zone. But you need to take better care of yourself from here on in, okay?"

"Yes, dear. Keep me updated on everything, okay? Call me from Austin. Call me anytime."

"Rest is your only priority. That's an order, from the new team owner." I smooth the blanket that's bunched up near his hip. Papa's chuckling now.

When I look up Max is there holding a cup of coffee. Thank goodness; that mushroom "coffee" was not at all satisfying.

"Okay, we're leaving, Mumsy's staying here," I say to him.

He smiles, as if this is all the most normal thing in the world. And oddly, it kind of feels that way. Like Max is the one who should be at my side during a crisis. Like he's part of my family. I decide not to dwell too much on that feeling and wave good-bye to my parents.

Max hands me the coffee and bends down, giving my father and awkward hug. He then rounds the bed and smooches Mum on the cheek. She clamps him in a big hug, as Papa and I watch.

Max and I say our final good-byes and make our way out of the room and down the hall. His two bodyguards are outside, and they join us.

I immediately begin babbling nervously.

"Dr. Patel said that Papa's left ventricle was nearly entirely blocked . . ." I go on about my father's heart while we step into the elevator and all the way down the ten storys to the bottom floor. I tell Max details about the heart that would impress a surgeon, and all he does is listen soberly and make eye contact, as if I'm telling him the most fascinating details about Michael Schumacher or explaining how a new braking system works.

Max truly appears as though he's riveted by what I'm saying, and that makes my face flush with warmth. Having his undivided attention in this cramped elevator makes my stomach flutter. Max is being his usual self: unfailingly polite. An angel. He's not showing his other side, the devilish side, right now. But I know it exists. I've seen it up close, in bed, and I've read about his exploits over the years with women.

Must. Be. Careful.

The bodyguards flank us as we make our way to the hired car. Outside, the humid Miami air slaps us in the face, and Max winces. "I can never get used to this weather," he says softly. Is that a subtle jab at my new hometown?

I'm about to retort with something snarky about the dismal weather in Germany when we're ambushed, literally descended upon by a herd of reporters brandishing cameras and microphones. This again.

"Oh shit," I mutter.

There's no escaping them because we're standing on a sidewalk, with a busy street between us and the car. Clusters of people are stopped nearby and on the other side of the road, taking pictures and video of the unfolding scene. They probably came to see their sick loved ones, but we're now the main attraction. This is a moment for TikTok, Instagram, the world.

The reporters don't care that people are watching. They shout question after question at us. The noise is so loud I can barely hear anything, and blood whooshes in my ears, making me unsteady on my feet.

"The driver's pulling the vehicle around," one of the bodyguards says to Max.

His gaze rakes over the assembled press. It's obvious he's not thrilled with this situation, and neither am I. My heart rate is spiking, my palms are sweaty, and I suspect all the photos and videos will show me looking dazed, if not outright fugly, wearing the same clothes as yesterday.

We're barraged with questions, and at first Max and I both stay silent. After thirty seconds of total pandemonium, I snap.

"Okay, okay. If you all shut up, I'll give you a statement." I hold up my hand.

Max looks uncharacteristically startled. When we were together I never said anything to the media, and in fact went out of my way to avoid them by using disguises and fake names. There's none of that now, though. Not while I'm running a Formula World team with the universe's most popular driver on the roster. It's time to woman up.

"Stand back. Give us room." I'm trying to channel my inner crisis mode. It's so much easier when I'm doing this for someone else.

The reporters back off about six inches, and I scan their sweaty faces. Tanya would probably want me to read from a prepared state-ment, but there's no time for that so I must improvise. "My father had a heart attack at the track yesterday. He underwent surgery and is now recovering well. Because it was a major operation, he'll need to undergo physical therapy and requires some time away from the team. I'll be taking his place running Team Onassis, and will be heading to Austin this afternoon. I can take a couple of questions, but we've got to make this quick."

"Lily. Lily!" It's Gordon, the Sky News beat reporter who does the on-track interviews. He waves his pen in my face, which makes me want to grab it and snap it in two.

"Yes, Gordon?" I'm dipping into a well of patience that I never knew I had. The reporters step closer, and a claustrophobic panic wells inside of me. It goes along with the hugging thing—I despise strange people in my space.

"Why are you the one to take over the team? Why not Jack or one of the other team principals?"

It's a fair question. "My father trusts me. I grew up around Formula World and am intimately familiar with my father's wishes. The team is an excellent group of professionals and I'm there to help manage things and cheer them on until my father is back in top shape. And he will be back, so don't get any ideas that this is permanent. One more question."

I point to a woman whose voice is barely audible above the other reporters' shouts. "Yes, you. Where are you from?"

"Lyn Eckfeldt from *Autoweek*. Ms. Onassis, will your prior relationship with Max Becker pose any problems when you assume your father's duties as team owner? How does that square with your crusade at your former employer to root out sexual harassment?"

I should've known this question was coming. I lick my lips, hating myself for hesitating. What I want to do is snarl and say it's no one's business what happened between Max and me all those years ago. But that would fan the flames, so I smile.

As I'm about to answer, Max steps forward, but I gently touch his arm and speak. "Max and I are great friends, and he's simply a brilliant driver. I'm sure we'll work well together. Isn't that right, Max?"

He flashes a rare grin for the media. "Lily's experience in the corporate world and her knowledge of the sport means she's as qualified as anyone to run a Formula World team. I'm thrilled to be her driver, and she will do an excellent job. We only focus on the present, because the only thing that's important is winning in Austin, and Montreal, and the championship."

"The car's here," one of the bodyguards shouts. He holds his beefy arms in a *T* so Max and I can walk through the swarm of media. They shout questions as we hustle into the waiting car, and I only exhale when we're well away from the hospital and on the road.

I stare out the window, wondering what the hell I've gotten myself into. My plan for the summer was to get my head on straight. Look for a new job. Try to regain my equilibrium and dignity after being fired.

"You did great," Max says in a voice reserved for upset children and feral kittens.

I turn to look at him. His eyes are soft, and I swear they're something resembling tender. "Thanks. It doesn't get any easier, dealing with them."

"I was pretty impressed. You'd have never acted that calmly seven years ago."

"I've learned a lot." My statement hangs in the air as we stare at each other. Learned how to tamp down my emotions, learned to ignore my instincts and operate on autopilot.

The driver's voice interrupts our conversation but not our eye contact. "Ms. Onassis, are we going straight to the executive airport?"

"I'd like to stop at my condo downtown. Thank you." I give the address without tearing my eyes away from Max's. "I appreciate you answering that question for the media back there, the one about us."

"No need to thank me."

We smile at each other, and the temperature in the limo rises about fifty degrees. I should stop staring into Max's eyes. Should stop remembering what it was like to kiss him. Shouldn't recall how it felt when he held me. But I can't, and it's making all the dopamine and serotonin in my brain ping around. I almost feel high, and yeah, a little happy under these messed-up circumstances.

"Your father asked me to help you, and that's what I was doing. Simple as that."

He breaks our eye contact and turns to look out his window. That's when my heart fractures a bit. He wasn't doing that out of kindness, wasn't coming to my rescue with the press out of anything but obligation.

All of that happiness evaporates, and I turn away, biting my lip in to keep from crying in front of Max.

CHAPTER ELEVEN

MAX

We pull into the circular driveway of a massive condo building in Miami's downtown. It's all sleek glass and concrete.

"This is where you live?" I don't mean to sound incredulous, but it seems so unlike Lily. I'd always taken her for a stand-alone home, something smaller and cozy, filled with books. This is cold and severe. Not terrible, and I'm sure it's luxurious, but different than I would've imagined.

"Yes. I'm renting for now." Her brow furrows. "You can stay here while I pack."

I stare at her. "In the car?"

"Yeah. Or go get lunch or something."

We lock gazes. There's so much pain in her eyes, all I want is to hold her. It's remarkable how all the tender feelings I had for her are back with a vengeance. I wish she'd invite me inside, because I'm dying to see her place.

"Okay," I say.

She lets out a sigh. "Or, if you want, come up and hang out in my living room. You can watch TV or whatever."

"That sounds great," I say quickly, hoping she doesn't change her mind.

The valet takes the keys and we troop into the lobby and the elevator, flanked by bodyguards. From the looks Lily is giving the two guys, I can tell she's uncomfortable about having strangers in her house.

She unlocks the door. "Sorry for the mess. I left in a hurry yesterday. I'll make this quick. I don't want to hold everyone up."

The colossal, gleaming windows with an ocean view gives the living room an airy sense of freedom. Tall potted plants are nestled in sleek pots, their deep-green leaves popping against the white walls like wide green wings. The living room is light and open, like the Miami breeze. "Wow. I didn't expect any of this."

"Any of what?" She tosses her purse on a tan leather sofa that's angled toward the windows. A fuzzy gold throw blanket is bunched in one corner of the couch.

I lift my shoulders. Considering I keep an apartment in Monaco—but didn't pick out any of the decor inside—and stay with my parents in Germany often, this place seems like a home for someone who has their shit together, which Lily obviously does.

"I don't remember you liking plants this much." She frowns, and I follow up with, "It's nice, really beautiful. Did you use a designer?"

"No. I did everything myself. I wanted it to look a certain way. Tropical, but warm. A lot of these condos can come off too sterile. I'm a plant person now, that's kind of my hobby. Anyway, make yourself at home, the kitchen's over there, the remote's on the table if you want to watch TV. I'm going to pack." She presses the heels of her hands to her forehead and mutters aloud. "How long am I going to be gone? How much should I bring?"

She wanders down a hall and I follow. "Well, there's Austin, then Las Vegas, and Montreal. I'd pack for six weeks."

I spy a couple of nearly empty bedrooms, with only modern beds and white linens. She stops outside of a closed door. "Why don't you hang out in the living room? And eat whatever you want since I'm not going to be here for a while. Dammit, I'll have to get someone in here to clean out the fridge. Maybe Mum can do it, though."

She's grumbling to herself as she opens, then closes, the bedroom door. Funny, in all the times we slept together, I never saw the bedroom of where she lived. Back then she'd just graduated from college and technically still lived with her parents. We were always traveling from race to race, and our time in bed was always in a hotel.

"Okay," I say to the closed door, wandering back down the hall. I wander around the vast living room for a while, checking out her art (it looks like graphic Mid-century stuff to me, abstract concepts that I don't understand but she probably does) and her books (a wide range of genres, heavy on the romance). The large bookcase is impressive, and that's one thing that obviously hasn't changed. She's always loved to read.

I spot something on the shelf and lean in. Wedged between two hardcover books is an insert, a tiny diorama of a library complete with bookshelves, lamps, and a small cat. I grin and bite my lip. I'd given this to her back when we were together. It's a handmade wooden nook that lights up, crafted by an artist in my German hometown. The fact that she still has it makes my heart slam against my chest.

It was her twenty-fifth birthday. I wanted to impress the hell out of her. I figured a gift like this would prove how well I knew her, how well I'd listened to her soul.

She'd loved it. Got teary when she saw it. Threw her arms around me and kissed me for what seemed like an entire, delicious hour. That night, I could see my lifetime unfolding. I'd become a champion in the sport, Lily would be my wife, and eventually we'd have kids and a beautiful life. A few weeks after her birthday she broke up with me, saying that we wanted different things out of life.

She didn't want Formula World, and I did.

And now here we are, back together again. And not in the way I thought we'd be by this time of life. This was supposed to be the baby-making stage, by my old estimation. I stare at the little diorama. It's a bitter reminder of a perfect life that I once wanted, one that slipped right through my hands.

The fact that she'd kept it all these years is like a punch to the gut. If I was that important to her, if she wanted a near-constant reminder of me on her bookshelf in her living room, why did she end it? Why didn't she stand up to her father and fight for us?

She never gave me an answer, and now it's too late—and too inappropriate to ask, under these circumstances.

"Max!"

Lily's voice soars through the condo. I wander into the hall in time to see her poke her face out of her bedroom door.

"There are cookies in the fridge. They'll go to waste if someone doesn't eat them."

"You don't have to tell me twice." I head into the kitchen, hoping to push all the old memories of us and the conflicted anger into the corners of my brain. Cookies might help.

I ate a huge breakfast this morning at the hotel, but I'm still starving. The day after a race I'm always a bit off, dehydrated and hungry. I peek in her fridge and see a plate of cookies wrapped in plastic. Grabbing those and the lone carton of milk, I make my way over to the sofa.

The cookies are incredible. I take a guzzle from the milk carton, chiding myself for not getting a glass. Where are my manners? I shove a second cookie into my mouth, wondering if I should get a glass. One more sip—

"Max? Do you think I'll need . . ."

Lily's standing there, staring at me. I swallow and wipe my mouth. "Sorry, I didn't find the glasses. I'm an animal for drinking out of the carton."

She snorts a little laugh. "Don't worry. It's going to be tossed anyway. I can see you haven't changed. Still starving the day after races?"

I pick up a third cookie. "*Ja*. Hey, who made these cookies? They're amazing."

"Me. I made them while watching the race yesterday."

"Really?" I say through a mouthful. When did she become such a good baker? Back when we were together I don't think she even knew how to boil water. I'm dying to ask her why she didn't go to the race yesterday, eager to ask her a thousand questions, but since my mouth is full of cookie and she's already probably disgusted by me, I keep chewing.

She screws up her pretty face. "You're such a . . . guy."

"Sorry, they're so good. Don't tell Lucas, he'll be pissed that I'm eating too much sugar. Can't believe you made these. You never used to bake—"

"I'm a different person, Max."

"I can see that." I swallow and wonder if I ever knew her at all.

"Listen. I've decided I'm going to pack light and buy anything I need while on the road. But what are the formal events in Austin like? Since that's a newer race, I haven't been. What did Papa go to last year? I don't remember him talking about anything."

"Umm." I lick my lips, wishing I'd grabbed a napkin. "Last year there was a thing involving cowboy boots and hats. So bring those if you have them."

She huffs off, muttering something about how she hates hats. If I recall correctly that pre-race party last year was the one where two American football cheerleaders wanted to have a threesome with me.

There was a time, post-Lily breakup, that I would've taken them up on it. But that was the old me that had gone off the rails in the wake of my breakup with Lily. I stopped being that guy a couple of years ago.

I was tired of being judged and tired of the people I was attracting. I've been a good boy for a while now and hope to keep it up. Older and wiser, I'd like to think.

I jam another cookie in my mouth and ponder if any of this is even going to matter. I'm not getting back together with Lily and she probably resents me for my playboy reputation. Pining over her isn't going to make her want me again.

If she wasn't the acting team owner, though. . . . I finish the rest of the cookie.

If Lily wasn't acting team owner, I'd definitely tell her everything I'm feeling right now. Maybe explain how important she was to the trajectory of my life. How I screwed up by not fighting harder for her.

But she shares blame, too, so maybe it's better if we don't get into all that right now. She already seems distressed enough by the idea of taking the place of her father. It's not going to be easy as a woman in charge of a racing team. She doesn't need me mucking things up for her and causing any further controversy or scandal. God knows I've done enough of that in my career.

As much as Lily brings out emotions in me that no other woman has, it's probably best if we keep this strictly professional.

CHAPTER TWELVE

LILY

When we board our flight to Austin I immediately claim a table, declaring the need to spread out in the back of the jet. Seeing Max sprawled on my sofa, looking cozy with a plate of cookies and a carton of milk, inspired dangerous thoughts in my mind.

Thoughts of lazy Sundays together drinking coffee and kissing each other breathless. Dirtier thoughts too.

He starts to take the seat across from me. Since it's a private jet, the seats are arranged facing forward and backward, around tables. That's something I always loved about him—that he seems to fit in anywhere with his rakish smile. He never seems awkward or ill at ease, whereas I'm a bundle of anxiety. I must stop lusting after him like this.

"What are you up to?" he asks casually.

"Swamped with work," I say, covering the table with my laptop, notebooks, pens, and almost the entire contents of my purse. I wave my hand over all my stuff, hoping he doesn't want to sit with me, because I don't need the distraction.

He surveys the table with a scowl, probably because he's an orderly kind of guy. I used to gently tease him about this, back when we were together, about him being a stereotypically orderly German.

"Orderly desk, orderly mind," he'd say, and glare at my mess. Exactly what he's doing now.

"Guess I'll leave you alone," he mutters. He's holding a little paper bag filled with my cookies. He insisted on bringing them with us. What a weirdo. As one of the richest athletes in the world, he could've stopped at any number of gourmet bakeries in Miami, but he wants those lumps of chocolate chunk cookies.

He turns and takes a seat closer to the cockpit, with his back to me. Thank god. A reprieve from his intense, sexy self. It's only now that I can exhale. We're the only two on my family's private jet because the rest of the team left for Austin already. I haven't been on this plane in a long time, preferring to fly business class when I was with the game company.

Something about private air travel makes me feel icky. It's too privileged for my taste, and that once used to be Max's opinion too. But from the looks of things, he's gotten quite used to luxury travel.

I turn my attention back to my computer, trying to push Max aside.

It's not like I'm lying about the amount of work I have. I do have a ton of things to do, mostly emails to various team principals. Others are personal, like to the concierge in my condo building. I plead with her to water my plants and clean out my fridge, and fortunately, she immediately responds and says yes. Mum can't be trusted with the plants. I also fire off a message to Mum with several bullet points about the house, Papa, and the top three cardiac rehabs in Miami. I'd researched those in the car on our way to the airport.

We take off, and the flight attendant comes to me first.

"Coffee. An entire carafe, please," I say, pressing my hands together in a pleading gesture. The attendant, a beautiful brunet who doesn't look a day over twenty-two, gives me a wide grin.

"How about I put a shot or two of espresso in the coffee as well?" She raises an eyebrow.

"You're a goddess. Thank you."

She then makes her way to Max, and I peek over my laptop screen and watch their interaction. A pang of shame mixed with jealousy shoots through me. Why I'm torturing myself like this is a mystery.

The attendant's body language says it all. Her chest is thrust out, her smile is glittering, her fingers flutter to his shoulder. He says something that I can't quite understand, and the attendant throws her head back, laughing like he told the best joke in the world. I hunch over my laptop and try to concentrate, but I can't.

When I first met Max he wasn't a flirt or a womanizer. He was a shy, polite twenty-two-year-old. It had taken a couple of weeks for him to speak in full sentences and not monosyllabic grunts to me. Then, when we became friends, I discovered that he was funny and sweet. After we started having sex, he was ravenous. But so was I.

Seven years in Formula World have turned him into a flirtatious fuckboy, apparently. Maybe all the tabloid stories about him are true. I stopped reading them a few years back, mostly because it was torture to know all the details of his hookups in Brazil with two models or his very public spat in Japan with an actress or the naked photos on a yacht with an Instagram influencer in Italy.

Even if I wanted to be with him now, how could I trust him?

With a sour feeling swirling in my stomach, I stop staring at Max and tap another message to Mumsy, asking for an update on Papa. For good measure, I send a third email with the name of a top nutritionist in Miami, and a PDF of what heart attack patients should eat. Thank god for Wi-Fi on planes.

My inbox is jammed with emails—how the hell did all these reporters get my personal email, anyway—and I spot five from Tanya, all sent in quick succession, and all with the word *urgent* in the subject line. Part of me wished she'd flown with us instead of going ahead to Austin. That way she could've acted as a buffer between me and Max.

"Oh Christ," I mutter.

"Everything okay?" Somehow Max has materialized in the aisle near my seat.

I look up, adjusting the glasses on my nose. Probably I'll have to shift to wearing contacts and sunglasses while at the track.

"Just peachy," I say.

He slides into the seat across from me, leans back, and spreads his legs. Just like he did when he was at my place, he comes off as very relaxed in my presence, all sprawly and comfy.

Like we've been together for years. This makes me act all the more rigid, for some reason.

"I love Austin," he says. "It's the whole Wild West feel about it. Last year we all went to this amazing Tex-Mex restaurant. The food was delicious. Maybe we should have dinner there."

I clear my throat. He continues, describing a dish he had last year before the race. "It was chili, but with steak instead of beans. And spicy. So spicy! Have you ever had it?"

Why is he sitting here, chatting casually about chili con carne? "Maybe once or twice."

"Being German, I don't usually like spicy food."

"I remember." I can't help but smile, thinking about the time we went for Thai food in New York. He'd never had it and ordered a four pepper–level dish. He spent the rest of the night guzzling milk and perspiring heavily.

"You'll be happy to know I love spice now." He says this almost triumphantly, as if he expects me to be proud of him.

"That's nice." I wonder why he's going to all this effort to chat with me when he could be laying the groundwork for a hookup with the flight attendant. "I need to, ah, send some work emails here, and it's hard for me to concentrate with you staring at me."

"Oh, right." He slaps his muscular thighs and stands. "I'll let you be. Think about that Tex-Mex place and the chili, though."

"Will do."

When he leaves I stare out the window at the clouds whizzing past. Chili? With Max? What. The. Eff? I imagine us eating together, laughing, talking about everything from books to the best racing documentaries to silly stuff like our favorite Japanese mascots. Like we used to. But as much as I want all of that, and more, I know it's not going to happen.

Can't ever happen. Because of my father, and because I don't think I'm in a place where I can handle another breakup.

CHAPTER THIRTEEN

LILY

Things move at warp speed when we touch down in Austin. Lucas is waiting to greet Max and whisk him away for an afternoon of interviews and physiotherapy, while Tanya and her team descend upon me. As we split into two groups going into separate cars, Max and I glance at each other. The corners of his mouth turn up and he shoots me a subtle wink.

A little jolt goes through me. Somehow the man is simultaneously adorable, goofy, and impossibly sexy all at once. Still, I hope no one saw that little display of flirtation.

In the back of the car, I ask if we're headed to the track or the hotel.

"Track," Tanya says briskly, then launches into a detailed list of what needs to be done, PR-wise.

"ESPN wants a one on one with you talking about your father.

That'll run during pre-race coverage. And German *GQ* wants a photo shoot of you and Max. I've scheduled the interview for this week but pushed the photo shoot to Las Vegas. Told them you had too much going on this week."

"Why do I have to be in a photo shoot?" I understand the need for an interview, and don't mind that too much—I can gush about my father all day long. But so much can go wrong with a photo shoot. I'm not great at hiding my emotions and being around Max is already difficult enough.

"It was originally scheduled for Max and your father. But they think it will be interesting to have you in it now, given the circumstances."

"Fine." I scratch my eyebrow. "Keep the interviews at a minimum, though. I have a lot of work to do."

Like talking to Jack about the engines.

"There's been an outpouring of support for your father. This is big deal, since he's a legend in the sport. Savannah and Dante Annunziata have sent their well wishes and have made a large donation to the hospital where your father is getting care, in his name."

I press my hand to my heart, touched. "That's really sweet."

She lists several other kind gestures, and then goes over the team obligations I'll be required to attend. When she gets to the Boots and BBQ–themed party this evening, I hold up my hand.

"I don't own boots."

"Noted. Tell me your size and I'll get you some."

For the first time, we laugh. "Seriously, Lily, you need to roll with this and have fun. I know how much you hate the press, but try to enjoy at least some of these events, okay?"

"I'll try. I promise."

"I know it won't be easy, given your past. We need to come up with messaging because we're getting a lot of inquiries."

All of the color drains from my face. "The gaming company scandal?"

"Well, that, and Max. Honestly, in the annals of Formula World scandals, it doesn't even rank in the top ten."

Good lord. I didn't think we'd reached scandal level. "What have you heard?"

She rolls her eyes. "That you two had a torrid affair during his first year of racing. That's all. Some called you a cougar."

"I'm two years older. Hardly a *cougar*." I shake my head. There's no winning if you're a woman in the public eye.

"Oh, and that you broke his heart."

That makes me I bark out a laugh. "*I* broke *his* heart?"

"Well, that you broke it off and he was never the same."

Oh, that's rich, given how much he slept around after we split. "News to me. It's more like he let out his true nature after we stopped seeing each other."

"Admittedly, that was his manwhore phase. Most drivers go through that in years two through four, when they realize they can get all the ass the want, anytime they want." She says this like it's a known fact. Maybe it is. Tanya's observed plenty of drivers at various stages of their careers.

"You've got it down to a science." I grimace, thinking of Max screwing his way around the world. I've tried to block that out for years, but now it's front and center in my mind, precisely when it shouldn't be.

Tanya continues, clearly relishing the topic. "Although for some drivers that phase lasts a lot longer. That driver from Argentina, the one on Team Praxis? He's thirty-three and still a horndog. Max has grown out of that mindset. He's really matured. Anyway, what do you want to say when the press asks?"

"The truth."

She arches an eyebrow. "Which is what, exactly?"

That I'm still wildly attracted to Max and that I have a lot of unresolved feelings that are almost wholly and utterly not reciprocated? No, that's a terrible idea.

"We were close friends when we were younger, that we remain dear friends, and we are excited to work together."

She scrunches up her nose and shakes her head. "That sounds either old ladyish or like you're still fucking. I mean, are you still fucking?"

"No, god. Never." I protest. "Say that we've been longtime friends and that I'm excited to work with such a talented champion and am proud to have him as the senior driver on Team Onassis. I'm certain that Max Becker will bring another season trophy to our team."

"Okay, I guess that works. I'll massage it a bit." She scribbles a note on her legal pad, then looks up at me.

I hold my head high, but something about Tanya's steely appraisal tells me that she believes my bullshit even less than I do.

CHAPTER FOURTEEN

MAX

"Okay, let's start from the top. What did you eat this morning?" Lucas taps on his iPad.

He hasn't said anything about me flying to Texas with Lily. Yet.

"This morning I had oatmeal with peanut butter, fruit, a protein shake, and some cookies as a snack." He's got me on a high-protein, whole-food diet, including a special powder formulated for vegetarian athletes.

He looks up, blinking. "What kind of cookies?"

I have a wicked sweet tooth. "Chocolate chip. I couldn't resist. They were homemade."

Now he's scowling, probably because he has me on a diet that's a far cry from my German favorites like schnitzel, bratwurst, and stollen. "Where did you eat those?"

I look out the window as we whiz down the highway. "They were at Lily's house."

He groans aloud. "Here we go."

It's not that Lucas dislikes Lily. Quite the opposite; they've always gotten along. But he also saw firsthand what the breakup did to me and to my driving performance.

"It's not what you think."

"You're having a great season. Don't let her derail you." Most men wouldn't want their friend delving into their personal business, but my relationship with Lucas is more than friendship. He's the main reason I'm a champion, a one-man support team who keeps me mentally and physically healthy.

Keeps me on top. Keeps me winning.

"I won't."

"I want to go on record that sleeping with your ex isn't a good idea."

A chuckle escapes my lips. "I'm aware of that. We haven't slept together. We had dinner last night."

"I saw the gossip sites. All the fan forums are speculating how this is going to affect your driving on Sunday."

"It won't affect my driving at all," I say sharply. "This morning I went to see Adrian in the hospital with her. It was the right thing to do, and then we stopped at her condo in downtown Miami. She'd made cookies and I couldn't resist. That was the only slipup."

Unless you count the dirty thoughts I'd entertained alone in my hotel room about Lily last night. But even though Lucas and I are tight, he doesn't need to know all those details.

There's a long silence in the car. I'm waiting for a reprimand about eating all those simple carbs, and I brace myself when Lucas finally pipes up.

"How's Adrian?"

Relieved that we're not discussing my diet, I tell him everything I saw and heard from Lily about her father's condition. Lucas inhales. "It's going to be a difficult few weeks, but he'll pull through."

We go over the plan for the afternoon: gym, stretching, massage, then two interviews. I'm glad he's not dwelling on the Lily situation.

"For tonight, I'd like you to take it easy in the hotel room. It's about as warm here as Miami, so I don't want you going into the week dehydrated. Sleep is a priority, especially in light of recent events."

Sleep is always a problem and a priority for me. "What events?"

"You know exactly what I'm talking about."

"Lily?"

"Mmm-hmm."

"I'm older now, dude. Mentally stronger. I've got this."

I pull out my phone, signaling that this conversation is over. But when I skim the headlines in *Der Spiegel*, Germany's largest paper, I spot a photo of Lily and me standing outside the hospital in Miami.

I don't read the article—I rarely do, and avoid the comment sections at all costs—but the headline is burned in my brain.

Ehemalige Liebhaber.

Former Lovers.

The word *former* triggers something in me, a sad, depressing feeling. It reminds me of the day Lily ended things between us. The day that defined me, inspired me, broke me.

It was two days after the season ended. I was twenty-two, and on top of the world because I'd come in second in the overall rankings that season, behind Dante Annunziata, a legend in the sport. A near unprecedented rookie season, in fact. It had been the twilight of Dante's career, and even he acknowledged that I was the future of this sport—and he'd been notoriously picky when he was a driver. I'd never confided in him about Lily, however—not even after Dante and I ended up on the same team and became friends.

Back when I dated Lily, we were in Dubai at the end of the season.

Lily and I had planned to steal away on a desert safari. She came to my hotel room that morning after having breakfast with her father. Her face was tear stained, and I drew her into my arms.

"What's wrong, Mausebär?" I always called her that in German because the translation—mouse bear—made her giggle, and I loved nothing more than hearing that sound.

"I can't do this," she'd said through her tears.

"We don't have to go to the desert. We can stay here and hang out." Back then, I was pretty dense.

"No," she cried. "This. Us. My father knows about us and he's pissed. He was furious at breakfast. And the press keeps blaming me for your performance this season. I can't handle the pressure, Max."

I kissed her forehead and told her everything would be okay. Told her that we'd work through it, that her father would eventually come around, to ignore all of the chatter from the press.

"It won't be easy, but we can do this together. I believe in us," I'd said.

But she wasn't convinced. And that was what hurt the most, that she didn't believe in us as a team.

"I need to get back to the States. To talk to my mom, to feel grounded again. I don't think this life is for me. All the travel and instability. I'm sorry, Max."

Then she kissed me good-bye, and I was left heartbroken, alone in a hotel room.

◊

LILY

Late in the afternoon, when the scorching Texas sun is high in the sky, I'm alone in the makeshift office at the paddock, feeling a tiny bit better. One of the first things the crew assembles is the office pod, which kind of looks like a modular classroom or a mobile home. All I care about is that it's air conditioned in this Texas heat.

Now that Max isn't nearby—he is doing an interview with a German magazine this afternoon—I feel much more like my old self.

Organized, purposeful, and in control. I've already talked with Anh; she's coming to the Boots and BBQ party tonight, and I can't wait to see her. And Mum texts with good news: my father's met with a nutritionist and is in good spirits. My weird parents are apparently getting along well.

Don't worry about us, dear. Papa says to focus on the team.

She then sent a selfie of the two of them. A half hour later I spot the same photo on her Instagram. Which is probably good because the press will pick it up and dissect her caption, taking the heat off me for a bit. Thanks, Mumsy.

"Whatever works for them," I murmur at my phone, then turn back to a lengthy recap written by Jack of the last race. Esteban needs to work on his focus, the team needs to prioritize tweaking the engine.

In reality, Jack writes, *we're not entirely certain how to unleash the potential for Max's car. Max's driving is in top form but we need to slice and dice the data, which isn't correlating with what Max is feeling and experiencing when actually behind the wheel.*

I take a minute to absorb this. When winning Formula World races, it all comes down to milliseconds. Sometimes it's driver performance, like breaking a fraction of a second too late. Other times it's the car and tuning it to get the most out of the combined petrol internal combustion engine and electric motors. Then there's the team and the pit stops, and if someone fumbles during a tire change, it can alter the course of the race.

Those aren't my decisions, though—it's why we pay top dollar for brilliant engineers to craft the perfect car. I'm merely my father's eyes and ears. Still, I love the sport and want to know what's going on. I love the technical details, and that's one of the reasons why I went to work for the racing game designer. I could be around the sport but not in it.

I fire off several emails about Max's engine issue in Miami. It's a complicated matter because any changes to an engine could result in penalties, such as Max being knocked down on the starting grid. It's essential we get these things clarified by the sport's governing body immediately.

If we make power unit changes to Max Becker's car prior to the Austin race, will we be penalized? I write in an email to Jack. There's also another issue: If we replace Max's power unit, must we also replace Esteban's? Doing so would cost the team millions, something I'd like to avoid on my watch. We're not a big team backed by a car company.

As I'm going over the sport's rules discussing at length which engine components lead to penalties, there's a knock on the flimsy office door.

"Come in," I call.

Tanya saunters through the door, holding a clipboard and a cell.

"Hey, there." I move my bag off a seat and she plunks down.

"You look happier," she says.

"Feeling much better. I've spent the last few hours reading through reports, getting up to speed. I think I can do this."

"You absolutely can. And I have some good news. The press release about you and your father is getting great play, and your mother's statement and photo on Instagram are playing well. We're also seeing a lot of positive reaction to you taking over the team. ESPN is already speculating about what it would be like to have you as the owner of your father's team. They're saying more women need to lead the sport. Even Savannah Jenkins weighed in."

"What did she say?"

"That she'd welcome you as competition."

I lean back in my chair, laughing. "It's true that the sport needs more women, but I'm probably not the woman to lead the charge. She is, though."

"We'll see about that." Tanya's eyes twinkle. "About the schedule. Tonight, at the Boots and BBQ event, you'll be meeting with the TelecomCo rep. That's a big one, since they're our largest sponsor and their company headquarters are here in Austin. I'll be there, and so will Esteban and a few team engineers."

Whew. At least I won't be around Max. I'm not sure if I can handle watching him flirt his way through a dinner party. "Location and dress code?"

She flips a few pages on her legal pad. "They've rented an authentic and well-reviewed taqueria, so I'd say business casual. In Texas that means jeans and a blouse, I'm told. Nothing formal. My intern is out buying boots for you now. The event begins in a couple of hours, so I suggest you shower and change here at the track in the team locker room. I'll clear the space. Saturday's the big pre-race bash."

I stare longingly at my suitcase in the corner. We'd come here directly from the airport, and I needed to freshen up and change. "Damn, I was hoping to get to the hotel and unwind a bit before any social obligations."

"Yeah, about that. We have an issue."

"What kind of issue?"

Her lips pull into a grimace. "There's a problem with the hotel."

"Okay . . ."

"You don't have a room. At least not for tonight. We think we can secure one at the team hotel for tomorrow through Monday."

"Wait, what? Why?"

"There was a mix-up, and our travel person canceled your father's registration because of his situation—"

Just then, the door flies open. Tanya and I look up to see Max in the doorway. He's still wearing sunglasses, looking impossibly cool and rested, even though he's been with a reporter.

"Hallo," he says cheerfully. "Sorry to interrupt. I wanted to tell you how today's interview went."

My eyebrows shoot up. Is this normal for a driver? Maybe it is. My father's a bit of a micromanager. "We're a little busy. We kind of have a situation."

"Okay, I'll wait." Max plunks onto the only other available chair and takes out his phone.

I try to catch Tanya's eye, as if to silently say WTF, but she ignores him and me. Maybe this is business as usual—I could see my father encouraging his drivers to lounge around his office, so I'm going to roll with it.

Still, Max's mere presence inspires a physical reaction in me. It's as if my skin tingles when he's nearby, like he's a pleasurable magnetic force field. It doesn't help that he looks impeccable. He's in perfectly fitted, well-faded jeans, a tight black T-shirt, and black sneakers. On any other man the outfit would look plain, but on him, it's irresistible. He slides his sunglasses off and his bright blue eyes look me up and down.

I'm sure I'm blushing, so I turn in Tanya's direction. "Anyway. What were you saying about the hotel room?"

"The Plaza's fully booked for tonight. Your father normally gets a suite, along with the two drivers."

"I don't need a suite. Any room will do. A closet is fine. I'm not picky."

"There are no other rooms at the Plaza. Everything's booked solid."

"I'm sure there are other hotels in Austin."

"All booked for race weekend."

"Every single one? That seems improbable."

"Unless you want to stay at a rent-by-the-hour motel an hour away." Tanya purses her lips. "We need you closer. We could ask someone to bunk with someone else."

I let out a sigh. The last thing I want to do during my first week with the team is disrupt their sleeping accommodations. That will only make me seem like a diva, but what other choice do I have?

"It's only for tonight?"

"Yeah, the hotel is going to bump someone tomorrow so you can have the suite."

"What about airbnbs—"

"I have a suite. You can stay in mine." Max leans forward, his elbows on his knees.

"Where are you going to stay?" I twirl in my chair to stare at him.

He shrugs. "In the suite."

I can't believe he's proposing this. "Oh, god no. You of all people need to rest during race week."

Back when he first started in Formula World Max had trouble on the track because he didn't get enough sleep. He used to be one of those people who couldn't sleep well in new places, and traveling around the world made it nearly impossible for him to get much needed rest. That detail even made the tabloids at one point, and in his home country the press dissected his slumber habits before and after every race. That would've annoyed me, but he let it roll off his back like water on a duck.

"It's no trouble at all. I have a big room. Surely we can find a space for you for tonight."

Tanya's face lights up like a Christmas tree. The idea of Max and me staying together in a hotel room is either titillating or thrilling to her, I can't tell which.

I swallow hard. "I don't know—"

"That's the best and easiest solution, because I don't have time to deal with such a minor problem," Tanya says, standing up. "Obviously, we'll keep this between us, because if it gets out then the press will have a field day. But thankfully the penthouse suites are on the top floor and accessible only to a few people, and they have their own secure entrance with a code. We'll get you a key to Max's room and you can bunk there. And that way, when we move you over to a suite tomorrow, it's less hassle because it's right next door."

Before I can protest, Tanya's walking out, directing Max to follow her so he can sign photos of himself for fans.

Max gives a little wave good-bye and when the door closes, I ease back into my seat. Things are going well, and now, I'm about to spend the night under the same roof with the man I've loved for years.

Well. This escalated quickly.

CHAPTER FIFTEEN

LILY

After a quick shower in the women's locker at the track—I'm not picky about stuff like that—I blow-dry my hair, toss on a white blouse and tight jeans, then turn to the box Tanya left for me.

When I lift the top and find a pair of scarlet cowboy boots inside, I crack up. And continue to chuckle as I pull them on. They're not me, but they're not terrible either. They are a perfect fit the moment I slip them on my feet. I take a few hesitant steps around the room, getting used to the stiff, rough leather so tight I can feel the pressure of my toes poking against the end of the soles.

In the mirror, I examine the combination of red boots, blue jeans, and white blouse. Unfamiliar, but not terrible. I twist and look over my shoulder, liking the way my butt looks in the jeans and how the boots make my legs look longer.

For an instant, I feel sassy, confident, even. I can do this. Go to a party, sleep in Max's room, help this team through this rough patch. This is nothing compared to what I experienced in tech. Actually, the boots are kick-ass, actually, and maybe I'll put them in permanent wardrobe rotation.

I strut to the SUV, where Tanya's waiting in the back. She's dressed in a similar outfit, only her shirt is plaid and her boots are black.

"Hey, cowgirl," I say as I slide in.

We discuss boots and Texas for a few minutes as we drive in heavy traffic to the downtown area, where the restaurant, and our hotel, is located.

"Let's get a little work done, we have quite a while before we get to the restaurant with this traffic."

"Sounds perfect to me." Tanya's sharp, and I appreciate her no-nonsense attitude, plus it's a distraction from the nervous anticipation buzzing in me from the knowledge I'll be seeing Max later. I lean forward to get my laptop out of my bag and set it on my thighs.

"Let's start with the press inquiries about your previous job." She scrolls through her phone.

My gaze darts to the window for a beat, then back to her. "I'm ready."

"One reporter asked if you'd like to discuss the circumstances of your fi—, er, dismissal. I told him no."

"Correct. That's off limits."

"Others wanted to know if you'd like to make a statement about women working in a traditionally male field, like tech or racing."

I shrug. "It might not be a bad idea. What do you think?"

"I need more details on your previous situation."

All the earlier badass feelings evaporate. "It wasn't one thing, one event. It was years of being a woman in the tech world, and multiple instances of sexual harassment. Everything from investors trying to get me drunk, to trying to kiss me in the office, and once, I was going over expansion plans and staff growth with an investor and he whipped out his erect, well, you know."

Tanya grimaces. "Eww. I once worked for a team owner like that. He was a Silicon Valley guy."

I can guess who she's talking about, but don't mention his name aloud. "I'm sorry," I say softly.

She lifts a shoulder. "Sometimes it comes with the territory."

"That doesn't mean it's right. That doesn't mean we should endure it." All of my old anger's back now, churning my gut. "At the game developer, I had issues with one guy in particular. He'd say the filthiest things to me at every chance. Once sent me a porn video. Then told me I'd be a good lay while we were at a conference. I was fed up and took a photo of him during the conference and tweeted about what he'd said. Definitely not my best moment, but I was fed up. That's why I'm quite sensitive to how I'm perceived around Max. I don't want to seem like I'm doing anything inappropriate."

"Understandable, and I'm sorry that happened to you. But your situation with Max is far different."

"How?"

"Because there's no real power differential. He's rich, richer than you, I assume, and you hold no real power over him."

I laugh. "Oh come on. My father employs him."

"True, but any team would employ him. He's a champion. You two have a history. Don't try to deny it."

A lump in my throat forms. "I'd rather not fan the flames of that story in the press."

"You and Max had a real connection all those years ago, didn't you? I've seen how he looks at you, and trust me, I've seen him look at a lot of women over the years. We used to work for the same team—coincidentally, the same owner who showed me his dick. I've observed Max many, many times, and I've never seen him as nervous or as captivated as he is in your presence."

"Please." I can't respond with anything more than that one word and a snort. None of what she's saying is true. I narrow my eyes and stare at Tanya. "I thought we were talking business here?"

She shrugs, and then points out my window. We're rolling up to the curb of a building that looks like a hacienda in the middle of a cluster of skyscrapers, a pink stucco two-story building with a red barrel tile roof. "Oh look, we're here."

We stay at the curb for a few minutes, not getting out, as we watch Esteban climb out of the vehicle ahead of us and saunter down the carpet to the front door. A half dozen photographers snap his photo, and he grins for each of them. Good lord, he's like Max: never met a camera he didn't love. Or that didn't love him back.

I let out a huff. "You didn't tell me there would be a red carpet and photographers."

"It's also news to me. I guess we're going to have to strut our stuff. Come on, cowgirl."

"Oh wait." I pull her back by the arm. "Can you make sure that no one gives me a hug?"

Her face crinkles. "Why?"

"I'm not a hugger with strangers. Don't like it."

"Sure." She says this like it's not the strangest request she's ever received, and I'm sure it's not.

We exit the car, and a photographer calls out my name. "Pose for us, Ms. Onassis? Wonderful boots."

I pause, put my hand on a hip, and channel my mom. But I'm not showing teeth so I'm certain I look constipated and not mysterious, like she does. Since no one wants Tanya's photo, I stick close by her, hoping people will think I'm her assistant.

She says she needs to chat with Esteban, and I'm left alone, so I wander toward the bar, my throat tightening at all the potential interaction with people. Then my gaze lands on a tall woman with a graceful neck, a killer body, and a megawatt smile, holding a bottle of beer.

"Anh," I cry out.

She sees me and her face lights up. I make a high-pitched sound of excitement as we get closer.

"I want to squeeze you," she says, holding her arms out. She's wearing what looks like a white leather jacket with fringe over what is possibly the tightest, most sparkly red tank and shorts ensemble. She's also wearing a white cowboy hat over her long black hair, and boots.

"You look freaking amazing," I cry.

"Please, can I hug you?" Anh has known me for seven years and is fully aware of my phobia.

I laugh and shake my head. "I wouldn't mind if it was only us, but I don't want other people to think they can embrace me."

"You are so weird as always! Let's get you a beer and go outside to the porch where we can talk in private." She wraps her perfectly manicured hand around my wrist and tugs me to the front of the line for the bar. Armed with her charm—and her showstopping cleavage—Anh secures a drink for me and leads me outside.

While there are groups of people out here, it's much less crowded, and I begin to relax. We settle onto a lounge sofa that's partially obscured by a potted shrub.

"I'm so glad you're here. There's a rich guy from Russia who keeps offering me money to send my models to his hotel room." She rolls her eyes and takes a sip.

"Eww. Gross. Some things don't change in Formula World. How are the drivers treating everyone?"

"You know, things have become less . . . active these past few years. And get this, I'm about to go on the road to hire more promotional male models too. I've got my eye on several Italians." Anh grins wickedly, and I laugh.

"How does Bryce feel about that?"

She waves her hand. "Doesn't care. He knows I'm crazy about him. He'll be here tomorrow, by the way. We should all hang out."

"Absolutely." I love being around the two of them because they're so bubbly and outgoing. Even though I have to lie down for a while afterward. They're both so *on*. All the time. "I'm so glad to see you. It's been a crazy day. God, it's only been a day since Papa's heart attack."

"Yeah, tell me everything."

Anh listens as I talk about my father. That's one of her best qualities, her ability to truly listen.

I was hesitant when I first met her. She was so beautiful and didn't hesitate to showcase her looks, whereas I was a twenty-four-year-old nerd intern. Still, she took me into her circle of friends, all models, and we'd had some amazing times together at places around the globe. We've ridden elephants, camels, and mechanical bulls. Swum in waterfalls, and danced until dawn in Spain.

"I'm so glad Adrian's doing better. How terrifying." She presses a hand to her chest. "And I saw your photo at the hospital with a certain driver. Or am I still prohibited from talking about him?"

A groan slips out of my mouth. There's no escaping the Max conversation. Not with my best friend. "Oh, get this. Guess where I'm staying tonight?"

When I tell her, Anh's eyes open wide and her mouth forms a perfect scarlet *O*. "In the same bed?" she whispers.

"No," I practically shout.

She raises her eyebrows and smirks, as if to say *yeah, right*.

"I'm serious."

"I am too. The way he was looking at you in that photo." She pretends to fan herself.

"Come on. I saw the photo and I looked sweaty."

"Dewy."

We laugh. "Honest. There's nothing going on."

"Look me in the eye and tell me you're not attracted to him." She fixes an unwavering gaze on me.

"I'm not . . ." My voice trails off and I dissolve into laughter.

She's not laughing.

"What?" I ask, taking a pull from my beer.

Anh shakes her head, still not convinced. "Babycakes, you can deny it all you want but I know that look when I see it."

She takes a sip of her fancy beer. One thing about Anh hasn't changed over the years: she can see right through my bullshit. Right now she's staring at me with a laser-like focus. It's time to change the subject.

"Who do you think will win the race?"

She purses her lips, aware of what I'm trying to do. "He didn't ever sleep with any grid girls, you know. In case you were wondering."

"Who?"

"You know exactly who."

I lean in closer. "He did sleep with a bunch of other women."

"Not recently, and only after you broke up with him. One model told me he said your name in his sleep one night." Anh is also up on all the Formula World gossip. If she says Max didn't sleep with anyone recently, it must be true.

"Come on, that's ridiculous."

"It's true."

I let this sink in. Max said my name in his sleep? I wonder when. "Well, whatever. Because we're not having sex. Tonight or any other night. I'm over him."

"Mm-hmm. We'll see," she hums.

Anh knows the incredible chemistry between me and Max and probably suspects (correctly) that I'm in denial.

"Nope. You know my dating record."

She snorts. "Max was way better than that string of tech guys you dated. Remember the time Bryce and I met you and that bro for dinner in San Francisco?"

I squint. "The guy who wore the stained hoodie?"

"No, that guy was kind of okay, even though he communicated only in monosyllables. I was thinking of the man who wouldn't stop talking about Steve Jobs. Remember how he showed us all those photos of the time he went to Jobs's house? Then he seemed offended when he said his company was selling for ten million, and we weren't superimpressed."

I grimaced. There had been a time when I tried, hard, to find a partner in Silicon Valley. "It was difficult to be impressed when the man ate pasta with his hands."

Anh folds over with laughter, shaking and snorting. She's one of those people whose laugh is infectious, and I can't help but chortle.

"They were all losers. Max isn't a loser, but our romance is firmly in the past. I'm serious."

"Okay, fine, I'll believe you for now. But I want a full report every day, because I have a feeling things are going to change. And Max has impeccable table manners, so keep that in. mind. Listen, I have to meet up with a sponsor. Coffee, tomorrow? Text me."

We do an exaggerated air kiss, keeping a foot away from each other—we'd done this for years—and she bounces off.

For the rest of the party her words echo in my ears. Is it possible that Max is truly a reformed fuckboy? And why do I care so much?

CHAPTER SIXTEEN

MAX

I flop around on the sofa in the hotel suite, trying to get comfortable. It's ten at night and I haven't yet heard from Lily. Her stuff was delivered two hours ago, and Tanya had told me earlier that Lily had showered at the track and gone directly to the sponsor dinner, and that she had a key to the suite.

I really shouldn't care so much, but I do. I'm kicking myself for inviting her here, and haven't yet told Lucas. He's at a meeting with the other driver's assistant tonight, and has expressly told me to stick to my diet and get a decent night's rest. My Tex-Mex dinner of vegetarian chili con carne was outstanding, although eating it alone in the hotel room was a bit of a downer.

Annoyed at myself, I flip through the TV channels, wishing I'd been assigned to that dinner at the taqueria. But according to my contract I only have to do two sponsor dinners per race, and this isn't my night. I'd insisted on two nights off before each race, and normally I like the downtime, chilling in the hotel room, meditating and exercising, and catching up on much needed sleep.

I flip to ESPN, and the talking heads are chattering about basketball. I only half listen, because I'm wondering how Lily is doing at the party. She's not really a social creature, and she normally shied away from such events back when we were together.

There's a sound at the door, like the lock is disengaging, and I sit up and grab my water. Then I realize I look too eager, and set down the bottle and sprawl back into the plush cushions. Better to have her think I'm half asleep, or engaged in the program.

She peeks in and enters quietly.

"Hey, there," I say.

She jumps, startled, and presses a hand to her chest. "Oh! I didn't see you there in the dark. Gosh."

"Sorry that I startled you." I sit up.

Her eyes dart around the room, and I stand up, then realize I'm not sure what I should do once I'm on my feet. I'm wearing gray sweatpants so I can't even stuff my hands in my pockets. Holy shit, she looks incredible in those tight jeans and red boots.

"Someone from the team delivered your suitcases," I say, wanting to be helpful. As angry as I still am about our breakup, I'm genetically incapable of being nasty to her.

"Oh, good." She lets out a breath. "All I want is to take a real shower and go to bed. I feel a headache coming on."

"Those dinners can be really stressful. How was it?"

"It was quite nice. I caught up with Anh. The tacos were amazing. They were street tacos. I ate, like, ten of them."

Laughter slips out of my mouth. "You ate ten of those big stuffed things?" I hold my hands about a foot apart.

"No, silly, you're thinking of burritos. Street tacos are small." She smiles. "Anyway, everyone was quite gracious, and asked about Papa. People really love him."

"There's a lot to love. He's a good man who cares for his team and his family."

We stand there and smile awkwardly, me near the sofa and her near the door. She looks down at her boots, then looks up at me.

"I'm kind of embracing this cowgirl thing. I might wear these all weekend."

I imagine her wearing them with a pair of cutoff denim shorts and a wet T-shirt and almost groan aloud as my dick tingles to life. In my core, I'm a horny dog, like most men. I try to keep this under wraps, but Lily brings out that side of me. "Are they comfortable?"

"Very." She smiles. She's also wearing a low-cut blouse that shows off her cleavage. I force myself to stare at her forehead, because I don't want her to think I'm a total perv.

Even though that's exactly what I feel like.

I scratch my arm nervously. "Oh! I put your suitcase in the main bedroom. You can sleep there. I thought I'd take the sofa."

A horrified look crosses her face. "Oh my god. I thought there were two bedrooms in here. There aren't?"

"No, not in this hotel. I was mistaken. Last year we stayed at another hotel and those suites have multiple bedrooms. The suites here all have a big living room and a bedroom, and a little kitchen area. I'm sorry if it's awkward."

Her mouth opens, then closes, and I chatter on about the view and the minibar. I even go to the window and open the curtain.

"See the view, it's quite nice. Downtown Austin. There's the Texas Capitol building over there. And that's the University of Texas Tower." What the fuck am I, a realtor? A tour guide?

She rubs her forehead, still with a stunned expression on her face.

"You have to practice tomorrow, so you should take the bed. The sofa's fine by me."

"I couldn't do that, no."

"Why? Please?"

"Nope."

Her expression has morphed into exasperation. "Listen, I have a bit of a headache and don't want to argue. I'm going to shower. Where's the bathroom? Are there two?"

"Oh, uh, it's in here. There's only one, unfortunately." I walk quickly into the bedroom, and she follows. I point to the ensuite. The atmosphere seems charged with electricity now that we're both standing near a bed.

"Thanks again."

"I'll let you shower." I back out of the room, my heart pounding, and shut the bedroom door behind me.

In the living room, at the faint strains of a suitcase zipper, I pace and tug at my hair. That was so awkward. Terrible. As if we are strangers, and not two people who used to have sex a couple of times a night, in various places (some of them wildly inappropriate).

I guess I shouldn't have expected more. Shouldn't have thought we could go back to our old friendship or fall back into whatever we'd been doing before.

I flop down on the sofa and grab a blue blanket slung over the back, throwing it over my body in exasperation.

CHAPTER SEVENTEEN

LILY

This is a disaster, staying here. I'm in the bedroom with the door closed, shaking because my nerves are so jangled. I'd assumed that I'd at least have my own space, but dammit, this suite is actually miniscule. Like a small apartment in New York City.

I pull pajamas out of my bag and glance around the room.

It's decorated in bright red, pale blue, and white colors. There's a bright red chair stuffed into a corner. A blanket in a matching red southwest pattern is tossed over the back. It's like an American flag exploded, and the overall effect makes me feel even more jittery. There's even a framed black-and-white photo of an old man with a beard on the wall opposite the bed, above the TV, and suddenly it registers that it's country star Willie Nelson.

I plunk down on the bed, staring up at Willie, who is strumming a guitar in the photo. Who would want to look at that face while having sex?

More importantly, why am I thinking about sex while in Max's hotel suite, on the bed that he's supposed to sleep in?

I shake my head, hoping to rid my brain of Willie and Max and sex, and go into the bathroom. Fortunately, that's a much more soothing atmosphere, with a light gray and white decor.

I take a quick and unsatisfying shower. Something about the idea of being naked when Max is sitting in the other room watching TV is too intimate for my liking. My insides are already quivering, and the sight of him in those gray sweatpants makes parts of me warm and tingly.

I do not want to tingle in those parts. Not here with him, and not when I have a headache blooming.

Fortunately, I brought decent sleepwear—my favorite pink silk pajamas—and not my usual cotton tank and shorts. I brush my teeth, blow-dry my hair, and slap on some moisturizer. I wipe away the condensation on the mirror and grimace. The events of the past day have caught up with me, and I look worn out. Haggard.

I hate for Max to see me this way. But this is my face, and I'm going to have to make the best of this situation. Even if that means the sofa.

He's going to have to understand the importance of taking the bed, chivalry be damned. He needs to be in top form this week, and starting it with terrible sleep isn't a good idea.

I march out to the living room and find Max lying on the couch, partially covered by a hideous blue blanket. His bare feet are hanging over the arm. The lights are out but the TV's on, tuned to some Animal Planet show about wildebeests.

"Max."

He opens his eyes. "Oh, hallo," he says casually, like he didn't expect me to be here. My presence barely registers, obviously.

"Sorry, I didn't mean to wake you. Really, you need to sleep in the bed. I know how you have, ah, had, sleep issues. You need to be at your best this week, especially after that Miami race. Please?"

He sits up. "I feel ungentlemanly if you take the sofa."

I can tell he's tired as well, because his German accent is a little more pronounced. "I won't hold it against you, I promise. It's more important that you're rested. That's an order. From the team owner."

"Okay, fine." He flings off the blanket. "Can I at least get you a pillow?"

"Sure."

We pass by each other, and I catch his masculine scent: the faintest whiff of aftershave and the unique smell of his skin. It smells like ocean sunrises and sea air, luxury hotel suites and pure sex.

The sensation of blood rushing in my ears makes me unsteady. I sink into the sofa, the cushions still warm from his body. The fibers of the sofa smell like him too. There are those tingles again, all concentrated in one bundle of nerves between my legs. If I was home alone, I'd take care of myself with my vibrator.

That's obviously impossible tonight, although the thought of doing so on the sofa while he's in the other room makes me even more aroused. I am a deviant.

Max pads back out, his footsteps soft. He's not holding a pillow, and gestures with his thumb behind him. "You know, this is an enormous bed. We can both sleep there. I'd hate for you to toss and turn with a headache tonight."

I take in his athletic frame, the muscles that ripple beneath his tight T-shirt, the way the fabric stretches over his chest, and how his eyes glint in the light coming from the bedroom.

My temple throbs, signaling the escalation of my headache. I look at the narrow sofa, its red cushions picture perfect, its fabric a luxurious crushed velvet. It's nice looking, but not designed for sleeping. It's also hard as a rock.

"Fine."

He smiles, but it's not a lascivious expression. It's a mixture of relief and, possibly, happiness. "I'm watching this program about animals, so I'll be in later. But, uh, feel free to sleep—"

"Yeah, I'm exhausted." I interrupt him. This is getting way too awkward for my liking and all I want is for both of us to stop talking. "Night."

"Night night," he says, shutting the door.

In the bedroom, I turn off the bedside lamp and slide between the luxuriously soft white cotton sheets. I roll onto my side, as close to the edge as I can without falling off, facing the window. I do not want Max to think I'm doing this for a hookup.

The thought of building a wall of pillows between us comes to mind, but I chide myself. That's absurd. We're adults, teammates, and we can bunk in the same bed in an emergency. This would be no different if it was Tanya or Anh.

Come to think of it, why didn't Tanya offer to put me up in her room, with her? As I pull the fluffy duvet up my body, over my shoulder, and cover my ear, I ponder this. Whatever. What's done is done.

The bed is sinfully comfy and I drift off, trying to will my headache away and not think about the moment when Max lies next to me. Many hours later, a soft buzzing sound stirs me awake. It's the air conditioner, kicking in. My eyes flutter open, and for a moment, I'm not sure where I am.

Oh right, the Plaza, in Austin. In a comfy bed inside a dark room. The temperature is perfect for sleeping, not too cold, not too hot, and . . .

There's a muscular arm around me.

It belongs to Max. Oh my word, we are spooning. He is the big spoon, and he's wrapped around me, his nose pressed into the nape of my neck. Our legs are tangled together, and his hand is sprawled across my belly.

My mouth opens in a silent gasp, while he snores away, the soft vibration causing little goose bumps to form on my neck. I turn my head to the left a few inches and spot the sleeve of his T-shirt. We're both clothed.

My heart is jackhammering against my rib cage. I don't remember when he came to bed, probably because I'm a deep sleeper. I also don't recall when we started spooning. Max is one of the few people I can hug without feeling odd. Even with some of the men I've had sex with hugging and nonsexual intimacy have been difficult.

It never was with Max.

I blink a few times in the dark, wondering if I should get up and sleep on the sofa. Or wriggle out of his embrace. I'd been sleeping so well until now, perfectly comfy in my little cocoon.

I shut my eyes and exhale. This feels amazing. Like it used to, when Max and I would sneak into each other's hotel rooms and fall asleep together. No, it doesn't feel amazing, it's perfect. A ripple of happiness goes through me, and I nestle closer to him. He squeezes my stomach with his hand and presses against me. We melt into each other.

Nothing about this is sexual. It's more intimate than that.

Forget the sofa. I don't want to be anywhere but where I am right now, in Max's arms.

CHAPTER EIGHTEEN

MAX

I haven't even opened my eyes and I feel a desperate ache in my cock. Holy shit, I'm horny. More so than I've been in years. I'm as hard as a rock and I can't figure out why. I haven't had sex in a while, so maybe that's it. Maybe I'll roll over and take care of myself, entertain a little fantasy of Lily in those tight jeans she was wearing yesterday . . .

When I open my eyes, I realize that's the issue. I'm pressed against Lily like she's a life preserver, my face in her hair, my arm around her waist, my hips nestled against her curvy, soft ass, which is covered in sensual silk pajamas. How long have we been like this?

Last thing I knew, I crawled into bed after watching that animal program. Lily was asleep at the far side of the mattress, and I stayed on my side, on my back. Even though I was nervous about sharing a bed with her again, there was no way I was going to make a move. It would be unprofessional, even predatory, and I'm definitely neither of those things.

Horny, yes. Harassing, never.

But sometime in the night our bodies found each other like magnets, and my conscious mind wasn't even aware. Or maybe Lily nestled against me.

The thought sends more blood into my dick. Does she want me? No, if she did, she would've done more than cuddle. At least, that's what she used to do when we were together, start kissing my neck when I was asleep.

I want so badly to press my erection against her, but considering I'm not certain when or why we're cuddling, that would probably be a terrible move. Inappropriate for so many reasons.

But her hair smells so good, like flowers. And it's so silky. Her body's warm, and memories of us having morning sex flash in my mind. When we were together, all it would take was a little thrust of my hips, and she'd make an adorable little *mmm* sound then take my hand and shove it down her pajama bottoms.

No.

I'm not twenty-two anymore, and we're not together. I'm supposed to be angry at her for breaking up with me. Plus she's my boss, for god's sake. A *thirty-one-year-old* woman. It was merely some kind of sleepwalking that led us to this position. Well, not walking exactly. Sleep spooning. Sleep cuddling.

I slide my arm away from her midsection and scoot back, not wanting to wake her. The clock radio says it's quarter to six, and I need to get to the paddock by seven thirty for a massage and stretching session.

Lucas is going to be at the door pretty soon, too, and I can't let him see that Lily's here. I don't want to deal with all the questions, not today.

As I'm sliding off the bed away from Lily, she flips over. Her eyes spy my hard on, which is tenting my sweatpants.

"What the . . ." She licks her lips, then shifts her eyes to my face. She squints. "I can't see. Where are my glasses?"

"Oh, uh . . ." I pretend to look around, in hopes my dick softens.

"The nightstand." She points, and I hand them to her.

She dons them and stares at me again. A flush creeps across her cheeks. "Oh dear."

"Sorry. Uh, we ended up . . ." I can't finish my sentence because I'm too embarrassed. Even though I'm fully clothed, I hold a pillow over my crotch.

"We ended up spooning. I'm not sure how," she says, a touch of annoyance in her voice.

"I'm not either. My apologies. Is your headache gone?" I want to talk about anything but what we were just doing in bed. Or think about what we could be doing in bed if things weren't so weird and awkward.

She stretches, and the hem of her silk pajama top rides up so I can see her belly button. I clutch the pillow against me for dear life.

"Why are you holding a pillow over yourself?" She sits up, staring at me with a dubious expression. Her long hair is messy, and her eyes heavy lidded from sleep. She's so beautiful that I want to collapse onto the bed and beg her to pet me like a dog.

"No reason. I'm going to take a shower. Have to get to the track. Practice day. And stuff. You know. Gotta go work out." I stand up and back away, babbling and still holding the pillow like a fool.

I quickly change into workout gear in the bathroom and walk into the living area, where Lily is already sitting at the desk, staring at a computer screen. Her leg is bouncing up and down, which tells me she's feeling as awkward as I am.

There's a knock on the door, and Lily whirls. "Were you expecting anyone?"

I'd hoped she would stay in the bedroom. "I'm sure it's Lucas."

A quick peek through the peephole reveals it is, indeed, him. I swing open the door a few inches. "Hey. I'll be right out."

He tries to peer around me. "Have you eaten breakfast?"

"Not yet. Maybe we can downstairs. Lemme put on my shoes."

I shut the door in his face, feeling awful for being so rude. I quickly lace up my sneakers and glance up at Lily's back.

"See you at the track," I say.

She looks over at me and gives a little wave good-bye. It's difficult to decipher her reaction to our physical closeness this morning. All I know is that I can't shake the feeling of her body next to mine.

I slip out of the room, making sure Lucas can't see inside. In the hallway, he hoists a large gym bag higher on his shoulder.

"Did you have a guest last night?"

It's an unusual question. When I was sleeping around he never asked me about the women, or who I spent the night with. I'm a terrible liar, so I sigh.

"Yeah. Lily."

His eyes widen and his mouth opens, and he's going to say something, but the elevator doors slide open. We step inside and the tension is thick between the two of us. The elevator stops on the next floor down. An entire family enters: mom, dad, and two teen boys.

"Oh my god, it's Max Becker," one of the kids says. "We're headed to join the line for this morning's event at the track."

I make a show of checking my watch. "At five forty-five in the morning? That's dedication."

The mother laughs. "That's what you get when you live with three Formula World stans."

Everyone in the elevator chuckles.

"How about an autograph," I say, happy to have interrupted the conversation with Lucas. He extracts a Sharpie and two printed photos of me from a folder in the gym bag—he always carries them because fans always want an autograph—and I sign them, using the backs of the kids as a table. They're overjoyed and ask me a few questions about the race.

When that's done, Lucas and I hit the gym in the hotel. It's reserved for us, and once inside, he takes out a pair of suspension trainers.

"Listen, your sex life is private. I've never once cared who you're sleeping with. But Lily? Come on, man. You know she's bad for you."

"We didn't have sex." I take the straps from him. "She didn't have anywhere else to stay because of a screwup with the hotel."

He shakes his head. "How can you forget what she did to you? How angry you were?"

I attach one suspension trainer around the metal post of a weight machine. "I'm still angry. But it's complex. I care for her, and can't shut her out. She's also my boss. Our boss."

"That doesn't mean you have to get cozy with her."

No, it doesn't. But I want to, and I know that's a problem.

◊

The next day my luck runs out. It's the second practice of the week, and I'm exhausted as all hell.

"Max, what the shit was that?" Jack says to me as I hoist myself out of the car and pull off my helmet. "I haven't see you drive that poorly since your first year in the sport. Christ."

Lucas stands by and stares in silence. I know exactly what he's thinking.

Jack sputters and follows us into the garage, where I guzzle down some Gatorade. "Was it the car? I don't think it was the car. Or was it the fact there was some dust in the air? Olivera went into the gravel before you and there might have been some debris—"

"No." I cut him off. "It's me. I feel like crap."

"Oh Christ, are you sick? You seemed fine this morning." Jack puts his hand on my shoulder.

I shake my head. "No, not sick. Had a really awful night's sleep last night."

After the previous night with Lily, when I'd slept better than I had in weeks, last night was spent tossing and turning in my own bed, alone, and I barely got a wink.

"Were you out late last night? I thought we talked about that when you came on the team. No late nights with girls."

I shake my head vigorously. "I'm done with all that. I've been done with that for a while."

"But you were at the sponsor party, right?" Jack eyes me carefully.

"Yeah, but only for a couple of hours." I'd put in my time with the sponsors, smiled and posed for photos. Lily was there, too, but we barely said a word to each other. In fact, I'd been trying to avoid her since our evening together.

Once Lily left the party, though, I had little interest in staying. Afterward, I'd gone to my room, tried meditating, stretching, reading.

Jack covers his face with his hands, his fingertips rubbing his eyes. "We need to do better tomorrow during quali, mate. Don't stay out late at that party tonight, okay? I know you have to attend and all, but skip out the minute you can. No screwing around, you got that? Lucas, make sure he gets rest."

He and Lucas murmur to each other and study my laps on the track on a computer monitor. I continue drinking the Gatorade, parched.

Jack thinks I'm reverting to my old days, in my third year in the sport, when I was teammates with Jack's old driver, Dante Annunziata. I'd been a wild man back then, and somehow managed to win on a few hours' sleep. Now, though, age has settled in. There's a big difference between twenty-two and twenty-eight in this sport because of how hard it is on a body. G-forces, dehydration, muscle strain . . . it's all amplified the older I get.

"Max, I'm serious. No women. No wild shit." Jack looks angry enough to coldcock me.

"I know, I know," I mutter, then stalk off to my dressing room. Now I'm angry, too, because I'd finally figured out how to balance travel and sleep and racing, and then Lily came back into my life, upsetting that delicate balance.

CHAPTER NINETEEN

LILY

It's our third night in Austin, and I can say with confidence that the week is going fairly well. The high point has been my daily coffee meetings with Anh, who has tried to catch me up on the gossip. Unfortunately, since we're both busy, that's only taken about an hour out of each day. She's gone out of her way to not mention Max, or ask about him, and for that I'm grateful.

Another check in the good news column: the team can replace the power component on Max's car without incurring an on-grid penalty. And Jack doesn't think we need to replace the power component in Esteban's car, saving us buttloads of cash—a fact that Papa has already praised me for in an email.

Tonight I'm at yet another party, once again wearing my red boots. Only this time they're paired with a little cream minidress, something billowy and boho that my mother would wholly approve of. I even took a photo for her before I left the hotel suite, and she messaged me back, asking if she could post it on her Insta.

Absolutely not, I want to reply. How I'm her offspring is sometimes a mystery to me. Instead, I tell her she can post away—Tanya had emailed me encouraging me to get Mumsy to post about me on her popular social channels. Gah.

I spot Max by himself for the first time tonight. He's leaning on the iron railing of the terrace, his silhouette framed by the city's skyscrapers. The entire outdoor lounge area smells like chlorine from the pool and exhaust fumes coming from the street below, tinged with expensive cologne. It's so hot that the scents hang in the air, heavy and oppressive, kind of like how the team feels after Max's dismal practice today.

I approach and mimic his stance but say nothing. Maybe it's because we're looking over the street, or because there's a pool behind us, or due being smack in the middle of the city, but it's swelteringly hot, even for nine at night. My cotton dress feels sticky against my back.

"I was going to say something about the weather, but it's pointless," he says softly.

His tone tells me everything I need to know; he's despondent about today's practice.

He glances at my hands. "Would you like me to get you another drink?"

"Thanks, but no. I'm thinking about heading to my room. This heat is sapping what's left of my energy."

I'm greeted with silence. There's no point in ignoring the obvious.

"Max, what happened today during practice? It wasn't the car."

He shakes his head while staring at the skyline. The light from the buildings gives enough illumination for me to see the angles of his face, the stern furrow of his brow, and the slight downturn of his lush mouth.

"It was all me."

"I see." But he'd done so well in practice on Tuesday. Yesterday wasn't so great, and neither was today. He knows it, I know it, hell, the entire team knows it.

"I got about an hour of sleep last night. Today I wasn't at the top of my game. I'm sorry."

That's when it hits me. He'd done so well on Tuesday because he'd gotten great sleep. Next to me.

"You've overcome the sleep issue before. How did you do it?"

"I worked with a sleep specialist. And was doing so damned well until—"

He looks at the bottle of sparkling water in his hands. The muscles in his jaw bunch and he looks on the verge of regret. He shakes his head, staring at the skyline. His face is a silhouette cut from marble, a perfect beauty that would've inspired Michelangelo.

"Until?"

"Until you came back into my life." There's an uncharacteristic bitterness to his tone.

"Oh god," I whisper, my stomach sinking. "Now it's my turn to be sorry."

We stand in silence for a beat, and I can't help but stare at his beautiful profile. I remember the way he felt when he was holding me two nights ago. And the taste of his lips seven years ago, the way it felt to have his hands on me, the way his tongue felt exploring me the nights we spent together.

My tongue tingles with the memory of him, his essence an addiction. I also feel a familiar wave of regret, because I hurt this beautiful, decent man. This is all my doing.

"Lily, it's my fault. My mistake. I invited you into my bed the other night and we ended up cuddling." The way he says the word *cuddle* is as if he's uttering a curse word. "And since then my sleep has been a mess. I'll work through it, I'll have to. I have an emergency video call with the sleep therapist tomorrow morning before quali."

"Do you think that will help?"

He turns to me. "Honestly, I don't know. So much of this is emotional, Lily. The off days are when I'm supposed to bring it all back into balance. My fitness, my eating, my sleep, my emotions. Two of those are going well. Two aren't. Lucas has some ideas on how to fix it."

"Does he know about us staying together the other night?"

Max grimaces. "He's not happy about it."

"And you? How did you feel about it?"

"What? Us sleeping next to each other?"

"Yeah." A thousand questions go through my mind, many of them about the women he's had sex with. Surely he's slept next to them during race weeks. Or perhaps not. Regardless, we must try to replicate Tuesday's incredible practice performance.

"It felt way too good to be real."

Those words slay me. Embolden me. Maybe even assuage my guilt a little.

I glance around, to check to see if anyone's nearby. What I'm about to propose would scandalize the team, my father, and the sport. "We need to fix this. I want you on that podium Sunday. It's my first race as team owner, or interim team owner, or whatever. I need to show everyone I'm serious."

"I'm in full agreement with that sentiment, but what do you suggest?" He huffs out a little laugh. "It's not like I can take sleeping pills, since they're testing me daily for every substance known to man. You know they're banned, and they leave me groggy." He takes a long sip of his water.

There's no one close to us, so I edge a few inches in Max's direction and lean in, so my shoulder is touching his. "We're going to try something tonight. Sleeping together."

This makes him swallow hard, then cough, and he forms a fist with his free hand and presses it to his mouth. "What did you say?"

"I know it sounds strange. But hear me out. Obviously, you got excellent sleep on Monday, and it showed on the track Tuesday. We're going to do that again and see how you do for qualifying. Exactly what we did the other night. Sleep in the same bed, cuddle, and spoon. Nothing else." I place firm emphasis on the last two words, as if I'm trying to remind myself of this fact.

His face twists in disbelief, then morphs into a slight grin, and then drifts back to shock. He looks so conflicted that I'm unsure whether he wants to accept my offer or tell me that I'm ridiculous.

"I want you to win, and if sleeping next to you will help, I'm happy to do it. My suite is right next to yours, I'm going there now. Feel free to join me. Unless you're more comfortable sleeping in your room. If so, call me. Text me. I'll come over. Think about it."

I nod in his direction, as if I'm a general giving orders during a war. Then I walk away. Tanya's at a high-top table, tapping away at her phone, and I have to pass by her to get to the elevator.

"Everything okay?" she asks, glancing up from her cell for a fraction of a second.

"It's perfect."

"Saw you talking to Max. Hopefully you were somehow inspiring him for tomorrow. He's looked pretty glum since practice. Not sure what's gotten into him. Look at him, all alone over there."

We both glance over at Max, who is still standing at the terrace railing, staring at the cityscape. He looks forlorn.

"I might have nudged him in the right direction," I say cryptically.

This gets Tanya's attention, and she raises an eyebrow. "Care to share?"

I shake my head and shoot her a coy smile. "I understand what motivates him, that's all. I'm headed to bed. Good night."

She hums a *hmmmm* as I walk away, and honestly, I don't care what she thinks—which is probably a mistake, but I'm operating on sheer adrenaline right now. My heart is beating so fast that I'm almost out of breath by the time I get to my room, and I let out a rueful, silly laugh.

This gives a whole new definition of taking one for the team.

◊

I'm perfectly calm as I shower and change into a T-shirt and a pair of soft cotton shorts. Whatever happens tonight is out of my control.

I made an offer to Max. An unorthodox, completely bananas offer, now that I think about it. I grab my book and climb into bed, trying to shove back my weird, conflicted feelings.

The book is a romance, and I'm getting to a sexy scene when I pause and set it down.

Will he think I invited him over for sex? Probably not. I'm well aware that like most drivers he doesn't have sex the day before qualifying or a race. At least, he never did before, and when we were together, it was the one rule we never broke.

There's a soft rap at the door and I fling the covers off. A look through the peephole reveals Max, biting his lip and glancing around nervously.

I fling the door open and stand aside while he comes in. He's wearing a plain white T-shirt and basic blue sweatpants, but with his tousled blond hair still looks like he's fresh off a *GQ* fashion shoot. No shoes, no socks. His phone is in his hand, and he grins a crooked, wicked expression that makes my heart race.

"I thought about it, and even though it's a little, uh, unusual, it's worth a try. Figured it would be better in your suite."

We stare at each other like we're firming up a business deal.

"I was reading in bed, so we can, you know." I point to the bedroom. It's like we're in a deleted scene on an episode of some bad reality TV program. Inviting a man that I'd had sex with on numerous occasions into my bed is suddenly more awkward than I could have ever imagined.

"Okay. Yep. We're doing this. I'm actually tired, so . . ." He runs a hand through his hair.

"Yes! Let's get to it." I clap my hands, feeling ridiculous.

We troop into the bedroom and stop suddenly, the large bed with the white duvet staring right at us. Like his room, the entire place is decorated in red, white, and blue. The pillows are of various sizes and seem to have multiplied in the last hour. The headboard is a bright red, plush and quilted. My mind goes to dirty places, imagining me on all fours, him behind me, my hand pressing against that headboard.

No, no, no. Bad Lily.

"Which side do you prefer?" I gesture to the bed, my index fingers dancing up and down.

"Umm." He strokes his chin. "Right."

"Cool." I go around the bed and climb in. It's the side near the closet. I stare at him expectantly. "Is the temperature okay?"

He looks around, as if that will help him decide. His gaze lands on the photo of Willie Nelson, and a slight frown flashes on his face. "It's acceptable."

"That's Willie Nelson," I point out helpfully. "You have one in your room too."

"Who?" He stares at me like I'm speaking a language he doesn't understand.

"The photo." I point. "You know, Willie Nelson. Country and

western. He's from Texas. 'On the Road Again'?" I sing a few bars and he stifles a grin. Yep. Nothing turns a man on like singing some off-key Willie. I know how to reel 'em in.

Good god, what am I doing? My palms are moist and I surreptitiously wipe them on the duvet, feeling out of control. "My mom used to sing that to me when I was little."

"Funny, I didn't take your mum to be a country fan."

He sets his phone down on the nightstand and pauses for a moment, probably wondering if he truly wants to go through with this silly idea.

"Can I test the pillows?" he finally asks.

"Oh. Yeah. Sure. Take whichever pillow you want. I'm not picky."

I sit up, and he climbs on the bed and kneels, leaving me dizzy from his proximity. One by one I hand him each of the six pillows. He inspects them, squeezing and plumping them with his hands, and I watch, wishing he was grabbing my waist and ass in that same way.

"This. This is the one." He holds a pillow in front of him with a small smile. It was the one I'd used last night.

"Perfect." I swipe one of the discarded pillows and set it at the head of the bed. To me, they're all the same. I toss the rest on the floor.

"I'm turning out the light."

So much for my book. As if I could concentrate on it anyway. "Okey dokey, smokey," I say. And then cringe.

He turns to flick the light out, bathing the room in darkness and his seductive scent. I lie, frozen, on my back, my arms at my side. I don't dare look at him—not like I could see him in this darkness—and feel him sliding between the covers.

I clear my throat. "Where do you want me?"

The question hangs in the air, filled with innuendo and memories. Just as my face is heating up with embarrassment, he laughs. The air is thick with tension, and the electricity between us almost makes me sweat. Great. Now I'm going to perspire all over him.

"Oh, Lily. Come here." He sighs and rolls onto his side, wraps his arm around me, dragging me toward him me so I'm the little spoon.

He buries his nose in my hair, breathes deeply, then holds me close to his body. With his thigh pressed against mine, I am uncomfortably aware of our differences. His long, lean muscles cut into my soft, rounded curves. His arm is like a strong, steel band around me, and I'm pretty sure I could stay like this for the rest of my life—even though I'll never tell him that. As far as he knows, I'm doing this so he'll win, not because I want to revel in his touch one more time.

It doesn't matter, because this moment is perfect. The steady thump of his heart and the feathery touch of his breath on my neck soothe me, and when he sighs contentedly, I allow myself to relax and enjoy.

I let go.

This is a bliss I haven't felt in so long. Several minutes later his breathing slows. It's the first sound of contentment I've heard from him tonight. But a feeling wells up in me that I try my best to ignore because it's more than a little terrifying.

I am still deeply, madly, in love with Max Becker. But I'll never tell him that as long as I live.

CHAPTER TWENTY

LILY

The good news is Max drives so well during qualifying the next day that he achieves pole position, which means for the race tomorrow, he'll be first on the grid.

The bad news is we'll probably have to sleep together again tonight so he'll win the actual race.

Or is that bad news?

I keep pondering this in the hours after Max's blistering qualifying laps. Watching him was pure joy, poetry almost, for people like me who love the sport and the art of driving. He handled every curve, hugged every wall, with a deft touch. Even Papa called me afterward, overjoyed. I gently chided him for not relaxing, but also felt secretly proud that the team was doing well in his absence.

Esteban came in third on the grid, so the team is in a cautiously optimistic mood as we head to that afternoon's press conference.

"You nervous?" Esteban asks me. He's so young and new in the sport that at thirty-one, I feel practically ancient next to him. We're walking with Tanya and Max into the press center on the track.

"A little. You?"

Esteban grins. "I love this part."

I wish I had his enthusiasm. This is the element I've been dreading. I've been able to handle everything else going sideways, like sleeping in the same bed as Max. But at least I've been able to stay out of the public eye. The press even ignored me on the red carpet and at that party the other night. But as is typical after qualifying, each team goes before the press and submits to a round of questions. Usually it's my incredibly quotable father here in the press room with Jack and the drivers.

We're all clustered in a closet-like room next to the press center, waiting for another team to finish up their media conference. Max tugs at my sleeve, and motions with his head to step to the back so we can talk.

"You're sure about this?" he asks in a low voice, sending a hum of desire through me. Despite our intimate sleeping position last night, we haven't so much as touched in a sexual way, but the tension remains—at least on my end.

Maybe not on his, a fact I was trying not to dwell on. As I'd pretended to sleep, he'd bounded out of bed early this morning and left without a good-bye. Neither of us wanted to make it any more awkward than it already was.

There had been his evident hard-on the other morning, an image that I hadn't been able to shake. Surely that happened to him every morning, though, regardless of whether he was sleeping next to someone or not.

"I'm good. Really."

"If there's anything you don't want to answer, I'll step in, okay? I know how to get the press off my back." Max is an expert at that. A glare and a two-word answer are all he needs to shut conversation down. I've watched him do it a hundred times.

"Thanks, but I'm okay." It's almost embarrassing to be this inept in front of the media, and surely Max thinks I'm ill equipped.

"It's time," Tanya calls, and we all file into the main room.

It's packed, lined with cameras and photographers from around the globe, and at least a dozen print reporters. My stomach coils into a tight knot. Maybe I'm not ready for this.

I paste on a smile and take my seat. Jack is at the far end, then Max, me, and finally, Esteban. As is customary at these things, Jack begins with a short statement about how the team and drivers did during quali. The rest of us sit and listen, drinking water or staring at the back wall of the room, over the reporters' heads.

A few reporters engage with Jack, all technical questions about the cars. Then Gordon, the guy who does the grid walk before each race, signals by waving his hand in the air. Jack calls on him.

"This is a question for Max. To what do you attribute your incredible qualifying times today? You were like night and day compared to yesterday's practice."

Max fixes his serious, icy stare on Gordon. "I had an off day yesterday."

"But what changed between yesterday and today?" the reporter probes.

I try to will myself not to blush and reach for the pitcher of water. It's shockingly heavy, like it's filled with lead.

"Nothing changed," Max says in a cool tone.

Another reporter, an older woman with a German accent, pipes up. "We are wondering if it's the presence of Ms. Onassis that's making your driving erratic."

At that, I fumble with the pitcher and spill a little on Esteban's leg. "Sorry, sorry," I whisper to him.

The sound of camera shutters fills the air as Esteban grins and Tanya appears with a towel. "Sorry, it's my first day drinking water," I quip, mortified. Naturally I'd have to do this right as an embarrassing question is asked.

"Next question," Max says.

"This is for Lily Onassis," says a reporter, who looks like a thin grandpa type, complete with handlebar moustache. "We're very happy your father is recovering."

My heart is thrashing against my chest as I lean into the microphone. Sweat slides down my back, and at this point, I don't even care if I'm making the table jiggle a little with my knee bouncing up and down. Why hadn't I brought my worry beads with me?

"Thank you."

"How are you finding running the team in your father's absence?"

I exhale. A softball question. I've rehearsed an answer that will fit for this one. "Many of the people on this team have been with my father for years, so it almost runs itself. I'm enjoying being back in the racing world. I grew up around the track, and watched my father build this team into what it is today, and I'm proud I can step in for him while he recovers."

The reporters scribble and nod. I allow myself to relax a little. Another journalist, one I don't recognize, pipes up with a British accent.

"How are you finding Max now versus at the beginning of his career?" she asks.

I turn to look at Max, who twists to stare at me. My tongue runs over my top teeth to stall while thinking of an answer. "Max has always possessed raw talent. But he's honed his excellent driving skills into championship form."

"And personally? How is your relationship personally compared to when you first met him?" the reporter probes.

I freeze. Is this journalist insinuating what I think she is? I open my mouth, but nothing comes out. Finally, as the silence hangs heavy in the air, practically crushing me with its weight, I say, "I'm not sure I understand the question."

"How is it being his boss when you used to sleep together?" the woman asks. "Especially since you were a crusader for sexual harassment reform in the workplace in your last job. Do you feel a bit hypocritical?"

I look around wildly, searching for Tanya. There's no way I'm answering that. It's a good question, however one I haven't entirely thought through.

"Well, Ms. Onassis, if you won't answer, then what are your thoughts, Max?" the reporters asks.

"My private life is just that. Private." Max's blue eyes have turned to a glacier-like hue, indicating that he's pissed.

Tanya rushes to the front of the room, as if blocking the reporters from us. She holds out her arms, then claps her hands. "That's all the time we have, folks."

We all file out to the sound of reporters shouting more questions but none of us say a word. Esteban peels off to sign autographs, and I expect Max to as well. I put my head down and walk quickly away, feeling shame deep in my core.

"Wait, Lily."

I turn to see Max calling my name and coming toward me. We stop in the middle of the walkway and stare at each other, but when people walk by and give us a glance, we step out of the way. We're sandwiched between the press center and a makeshift café that's open to all the teams.

"I'm sorry. I got so pissed at that question that I couldn't help but step in. I probably should've minded my own business but—" He blows out a breath and brushes his hair back with his hand.

"Don't apologize. This is the way it is for me right now. You know, the only way out is through, and all that."

"Yeah. Uh, about tonight."

"I have a sponsor dinner. You?" I didn't see his name on the list I'd been given.

"I'm with other sponsors at a cattle ranch."

"A cattle ranch?" A giggle slips from my mouth and I clap my hand over my lips, trying to imagine Max and his sexy European self around a bunch of Texas cowboys.

He grins, a dazzling smile that makes me swoon a little. His eyes practically glitter in the late-day sun.

"Nine p.m., your room?" he says in a low tone. Thank god no one's nearby. "Is that okay?"

I break out into a fresh sweat. "Sure. Nine p.m."

We say our good-byes and walk in different directions. Him to sign autographs, and me, well, I'll call Papa and find out how he's doing then head to the office to run this team. All while wondering where and how this is all going to end with me and Max. He's sleeping in my bed because he wants to win. I need to keep telling myself this.

CHAPTER TWENTY-ONE

LILY

That night, in my hotel suite after our respective parties, Max and I climb into bed.

"This feels like one of your routines," I remark.

He smooths the pillowcase and lies on his side. "What do you mean?"

I lie down, facing him. "You're treating this like another one of your race week routines. You know, work out, do fifty sit-ups, get a massage, eat a perfect two thousand calorie breakfast . . ." I almost say "Sleep next to a woman you used to have sex with," but don't.

"I wish it was a routine."

His simple declaration disarms my jumbled thoughts. "What do you mean by that?"

Our faces are inches apart, and if this was seven years ago I'd snuggle into his body and plant a kiss on his face.

He licks his lips. "I like sleeping next to you."

"Because it helps you on the track?"

"Sure. That too."

"Yeah." I flip over so I'm not looking at him. My tone is a bit frosty, and so is my body language. For some reason, I'm irked that he's sleeping with me because it might give him an advantage while driving. Even though it was my idea.

He scoots closer to me, and I feel the heat of his body pressing into mine. He wraps an arm around me. "The truth is a lot more complicated, Lily."

"Don't you think we should talk about it, eventually?" I thread my fingers into his.

"Weren't you the one who said you didn't want to rehash our past?" His lips are dangerously close to my neck, and wave after wave of need is washing over me.

"Yeah." That was stupid, in retrospect.

"Maybe we should talk about it after the race tomorrow. Before this goes any further." His voice is heavy with sleep. It's already late, later than he likes to go to bed the night before a race.

"Okay, tomorrow," I say softly, as I melt into his body.

◊

I'm wide awake at six thirty but don't dare stir because I know that on race days Max doesn't get up until seven. This extra half hour allows me to snuggle into his arms and exist in my cocoon of happiness.

But my overactive mind takes over, wondering what will happen after today. Will we be "sleeping" together before every practice, qualifying, and race from now on? Am I merely another of his support staff? He has masseuses, sleep specialists, nutritionists, and now a personal cuddler.

This thought makes my mind wander as I recall a TV show I once watched on professional cuddlers, who hug and sleep next to people for therapeutic reasons. My nose wrinkles at the idea. Gah. I can't imagine spooning with strangers. I snuggle deeper into Max's embrace.

I was even hesitant to sleep next to most of the men I've had sex with, and usually got out of it by saying I had early meetings. Well, most men other than Max, which should be a good indication that I'm potentially in deep emotional quicksand here. He's the only guy I'm truly comfortable being this close to. I'd tried with other men and had even enjoyed sex, but afterward I hadn't wanted to cuddle, for various reasons. One guy smelled funny; another guy had scratchy hair on his legs. A third breathed through his mouth with a weird whistling sound when he was asleep.

But Max feels so perfect next to me. Warm and strong. Protective and sexy. Familiar yet exciting. I let out a long, satisfied breath through my nose.

Max nuzzles my neck with his lips, sending a shower of desire through me. "Mmm, good morning, Mausebär."

It's hard not to grin when he says that word. Mausebär. When I first heard him call me this I was so confused and asked a million questions.

"Did the Germans run out of cute baby animals to use as nick-names?" I ask. It's something I used to say seven years ago to make him laugh.

Why he's treating me like he used to when we were together is a mystery, but I don't want to question it, or anything really, hours before a race. It all feels too familiar, too perfect.

He laughs and tickles my belly.

"Good morning," I whisper.

He skims his fingers over my arm and takes my hand in his, twining his fingers into mine and hugging my midsection.

"How did you sleep?" I ask.

"Like a milk-drunk baby." His breath is warm on my neck, and goose bumps flare on my skin.

We both laugh, and I roll over to stare at him. He brushes hair back from my face.

"You're going to have an amazing race today," I tell him.

He seems to be paying attention to my words, but with his eyes fixed on my lips, I don't think he hears anything coming out of my mouth. The sun beaming through a crack in the curtain casts a brilliant blaze to his blue eyes, and I can't help wondering if he can see the need and desire coursing through me; if he can feel my heart hammering against my chest.

"I want to kiss you." It's uttered as a statement, but knowing Max, it's a question. He wants to know if it's okay. It is most definitely okay, but my hyperactive, anxious mind has questions. My heart and other parts ignore the brain, though, and send up a resounding cheer.

My mouth opens, then closes. "If we kiss, I don't know if we'll stop. You never had sex on race days before."

"And I still don't. You don't think I have the willpower to stop kissing you?"

His thumb tenderly brushes my cheek. It's all I can do not to fling myself on top of him and rub against him like a cat in heat.

"I don't know if I have the willpower."

He chuckles softly and leans in, brushing his lips over mine. For a second I freeze, because it dawns on me that this is really happening. That my first love is kissing me. That it feels just as amazing; no, better, than before. Then I come to my senses and close my eyes, kissing him back, softly at first, mostly with a closed mouth and definitely no tongue.

For a moment I forget that we'd ever broken up, that I let him go despite all my instincts, and I'm kissing him back. That I'm letting him sink his lips on mine feels so right and so wrong at the same time, but I don't give a damn about the wrong.

He presses his hand against the small of my back and I arch against it, basking in the sensation of his body against mine. This is a dangerous line to cross, but I'm losing myself in this kiss.

The world around me melts away into a blissful haze where there is no team, no media, no race in a few hours.

But deep down, I know this is risky for so many reasons.

I shiver pleasurably when his hand cups my jaw and draws me closer. It's the kind of kiss that would make me so weak in the knees that I wouldn't be able to stand, so it's good that I'm horizontal. Or maybe it's bad, because I can feel his erection poking into my leg, and that makes me want him even more.

"Max, we shouldn't—"

"I know. I'll stop. One more kiss. Please?" he whispers against my lips, planting another gentle kiss on my lips. The kiss is so delicious, so intoxicating that I can't help but let out a soft moan, like a purr. It's a solid minute time before I realize I'm the one making that noise.

Right then, there's a loud knock at the door and we both freeze, our lips fused together. My eyes open, and so do his. We ease apart a few inches and I turn my head.

"Yes?" I call.

"It's Lucas!"

Oh shit, I mouth to Max, who squints at me.

"What are we going to do?" I hiss.

"We have to open the door." He flops onto his back as the alarm on his phone comes alive with an annoying ringtone. It's an air horn set to electronic dance music. I glance over, horrified, and he twists to shut it off.

"Okay, hang on," I holler, crawling over Max to get out of the bed, nearly falling on the floor.

I shut the door of the bedroom on my way into the living area of the suite, then fling the door open. Lucas is standing there with a stony face. Oh god, he knows.

"It's time for Max's breakfast. I've been trying"—he points with his pen—"to deliver his breakfast but he's not answering the door, probably because he's not in his room. Should I have it brought here?"

"Why would you assume he's here?"

"Cut the shit, Lily." He sighs, and I wonder what his problem is. Lucas and I have always gotten along, and even the other day in the cafeteria we had a nice chat about video games.

I run my tongue over my teeth, suddenly self-conscious that I kissed Max without brushing. "Yes, bring it in here," I say firmly, while standing aside to allow him to wheel the cart holding the food inside.

Once he's in, I shut the door.

"Max, I have your breakfast." Lucas's voice is frosty.

I stand awkwardly by the sofa as Max pads out in sweatpants and a hoodie.

"Guten Morgen," Max says, yawning. "Thanks for bringing this."

Lucas lifts the stainless steel lid off a bowl, revealing something that resembles scrambled eggs and home-fried potatoes.

"I thought he was on a plant-based diet," I say to Lucas, trying to diffuse the awkwardness.

"Tofu," he says curtly.

Sounds awful, but I say nothing. Max goes to the cart and swipes a potato chunk off the plate and pops it in his mouth.

"Yum," he says, reaching for a fork.

"Lily, would you mind if I had a word in private with Max?" Lucas says.

"Not at all," I chirp. "I should get ready anyway."

I scurry into the bathroom, feeling as though I've done something wrong. This is not the way I want to begin my first race day with the team.

CHAPTER TWENTY-TWO

MAX

"Seriously, Max. Why are you torturing yourself?" Lucas stares at me.

He's not asking in an accusatory way, nor does he seem pissed. He appears genuinely curious, similar to when people wonder why others climb Everest or tame lions in the circus.

"Sleeping next to her helps my performance. That's all. I wake up feeling refreshed."

Lucas is holding a cup of coffee and pacing around the small living room, the tiny space between the coffee table and the TV console. I'm at the little table in the corner, eating my bland scrambled tofu and wishing it was a giant bread roll with marmalade. When I leave this sport, I'm probably going to gain fifty pounds eating every carb in sight.

"I don't doubt that you feel that way, or that you're refreshed. But this isn't a long-term solution. What's going to happen when her father returns? When she's no longer with the race circuit?"

I lift a shoulder into a shrug and swallow. "I haven't thought that far ahead."

That's not a lie. I haven't. I'm the kind of guy to take things as they come, not worry too much about the future. It's always worked for me. Now that Lily's back in my life, it's almost easier to forget that I was ever angry at her, although those feelings sit uncomfortably below the surface, even as I am loving every second of being near her.

"Your top priority is your mental health. When she left you before—"

"Shh. Keep it down. She's in the other room."

Lucas comes and sits with me at the table. "When she left you before, you were in pretty bad shape. Thank goodness the breakup happened at the end of the season."

"I'm a different man now."

"Are you, though? She's like your kryptonite."

I take a sip of a green smoothie and grimace. Why is he bringing up the one topic that gets me worked up on race day? "Can we not discuss this now? I need to prepare for the race."

He grumbles an okay, and I shove everything to the back of my mind. The terrible food, the discussion with Lucas, the complicated situation with Lily. On race day it's essential to compartmentalize, to deny, to focus on one thing: the driving.

It's time to get into the zone.

CHAPTER TWENTY-THREE

LILY

The second Max speeds past the checkered flag everyone in the control room erupts in cheers. Jack high-fives me—someone must've told him about my aversion to hugs—and I do a little dance. Apparently, it wasn't only Jack who was told; word must have gotten around that I don't like physical displays of affection because the guys give me little pats on the back or shoulder squeezes instead of the big bear hugs they give one another.

Even that would normally make my skin crawl, but for some reason, the win makes everything around me positively sparkle. I'd forgotten this feeling, of being part of a winning team. Of the sheer rush of anticipation and exhilaration when a driver crosses that finish line.

I don't, however, go into the pit to greet Max when he brings the car to the garage. Even though I'm elated, I don't want to risk any public displays of affection with him. Not after sleeping next to him for two nights and especially not after our scorching kiss this morning.

Neither one of us can be trusted at this moment to not lock lips, and that's exactly the kind of thing the world *cannot* see during my first race. So I stay in the garage, congratulating every member of the team who wanders through.

"Fucking amazing job, Lily," Jack says to me, his hands on his hips.

"It was all your doing. I had nothing to do with any of this. You're incredible. The team's incredible. Thank goodness the engine fix worked and your tire strategy was brilliant."

He grins. "It was, wasn't it? Anyway, perhaps you're our good luck charm."

"I'll gladly take that role."

Tanya sweeps in and folds Jack into a big hug. I'm certain there's still sparks between them, but it's none of my business—unless it affects team operations, and then I'll step in. Certainly my father must know about their past. I'll have to ask him.

Papa.

"I need to call him," I blurt.

Tanya and Jack stare at me.

"My father. I'm sure he's watching from the hospital."

I find my phone and FaceTime my dad. He answers on the first ring, his eyes positively glittering.

"Kamari mou, I knew you could do it!" The top of Mum's head pops into the frame.

"Hi, you two! Can you believe it? We won! First and second place! Look at all the celebrating." I tilt the phone around the garage and call out, "Hey, it's my father, he watched from the hospital."

A roar of cheers goes up, and I peek at the phone. Papa's holding his fist up in a victory gesture, and I even spot tears in his eyes.

"Papa, I'll call you later. I wanted you to know we're all thinking of you. Love you."

"Love you too," he says.

Mum grabs the phone. "Lily, I saw you on TV earlier. Get your hair out of that ponytail before you do any interviews. You look so much prettier with it down. Trust me on this."

"Mum, I'm running a team here. Gotta go. Bye!"

I laugh out loud at Mum's silliness. She knows I don't give a flying fig about my hair right now.

Tanya approaches. "Okay, so Max and Esteban are doing their post-race weigh in, then they're going to the podium. I kind of figured you'd want to stay off the podium? Or do you want to be there?" She tilts her head, waiting for my response.

"Correct, no podium for me." As thrilled as I am with the race result, the last thing I want is to stand on a stage in front of tens of thousands of race fans and have Max, Esteban, or the third-place winner blast me with a magnum of champagne. It's fun to watch but participating in something like that is a nightmare.

"After the podium there's the press conference for the drivers. But ESPN would like a word with you in the meantime. I was thinking about setting that up in our lounge area so it's quiet and you can focus. I'll be in the room with you in case you need any help."

"I appreciate that. It all sounds perfect." I pause and squint. "Hey, do you think my hair should be up or down for the interview?"

"Oh, totally up. You look badass in a ponytail. Highlights your cheekbones."

Huh. Maybe Mum doesn't know everything. "Cool."

The next hour is a whirlwind of details, post-race certification paperwork, more congratulations from other team owners, and multiple opportunities to dodge hugs. At no point do I see either man who made today's celebration possible, because they've got their own routine down. I'm so busy getting ready for the ESPN interview that I don't even catch any of the podium celebration.

It's exactly the kind of scene Max loves, and I'm thrilled that he's happy. Hell, I'm happier than I've been in a long time, which is a new and unfamiliar feeling. It's like adrenaline is coursing through my veins at two hundred miles per hour and I can't stop grinning.

Even my interview with ESPN goes well. Tanya freshens me up with blush, lipstick, and a spritz of perfume. The reporter is a tall, former WNBA player who loves racing, and she asks softball questions about my first race as interim team owner. Tanya stands by, watching in the corner, in case I fumble or become overwhelmed.

Obviously, I give all the credit to the team, especially the pit crew. "They're the rock stars," I say. "Two-point-four second stops are the best any team has had all season. I couldn't be happier, and my father is so proud of everyone."

"And what about Max Becker? How do you explain his dismal performance during qualifying, and then this stunning, career-record performance today on the track? What's his secret sauce?"

Snuggling next to me all night? Sleeping a full eight hours? A scorching hot pre-race make-out session? Even I find it difficult to believe those are the reasons, but all signs are pointing toward those contributing to his mental state and win.

I still inspire him.

It's nearly impossible not to gush openly about this, I'm so giddy.

Of course, I know exactly the ingredients of the secret sauce, but it would be a scandal like no other if I said anything. "Max can do amazing things when he's in the right frame of mind. With a driver like him, performance is all in the mind. When he harnesses that combination of drive, focus, and passion, there's no limit to how well he can perform."

"It was an impressive day for Team Onassis. Thank you for taking the time for an interview," the reporter says.

"Anytime." Normally I wouldn't say that, but today feels different.

The reporter and her camera crew pack up, and Tanya checks her clipboard. "You have a bit of free time now, and then there's a celebratory party at the hotel. I'll see you back there in an hour or two. You know where to get the car to the Plaza, right?"

"I do. I think I'm going to grab something to drink first. I'm parched."

"Good deal. I need to meet a paper from Australia in the garage. Jack has his interview. See you around."

For the first time I'm alone, and I let out a pleasurable sigh. I did it, made it through my first race and won. Did my first solo interview and survived.

Go me.

Now it's time to congratulate the man who made this all possible. I wonder if he's upstairs in his driver room?

◊

My heart flutters as the woman at the front desk buzzes me into the private area, and I practically run up the steps to Max's space. Before I knock, I hesitate, my hand in the air.

Maybe he doesn't want to see you.

Maybe he's got a woman in there.

Maybe he's not even here.

Those little wicked thoughts fly through my brain. *No. Stop being insecure. You're here to congratulate him, and nothing more.*

I softly knock on the door. When it doesn't open immediately—it's not that big of a space, surely he'd open immediately if he was inside—I turn to leave.

The door flings open to reveal Max in nothing but wet hair and a towel around his waist. His eyes light up when he sees me.

"Oh," I whisper, suddenly shy. Everything I was going to say, all the congratulations, dissolve in my mind.

He reaches for my arm and pulls me in, then shuts the door firmly behind me.

"I wanted to con—" I can't even finish the sentence because he's pressing me against the door, cupping my face in his hands, putting his lips to mine. That's when I fall apart.

I allow him to pin my wrists against the door, high above my head. His kiss is intoxicating, debilitating, leaving my insides like jelly and my brain filled with fireworks and a lack of linguistic knowledge.

"Congratulate. You." I murmur this against his lips between kisses. "You drove. Incredible race. Celebrate. Us. Together. Alone."

"Lily, shhh." His voice is a feral, desperate whisper. "This is the only celebration I want, right here, right now."

He dips his head to mine and kisses me harder, then releases my arms. His mouth is hungry, and so is mine. We're standing here devouring each other like horny teenagers, and I am here for it.

I fan my hands across his bare chest, feeling the need and desperation vibrating under his skin, which is pleasantly warm and slightly damp from the shower. My heart skips a beat at the sight of him. His wet hair is slicked back, making his bright-blue eyes pop. His face is clean shaven and his skin tanned and smooth. There's a flush on his cheeks. Perhaps it's from the adrenaline rush of winning, or maybe he's genuinely excited to see me.

"I promised myself that if I won I'd kiss you until you told me to stop."

"Thank god you won, then. Because I'm definitely not going to tell you to stop."

While he chuckles, his hand gently skims and caresses my breast over the fabric of my dress. A button pops open and he slides his hand underneath, under my bra. A low groan forms in his throat, a sound so satisfying.

The combination of his strong lips and his soft touch is simply too much. I'm throbbing between my legs, and I don't think I've ever wanted sex as much as I do right at this moment.

My hands trail down his chest, over his taut, muscular stomach, and to the towel. I claw at the fabric and don't waste any time in undoing the tuck at the side of his hip, and now he's completely, gloriously, amazingly, naked. He also smells like some kind of delicious citrusy soap that makes me wants to lick every inch of his body.

I break away from his kiss to look down at his cock, and I actually let out a little gasp.

"It's larger than I remember," I blurt.

"Get the hell over here and kiss me again," he growls. I do, but I can't help my grabby hands and reach for his dick. He stops kissing me and hisses an exhale against my mouth as I slowly stroke him.

"Lily, do you see what you do to me? Look how fucking hard I am."

"I can feel. I want you inside me. Now." There's no point in trying to hide it or deny it. What we're doing is probably a terrible idea, but since he's naked and I'm impossibly wet and ready, I'm willing to throw all logic and good judgment out the window.

He puts his forehead to mine and moans. "Sweetheart, I don't have any condoms here."

"Oh no," I whisper, still stroking him, my skin tingling at his old-fashioned pet name, one he used to use for me during our dirtiest moments. The juxtaposition of the sweet and filthy never fails to turn me on.

And now, I need to feast. I need to taste. I need to surrender. To him.

"Max?"

"Yes?" He looks down at my hand on his shaft, then whispers, "Fuck. I want you, Lily. Right now. Here."

"I want you to sit on that sofa over there."

He looks up, into my eyes. "Can I ask why?"

I shake my head and grin. He dips his head for another kiss, then groans. "Okay, I love a surprise."

He starts to pick up the towel, and I clasp the end. "No towel."

"I like this even more." He walks the few paces, giving me a view of his perfect, muscular ass, and sits.

I follow and lean over to kiss him softly.

"What do you have planned?"

I sink to my knees, between his legs. I'm momentarily distracted by a large, intricate tattoo on his right thigh, and run my fingers over it. The image barely registers, though, because I'm mesmerized by his erection. I stroke it for a bit, and he's staring down at me, then I look up and meet his gaze.

"This is what I have planned," I say, and open my mouth, allowing my tongue to flutter over the tip.

He inhales sharply, and his hands find my head to undo my ponytail. I take him entirely in my mouth, and he lets out a whispered word in his native German. It could be an entire sentence, or one long word, I'm not entirely sure.

All I know is that he's extremely turned on and is getting more so with everything I'm doing.

He's so hard, inexplicably so. I lick my way up his shaft and glance up at him. He's staring down at me with his eyes half-lidded, his lips parted. Like he's swept away by what I'm doing.

"I love seeing you down there, you know. On your knees."

I hum against his flesh, once again taking him entirely in my mouth. He looks and tastes and feels so sexy that my entire body is probably vibrating with pleasure right now.

"Lily." He says my name more like a plea. "How do you know exactly what do to with me? I'm not going to last long."

I let go of his thick length with a pop of my lips and tongue, and look up at him. My hair falls over one eye and I grin saucily while I stroke him. "Didn't I teach you how to relax and enjoy this?"

"Uh-huh." I'm not sure my question actually registers, and he bites his lip. I return to what I was doing, slowly teasing, licking, and bobbing, knowing that I'm driving him absolutely wild. When we first started having sex, he'd often be too tense for oral, and said he didn't want to finish so fast.

While I'd like to take my time right now and savor this moment, I also have to be mindful that we're in the team headquarters and I'm not entirely sure if that door is locked. I pick up my pace, gliding up and down, sucking as if he's the most delicious thing I've ever tasted. Because he is.

"Lily—" He lets out a restrained breath and one of his hands fists my hair. "I'm going to—"

A guttural groan is followed by his hot, salty essence in my mouth. I swallow it all then lick him clean while he gasps for air and releases my head.

When I'm finished, I lean back on my heels and swipe my fingers over my lips, which are tingly from all the activity. His eyes are shut, his limbs sprawled, his skin a radiant bronze flush from his orgasm. How a man can be so beautiful is beyond me, and like I used to, I wonder how in the world a man this perfect ever chose me.

His eyes snap open and he reaches for me. "Come here. Please. Please?"

I try to sit next to him on the minuscule sofa—it's a loveseat, really—but he pulls me into his lap, mashing his face against the hollow of my neck. One of his hands is on my ass, gripping my skin with his fingers, as if he's holding on to me for dear life.

"I loved that," he mumbles.

His hand slides between my legs.

"Max, we probably shouldn't."

He lifts his head. "You don't want this?"

"Oh, I definitely want this."

"Mmm," is all he responds, his hand sliding from my ass to my hip, then to my inner thigh. His fingers make contact with the cotton fabric of my panties, and his hum turns to a low purr. I could almost orgasm from that sound. I'm about to protest, say that no, we've already risked so much here in this little dressing room. But his hot, naked skin, the feel of his lips on my neck and his fingers grazing that needy spot, make me part my legs and give him full access to me.

"Good god, you are so wet."

I'm not just wet, I'm drenched. He strokes gently and I let out a short puff of breath.

"You know how I like balance, Lily. You did something for me, now I'll do something for you. I won't be satisfied until you're satisfied." His nose nuzzles my neck and I'm trying to hold it together, trying not to ravage him the way I want. It's not the time or place.

I lick my lips and taste him, and this sends another rush of wetness between my legs.

His fingers locate the elastic waistband of my panties and he's about to delve into me when there's a knock at the door.

"Max?" It sounds like Tanya. Damn her. We pull apart and stare at each other, but he keeps his hand firmly on my flesh, under my panties. His fingers are so close to my entrance. So. Damn. Close.

I'm not here, I mouth, shaking my head frantically.

What? he mouths back.

"Hey, I'm not dressed, can you come back," he yells, his hand moving in slow motion toward my clit. He's teasing me, and he knows it.

For some reason this all strikes me as hilarious, mortifying, even, and I press my face into his shoulder, trying not to cackle.

"Okay, no worries. We need you in fifteen for an interview," she says in that bubbly tone of hers.

"Will do," he says, his fingers edging closer and closer to my folds. He's about to dip his middle finger into my . . .

"Oh, and have you seen Lily?"

Max slides a finger into me, skimming my clit and making every nerve in my body sing with glee.

"Not lately," he calls out while circling my clit. "Sorry."

"Okay, thanks. Meet you downstairs."

Max continues to stroke me, and I'm trying hard not to laugh, orgasm, or implode.

"We need to stop," I hiss.

"Why? We have a few minutes. You don't want to finish?"

I wriggle out of his arms, away from his fingers, which are tormenting me. I'm desperate to finish, in fact. But now isn't the time. "I can't, not when there's time pressure."

He leans in and kisses me on the mouth. "Okay. No worries. We'll pick up where we left off tonight, after the party. In a proper bed. I'll bring the condoms."

I stand, straightening my skirt. The full force of what we did in his locker room—and what he's fully expecting later tonight, after we meet our team obligations—sinks in. It makes me a little dizzy, and I rake my fingers through my hair, knowing that this time, I'm not going to say no to anything Max wants.

CHAPTER TWENTY-FOUR

LILY

I've been to a lot of team parties, starting when I was a child. Mum used to take me for an hour or so before the real fun started, and when I interned for Papa, I'd often stay up all night, partying with Anh and the grid girls and the other interns.

Tonight's party, held on the rooftop bar of our hotel, is one of the most jubilant I've been to, or perhaps that's my mood. Probably it's because we had such a great showing in today's race, or because of our incredible comeback from last week's circuit. Or it's because I'm the de facto team owner and the victory is that much sweeter.

But everyone I see is laughing and drinking. The mood is so positive—with the added sweetness of my hookup with Max earlier—that I'm giddy when Tanya pulls me aside to a high-top table.

"What's up?" I ask, clinking my glass of champagne to hers.

She takes a sip and eyes me up and down. "Cute dress," she says.

I'd worn the one bodycon dress I'd packed. It's essentially a tube of black fabric that hugs my body, paired with some strappy heels. At first I wasn't sure, but when I spotted Max's eyes grow wide when I walked in, I knew I'd made the right choice.

As I'm thanking Tanya for her compliment, she interrupts.

"Don't freak out, but I have some news."

I pause and stare at her over the top of my glasses. "You've pretty much guaranteed I'll freak out now."

"I'm hearing rumors about you and Max. But it's okay! I've asked around and no one seems to have anything on you. I think it's because of that reporter's question the other day. That inspired some gossip."

"Hmm." I sip my champagne, turning this information over in my mind.

"Please, be discreet, is all. I'm going to come up with messaging. I was kind of thinking. . ." Her voice trails off and she stares into the distance.

"Thinking what?"

"How would you feel about going out on a fake date with someone? Like a sponsor?"

"What?" I yelp.

"It could deflect attention. It's a common PR tactic."

I'm shocked that she's mentioning this so casually. "Seems weird."

"It's only dinner. I have someone in mind."

My expression contorts into a grimace, the kind that my mum used to claim would freeze on my face if I made it too often.

"He's from a beer company. One of their executive VPs who deals with brand partnerships. Seems like a decent guy. I was thinking that you could go to dinner with him in Las Vegas before the next race, we could tip off the paparazzi, you know, that kind of thing."

That kind of thing that I absolutely loathe. I roll my eyes.

"Let's go meet him. He's right over there."

"Do I have to?"

She shoots me a reproachful look. "It's one dinner, all for show. It also helps to schmooze with the sponsors. Your father does it all the time."

Tanya starts to walk away but I reach for her arm. "Wait. Does he know it's all for show?"

"No."

"Isn't that bad? Disingenuous? I'm a terrible liar."

"Look. As far as he's concerned, he'll think he's having dinner with a business connection. And he is. Look at it as a networking dinner, except that some photographers will capture you together. I'll make sure of that. It'll be two hours, maybe three."

"You mean you'll tip off the paparazzi."

"Something like that. Come on, I'll introduce you."

Because I'm in a good mood, I follow Tanya, if only to humor her. She stops at another high-top table across the terrace, where two men are chatting. Both are wearing white shirts and jeans, as if they shopped at an identical store. One is a bit taller than the other, and the shorter one has dark hair, dark stubble, and dark eyes.

"Lily, this is Rob McDowell. He's the VP of brand partnerships I was telling you about." Tanya goes on for a solid thirty seconds about his beer company, which is one of the sponsors of our team.

I tell Rob that it's nice to meet him and we shake hands. Under normal circumstances I might be madly interested in the handsome and well-employed Rob. But not hours after I was on my knees for Max.

Oh, Max. I glance around but don't see him. It's so packed and dim up here on the terrace that it's hard to tell where anyone is, though.

Rob gushes about the race, the team, and today's win.

Tanya interrupts. "I need to go talk with someone. Lily, think about what I said, okay? We'll talk tomorrow."

She melts into the crowd, and I'm left alone with Rob.

"What are you supposed to think about?" Rob says, with a flirtatious grin.

"Oh, some team stuff. Business, you know." I wave my hand helplessly in the air, wishing I could dive into a gallon of champagne.

"You're doing a great job with the team," Rob says, and I beam. "Your father's quite the guy. I've had dinner with him a few times, and boy, is that man entertaining. How's he doing, anyway?"

I relax a little, because this is a topic I'm comfortable with. I launch into an update about my father's health, and Rob seems genuinely interested.

"He won't be back before Las Vegas, and possibly for a few races after that," I say, referring to the upcoming calendar. As we speak, some of the team is packing up here in Austin, getting ready to haul the trackside garages and modular buildings thousands of miles north.

"When do you get to Las Vegas?"

"I'll be there tomorrow," I say, praying that he doesn't probe any more about my life.

"Me too. Have a bunch of meetings in the morning. How about we have dinner tomorrow night? I know of a great steakhouse on the Strip." Rob's eyes crinkle at the corners.

Tanya will kill me if I say no. But isn't it wrong if I do? How much am I willing to do for this team? Then again, one dinner with a sponsor won't kill me, although the way Rob's leaning toward me and making deep eye contact makes me think he wants to discuss something other than business.

"Sure," I say breezily. "Tanya can set up a time with your assistant."

At that moment, I feel a familiar hand on my back, and Rob's eyes widen with excitement.

"Max Becker, bro, you drove an incredible race today!" Rob extends his hand and Max takes his hand off my spine to shake it.

"It was all my team, man. They're incredible. From the top on down." Max slides a glance at me and remains close by my side. It's an unusually flirtatious gesture, possessive, even. Especially for a man who doesn't often show emotion in public.

I chew on my cheek, wondering if Max heard Rob ask me to dinner. But that's ridiculous. We're not in high school here. I do have team obligations. It's not like Max and I are a thing, despite what happened earlier today. And yet.

"Lily seems like a natural as a team owner, doesn't she?" Rob says to Max.

"She sure does." Max is all smiles, and I'm guessing that he didn't hear my exchange with Rob. Or if he did, he doesn't care.

"Don't get too used to me, I'm only here for a few more races." I grab a champagne from the tray of a passing waiter.

"A shame," Max murmurs, looking at me through his lashes.

"Definitely a shame," Rob says, raising his glass of his brand of beer. "The sport needs some estrogen, doesn't it?"

I smirk, wondering if he's being patronizing. Maybe I'm hyper-aware of comments like that because in my former job those were usually the kind of gateway words to things far more offensive.

"Oh, there's Stephen." Rob looks toward the door, at the team's manager of brand partnerships. "I've got to have a word with him. Max, congratulations again. And Lily, we'll be in touch."

I give a little finger wave and Max slaps him on the shoulder, all gruff and macho like men in this sport sometimes do.

Now that Max and I are alone at the table, I shift away from him, acutely aware that people might be watching.

"You look gorgeous tonight," he says in a low voice. "That dress. It does something to me."

Clearing my throat, I try to will away the hum of desire coursing through my veins. How is it possible that I'm hornier for him now than when I was younger? I can barely glance for too long at him, because he's looking adorably hot in a deep-blue team T-shirt and black jeans.

We're a respectable distance apart, but it's as if our hookup in his dressing room crackles and sparks in the air between us. It's been on my mind for hours—I somehow still can't get his scent off me, even after a shower—and it's obvious from his intense gaze that he's thinking of it too.

"How do you feel? Any post-race exhaustion?" I ask. It's almost a tease, asking this question.

"Hmm." He ponders, staring into his drink, then looks into my eyes. "I feel unbalanced."

"Unbalanced?" This answer is a bit of a surprise. I repeat the word. "Why?"

A playful smirk spreads on his face. "I feel unfulfilled when I'm, ah, satisfied, and others aren't. It doesn't seem fair, and I'd like to make things right. Balance is essential, Lily. It feels like the cosmic order is out of whack. I need to fix this tonight."

It dawns on me that he's talking about us earlier, and how he'd orgasmed and I hadn't. My face grows hot, and other parts too. I look around at the people and the party. It's in full swing, and it's likely no one will miss us or notice that we're both gone. Drivers leave parties early all the time, especially the ones right after races.

"I'll meet you in the room," I murmur.

He responds with a single nod, the corners of his lips turning up. I say my congratulations and good-byes to the rest of the team, apologizing for turning in early. I explain that I'm feeling a bit exhausted from the excitement of the day, then weave through the party to the elevator, which is also crowded.

A few people recognize me, saying they're thrilled about the day's results. Another couple, in town from London for the race, ask about my father.

"He's doing so much better, especially after today." I flash a genuine smile, feeling feverish and a bit out of control. Probably I look so eager and manic about meeting Max in a few minutes that it's obvious on my face.

"Max looked amazing out there today. He is so proficient," the man from London says, and his wife agrees with a little squeal.

Now, I'm probably as red as an overripe tomato. "That's a good word for him."

The couple gets out on the floor before mine, and once I'm alone, I lean against the back wall, unsteady and flying high from what I'm about to do.

Max is so proficient.

This makes me giggle aloud as I exit the elevator and walk the few paces to my suite door.

Max is proficient, all right. Because I taught him.

CHAPTER TWENTY-FIVE

LILY

Inside the suite I slip off my shoes, rinse my mouth out with mouth-wash, and brush my hair. Or maybe I should keep the shoes on. They're about four inches high. Supersexy. Nah, my feet feel much better without them.

It's been all of five minutes and there's a soft knock at the door.

I make a mad sprint to the door and fling it open. Max tumbles in, reaching for me. We're both laughing as we kiss. When our teeth clash, we break apart, grinning.

"What are you laughing about?" I say while he gently bites my chin.

"I'm happy. That's all. Happier than I've been in a long time. Why are you laughing?"

I wrap my arms around him and we hug tight. "Someone in the elevator called you proficient."

He pulls back and looks at me with a mock shocked face. "I am very proficient on the track."

I shake my head. "I know you are, silly. But I was thinking about you being proficient in other things."

He reaches for me and trails kisses on my neck, making me whimper aloud. "You question my proficiency in bed?"

"I'm aware you are quite proficient there, as well," I tease, going to unbutton his shirt. "But I do remember when you used to strum my clit like you were toggling a Nintendo console button."

He tips his head back and chortles. "Oh god, I did, didn't I?"

I undo a second button and lean up to kiss him. "You did."

"But we learned together, didn't we?"

"Oh, yes, we did," I purr.

"And I'd like to think I've picked up a few tricks—" His voice stops abruptly and his expression falls. I cease unbuttoning his shirt. "Sorry."

"What?" I look into his eyes, which are filled with regret.

"That was a shitty thing to say, I shouldn't talk about that with you. My past. Or the time between when we were together and now."

I take his hand and lead him to the sofa, pulling him to sit next to me. "I'm not jealous."

"You're not?"

I tilt my head. "I don't like to think about you being with another woman. Or women. But I also knew it was going to happen, and I understand. Temptation is difficult to avoid in this sport. I'm not naturally a jealous person."

His nostrils flare. "But I am. I'm jealous of the men you've been with. I'd hear or read about you being with a guy and I'd get pissed. I'd be annoyed for days. Like when you were with that tech guy, the one with the bad hair. I saw you in *Vanity Fair*, while I was on a plane."

Which tech guy with the bad hair, there were so many, I almost say, but don't. For some reason, his reaction shocks me, and I open my eyes wide.

"What? You never imagined I'd get jealous?"

I shook my head. "I didn't think you cared that much."

Didn't think you cared because when I broke it off you let me go without a protest. You didn't try to get me back. You accepted it, and drove the next race. Then you moved on to supermodels, actresses, and pop stars . . .

He licks his lips and looks at his hands, and for the first time since Miami he looks like the younger guy I once knew. "We have a lot of time to make up for, Lily."

His words leave me breathless; I'm astonished that he's capable of such depth of emotion—and all for me. My thoughts are filled with memories of us together, and I launch myself toward him, so I'm straddling his lap. He catches me easily, and we're devouring each other in seconds.

We kiss deeply, fumbling with clothing and buttons. He's trying to pull my dress over my head while I'm tugging his shirt off his body. Somehow he gets tangled in a sleeve and we break from the frenzy of undressing and laugh.

This only ends up making us kiss more. When he's finally free from the sleeve, his hands reach around my back to fumble with my bra. He struggles to unhook it, which is kind of surprising. I figured he'd gotten quite good at that given all the women he'd slept with since we first met.

"I need help, baby," he pleads.

I oblige. The moment the bra comes undone, I slide it off and toss it to the floor. He sucks in a breath at the sight of my naked breasts, then cradles them in his hands. The way he caresses them with the lightest touch, then digs his fingers into my flesh, proves he definitely wants to make up for lost time.

My hands are in his gloriously thick hair, tugging while I kiss. And his hands are around my waist, moving my body, no, grinding me over his erection. All I want is for us to be magically naked this second because of all the pent-up lust that's built up over the last week.

"Can we move somewhere more comfortable?" I ask as I fiddle with his belt buckle.

"Mmm-hmm." The question doesn't seem to register because he's caressing my hard nipples with his thumbs and staring at my breasts. His eyes have glazed over, like he's in a trance.

"God, I've always loved these. They're fucking perfect."

I finally undo his belt and the top button of his pants, then squirm out of his grip to stand up. "Bed?"

He launches himself to his feet and we kiss while standing, my bare breasts brushing against his fever-hot skin. We take a few steps and kiss. While he's pinning me against the wall, I unzip his fly, and by the time we get into the bedroom, we're both not wearing anything.

"Oh crap. Don't let me forget." As we're about to fall into bed, he rushes out. I see him grab something from his pants pocket, and when he returns he's brandishing a sleeve of condoms.

Those get tossed on the nightstand before he eases back onto the bed with a little groan. It's not a sexy sound, though.

"You okay?" I ask, ogling his muscular body.

"Yeah, I'm fine. It's an old injury. From that crash a couple of seasons ago in Italy." His hand goes to his neck.

I sling a leg over his hips and straddle him, leaning down so I can kiss his mouth. I need to be careful because we're both naked and he doesn't have a condom on, and I'm so damned wet that if I move my hips a few inches, I could slide right down onto his erection.

"I remember that crash. I spent an afternoon crying in my living room wondering if you were okay."

His hands gently work their way into my hair, brushing it back from my face. "You did?"

I nod. "I even texted Anh during the race."

"You did?" He draws me closer into a kiss.

"She told me you were okay, but I was still upset."

He cradles my face in his hands and we stare at each other. It's almost too intense. The light pouring in from the other room is a touch too bright, and I swallow away a lump in my throat.

"Max, what are we doing?" I whisper.

"Making love." He says it in a matter-of-fact tone, and coming from him, it doesn't seem like a cheesy phrase.

He gently pushes me up so I'm sitting, actually hovering, over his erection, while his hands skim my skin. I move back, away from his touch, so I can run my fingers over his muscular chest, down his stomach, and lower.

I see the body I've loved for years, his tan skin smooth and taut from all his conditioning. His sculpted chest rises with each breath; his teeth are bared in a feral, sensual grin.

My intent is to stroke and tease, but I'm distracted by a tattoo on his thigh.

"I saw this earlier but I didn't get a good look at it." I run my fingers over the tattoo. "I was too dickmatized."

He chuckles at my made-up word and plays with my hair as I kiss his leg. I pull back and inspect the tattoo. It's an intricate design of a flower that snakes over the hard muscle of his thigh. I trace the riotous orange-red flower with my finger. It's almost the color of his first race car, and initially I think that's why he's chosen that design, and then I gasp.

"Max. This is a . . ."

"Lily. Yes. My Lily." His hands are still in my hair.

I look up at him, awareness sending goose bumps over my skin. "When did you get this? Where?"

"A few years ago. I was in Paris for a long weekend and met a tattoo artist at a party. I'd been thinking about it a while and told him, and he hooked me up."

The tattoo is gorgeous, one of the nicest I've seen. It was obviously done by a talented artist from the looks of its bright colors and layers of shading. That he would tattoo the flower I'm named after on his body, sit for probably hours and endure such pain, astounds me. I explore it with my fingers, skimming every inch of his thigh. The tattoo is large and takes up almost his entire upper thigh from stem to petal.

"It's a reminder of you." His voice is solemn.

I sit up, allowing this information to sink in. His hands cup my breasts, sending a shiver through me.

"Why did you . . . why?" I finally stammer.

"Because I've never stopped thinking of you. I wanted you to be with me always."

Now I'm totally at a loss for words. All I can do is melt into him, dissolve into his kiss.

He flips me over and cages me with his arms. I shiver pleasurably as he kisses his way from one breast to the next, taking time to gently bite and nibble. He knows exactly how to tease me, precisely how to get me hot. My skin breaks out in goose bumps, the feeling is so intense. My thighs are shaking, my hands are trembling. I grip the duvet hard and ball up my fists, craving the release but also wanting this moment to last forever.

By the time he's kissed his way to my stomach, I've already opened my legs for him, and he groans when he skims his fingers between them.

This time, it's a sexy sound. "So wet," he mutters, stroking me, then saying something in German.

I feel like I'm dissolving into the bed as he kisses his way to where his fingers are. His tongue, soft and warm and wet, glides across my folds, parting them, exposing my entrance. I want to push all my thoughts and doubts about this situation far away. I'm not the team owner, he's not the driver. We're two people with incredible chemistry and a complicated past.

I bite my bottom lip and smile, remembering how I used to tell him to trace the alphabet down there with his tongue. His tongue on me again feels like a brush of ink across a white page, like a new beginning or an ending.

Like fate.

Now he's not merely tracing letters, but an entire book. *Damn.* Max has gotten amazing at this. Not that he wasn't pretty wonderful before, but now he's . . . my thoughts disappear as I allow myself to surrender to him.

"Wow. Oh wow," I blurt. My moans carry with them full-body shivers as his tongue laps at me, hitting every sensitive area.

"It feels good?" he asks, between swipes of his tongue.

"Um. Yeah. It does. So good." I can barely gasp the words out because he's taking me to the brink of orgasm with his tongue. When we were together before, this was what he'd do to get me wet, then finish with his fingers.

"You seem really close," he says, replacing his tongue with his thumb, circling and tantalizing.

"Please. Your mouth. I need your mouth down there," I manage to say.

"Oh, you really liked that, didn't you? Such a good girl, getting so wet for me."

My fingers find his hair and tug as he pulls me right to the edge, then pushes me over. I cry out as I come, squeezing my eyes shut and gasping as I feel like I'm exploding into a million pieces. And when he takes his tongue off my clit he moves up my body, kissing the way he came while touching me gently with his fingers.

This makes me have wave after wave of orgasm, and my mouth opens in a silent scream. The only noise that's audible is my own breath, then an anguished final cry as I come.

CHAPTER TWENTY-SIX

MAX

I'm fumbling for a condom on the nightstand, and shaking. The taste of Lily is fresh on my lips, and I can only hope that I satisfied her as much as she did me earlier.

Never have I wanted to please a woman so much. I've been planning tonight all day since the encounter in my dressing room. It's all I could think of throughout post-race interviews, autograph sessions, and that tedious party.

I imagined peeling off Lily's clothes, teasing her for hours. In the end, we tumbled into bed laughing, and now she's naked and wet and ready for me. She's still panting, her hair a mess. Looking so fucking perfect while she stares at me with a mixture of desire and shock.

Yeah, I've learned a lot since we last were together, and I'm going to use every trick at my disposal. Or maybe not, because the way she responds to me—and the way I'm treating her, with reverence and need and something deeper that I can't put a name to yet—feels perfect.

Effortless.

All of the anger over her leaving me is nearly dissolved, or it's been replaced with sheer unrelenting want. It's not time to analyze feelings now. I finally tear the foil packet open with my teeth and slide the condom on my dick, which is positively aching to be inside her.

"Come here," she murmurs, guiding me on top of her. From her curves to her freckles to that little mole on her inner thigh, everything about Lily is perfect. My catnip.

The way her eyes light up when she sees me naked. The way she swallows hard and licks her lips when she looks at me like that.

I study her face for a second, our eyes locked. Her thumb skims my lips.

"I can't believe we're doing this," she whispers.

"This is what you want, right?"

She doesn't answer for a split second, and in that moment, the bottom falls out of my world. This is all I want, being here in bed with her. Screw races, trophies, championships. I've been chasing this feeling I had with her for years, only to find that my feelings had everything to do with her.

That she wasn't interchangeable with any other woman.

"Yes. A thousand times, yes."

I let out the breath I didn't know I was holding and dip my head so I can devour her mouth. While we're kissing, she gently guides my dick to her entrance. Something about the way she smells, like jasmine and sex, makes every pleasure center in my brain light up.

I sink inside of her, my lips hovering over hers. She's warm and so deliciously wet, and when I groan in pleasure, she gasps a little.

"Lily? Are you okay?"

"Yes, it feels . . ." She squeezes her eyes shut and buries her head into the hollow between my neck and shoulder.

"Too much? Does it hurt?" I'm fully in now, balls deep. It feels exquisite to me, but for her, I'm not sure.

"No, it feels perfect." Her voice cracks, and I ease out a little, then thrust back in.

That's when I notice her eyes are glistening. And one of her cheeks is wet.

"Baby? Mausebär?" I say hesitantly. "Are you crying?"

"Yeah, a little. But not because it hurts. It's really emotional, doing this with you."

"I know. I know." My voice is hoarse now, and all the emotions I've bottled up inside over the past seven years are threatening to break free.

I try to kiss the tears away. She's shaking all over, but I still don't know what to do. I take a deep breath and thrust harder. My mind is numb from pleasure and emotion, and all I can do is to focus on the feeling of her wrapped around me. The feeling that I finally have everything I want.

I repeat her name a few times between kisses, in time with my thrusts. Of all the things I expected tonight, her crying wasn't among them. I'm not even sure how to feel right now, so I keep kissing and pick up my pace, losing myself in the feeling of her.

"Yes," she breathes into my ear. "Like that, Max. Fuck me exactly like that."

She kisses me as fiercely as I'm kissing her, and now I'm hammering into her, hard and deep. Her legs are wrapped around my hips, her heels digging into my ass. Her tears are gone now, replaced with an expression that's contorted with pleasure.

She cries out and scrapes her nails into my back. Our bodies slap together in the semidarkness. We are finally together again. I'm a little afraid.

Afraid of what these scrapes will leave behind on my back, afraid to know where this will lead.

Or where it will end.

I move in and out of her like a piston, in rhythm with her own thrusts beneath me. It doesn't take me long to feel the familiar tingle in my balls, telling me I'm about to explode. When it happens, it almost takes me by surprise. I've lost all control, it seems.

I come inside of her, my body shuddering with pleasure. It is like sliding through warm cream inside of her, my every cell screaming with pleasure. I can only do one thing: laugh out of sheer joy, because we're making the greatest kind of magic.

She's laughing, too, pulling me down, so my full weight is on her body.

"Oh my god," she says, between giggles and kisses. "What the hell just happened?"

"I have no idea," I reply.

All I can think of is when we'll be able to do it again.

CHAPTER TWENTY-SEVEN

LILY

Early the next morning, both of our phones are practically levitating off the nightstand from all the texts and calls congratulating us on the race win.

But Max and I are ignoring everything because we're snuggling after another round of sex. We've had the most incredible night together, not talking about anything substantial, staying in our own little carnal world. All we've done is laugh and screw, and it's been heavenly. I'd forgotten what fun he was to be around, away from the hectic day to day of Formula World.

"What should we order from room service? I can get anything I want this morning." He twists away from me to grab the menu from the nightstand then scoots back into position next to me. I fold myself in the crook of his arm and we stare at the extensive offering of food.

"That huevos rancheros platter looks good. I'll take that. And a coffee," I say.

"Lots of coffee." He kisses the top of my head. "Let me call in the order."

He somehow manages to keep me close while reaching for the phone and talking to the room service people. He orders for me first, then himself. "I'd like a breakfast burrito and the blueberry pancakes. And some tomato juice."

Stifling a laugh, I bury my face in his side. When he hangs up, I kiss him on the lips. "That's quite a combination."

"I can't resist pancakes. Just like I can't resist you." He rolls me on top of him and squeezes my butt. "What's your schedule today? Want to do something fun, like, I dunno, go to a ranch or something?"

"I'm scheduled to leave for Las Vegas at noon." I spare Max the boring details of how I'm supposed to review reports from various departments today. I figured it would be easier to do that in Las Vegas, where a veritable circus awaits. It's only the second Grand Prix in that city, and there's an entire week of festivities scheduled before the race in six days.

"In that case, I'll go to Vegas too. We could have dinner tonight or see a show. Maybe one of those magicians."

I shift so I'm sitting up, and hold the sheet over my bare chest. My stomach tightens. "Max, I don't know if that's a good idea, going to dinner in public together. The last thing I want is more rumors, more tabloid stories, more questions from the press. And I definitely don't want to worry Papa."

He scowls. "It wouldn't be that strange for the team owner and the driver to eat together."

"But to see a show together?" My conversation with Tanya and that fake date with the beer guy comes to mind. Ugh. "That might be a little much, don't you think?"

"You think we should sneak around, like we're doing something wrong?" His blue eyes are unwavering and icy. "Maybe we should be straight with your father. Maybe if I had a man-to-man conversation with him, he'd be fine."

I open my mouth then close it, wondering how this cozy morning took a wrong turn. His suggestion of a "man-to-man" talk with my father also irks me.

"We *are* doing something wrong. I'm your boss. I promised my father there would be no scandals. After what I went through with the game company, all I want is to be viewed as a competent temporary placeholder for my father. That's the best I can hope for. You know as well as I do that if this got out I'd be raked over the coals because I'm a woman, and you'd be celebrated as some kind of virile hero."

"Fine. And afterward? Will you still feel ashamed to be seen with me?" This conversation has gone from zero to bitchy in no time.

I rear back, shocked at the bitterness in his tone. I'm also surprised he's planning a future for us. "I don't know what to say to that, Max."

He lets out a sigh. "I guess I'm wondering when you're going to run, like you did before. Will you wait until the season end?"

"Excuse me?" The hair stands up on the back of my neck, like I'm a cornered and annoyed cat. "I had reasons for breaking things off before."

"Flimsy reasons." He climbs out of bed and tugs on a pair of black boxer briefs. They highlight his perfect, taut ass, which only somehow annoys me in this moment.

"Excuse me for not being as willing or capable of dealing with the press as you are." I slide out of bed and stomp to my open suitcase in the corner, which is exploding with clothes. I pluck a robe out of the mess and put it on.

"Did you ever once think about how the breakup affected me?" He pulls back the thick curtain and stares out the window. The morning sunshine makes his hair look like spun gold.

I snort aloud, knowing I shouldn't because it will escalate the situation. "Yeah, it affected you so much that you hopped into bed with women on literally every continent."

"I didn't sleep with anyone for months after you. But I'll admit that I did fuck around later. Sure. I was so pissed, Lily. So hurt. I tried to find someone who compared to you. Tried to work out my feelings with other women. I'm not proud of any of that. Which is why I stopped fucking around a couple of years ago. Trust me, I tried to find a stable relationship with someone who made me feel like you did."

I stare at him, open mouthed. He'd never told me any of this before. "If that's how you felt why didn't you call me, email me, visit me, tell me in person? All those times we saw each other at events you barely spoke to me. After I left you at the end of that season, I never heard from you. You didn't fight for me, Max."

"Did you fight for me? Did you stand up to your father? Did you try to deal with the press, like everyone in this sport does? No. You didn't fight for us." He shakes his head. "I didn't talk to you at those events because I was angry, Lily. I didn't want you to see my anger."

"You obviously want me to see your anger now," I snark.

"This conversation is long overdue."

The reality of his words hangs in the air, and I feel like shit. I also have a deep desire to hear him say he's sorry too. Maybe it's something we both need to say, but I'm not ready for that yet. Maybe I'm not ready for any of this. I do want to stop fighting, however.

"I don't understand how we went from last night to . . . this." I intentionally soften my tone.

"Last night was amazing. It reminded me of how perfect we are together."

My heart breaks at his words. I open my mouth to say something, but he continues. "Reminders of us, and how we're so good together, make me pissed, Lily. We could've had this for the past seven years. But we didn't. And I'm not sure it's something you want for the future, which makes me even more upset. I don't think you've dealt with the past, which means we can't move on. I was hoping otherwise."

He turns to stare at me. We're about six feet apart, but it feels like the Grand Canyon separates us.

Finally, he sighs. "I'm going across the hall to my room. Please send my breakfast there."

I watch, stunned, as he walks out the door.

CHAPTER TWENTY-EIGHT

LILY

"Can you believe that crap? That I haven't dealt with the past? That's what he said."

It's nearly ten hours after my fight with Max in the hotel suite in Austin. I'm now in Las Vegas, sitting at the hotel bar with Anh. In exactly half an hour I'm supposed to meet Rob, the beer guy, at the steakhouse in this hotel, but I figured a pre-game cocktail with a friend would help calm me down. She brought me up to speed on the gossip involving the grid models, and then I unloaded on her about my earlier fight with Max.

"You're pretty worked up about this." Anh sips her gin and tonic. "And you know I'm on your side, but, is he wrong?"

"We had a night of incredible sex and laughs and he . . . imploded. We were cuddling, we ordered room service and then bam! We were fighting." I've been fuming about this all day. Part of me expected him to text or call, but since he hasn't, I'm even more baffled. "If he was so angry with me why did he sleep with me?"

"You want my opinion?"

"Lay it on me." I take a bracing gulp from my glass of Cabernet.

"You were his first love and you broke his heart. Simple as that. He can't resist you, which is why you to ended up in the sack together. But he knows he still has feelings for you, and that frustrates him. He can't control what you do, or his feelings. In men, frustration reveals itself as anger."

"Hmph." I wad up the cocktail napkin.

"How did you two leave it?"

"Dunno. He left, I barely ate breakfast, then I had to catch my flight to come here. I saw a team email saying that he and Lucas were going mountain biking in Utah today or tomorrow." It wasn't uncommon for drivers and their trainers to do something physical at the beginning of the week prior to the race.

"You need to have a serious, adult conversation with him. You're not in your early twenties anymore. This isn't the first rodeo for either of you. He's slept around, you've slept around—"

"Not like he has," I grumble.

"Whatever. You haven't been celibate since the two of you broke up. If you both care for each other, then why not make a go of it? What's holding you back?" Anh always asks the direct, important questions. The ones that are hardest to answer.

"My father's health, for starters. I don't want to upset him."

"That's understandable, but only temporary. You're not taking over this team forever, and Max won't be a driver forever. He's probably starting to think of his post-racing life, since he's about that age when most drivers do. He's won the championship. And you, what do you want?"

"Stability. A life out of the public eye."

She presses her pink lips together and rolls her eyes. "Look, you won the birth lottery in so many ways. But when it comes to the press, you might have to put on your big girl panties and deal with it. There are worse things in life. And you have the resources to hire people as buffers, you know. Maybe he wants a life out of the public eye as well. Have you asked him?"

I've barely had time to ask myself difficult questions. Everything seems like a whirlwind since Papa's heart attack. "I managed to live a low-key life when I was at the game company."

"Until you didn't. And I totally support what you did because sexual harassers deserve to rot in hell. You need to be realistic. I'd hate for you to miss out on the love of your life again because you don't want to deal with some reporters. Don't let perfect be the enemy of amazing."

Damn. Now I feel like crap. Should I apologize to Max? "When you put it that way, it does seem silly. And I think the saying is, don't let perfect be the enemy of good."

"But what you have with Max isn't good. It's pretty damned great. It might not be perfect, but nothing is. Think about it." She drains her drink. "I have to get in the car so I can pick Bryce up at the airport, then we're headed to a party. And you have your sponsor dinner."

"That I do." *Gah*. This is the last thing I want to do right now. I stand up and she holds out her arms.

"Okay, a quick hug." I laugh. While I'm not a fan of hugs, I can tolerate them briefly with a select few people. Anh is one. I wrap one arm awkwardly around her shoulders. She always smells like expensive perfume, and I have to stand on my tiptoes to embrace her properly.

She embraces me with both arms for a millisecond and she laughs. "See? You're getting better. You can do this! We'll talk tomorrow."

I wave and grab my wine glass. It's time for me to meet Rob at the steakhouse, but all I want to do is hole up in my room and text Max. He's probably in Utah at some lodge, recovering from a punishing mountain bike ride. Or chatting up a sexy hiker woman. Even though I'm not normally a jealous person, the idea of this puts me into a funk.

I make my way to the maitre'd. Rob is already standing there, and grins when he sees me.

He's dressed in an upscale, business casual way, with a button-down shirt, nice jeans, and a dark blue sweater draped over his shoulders and knotted in front. My guess is that he reads *GQ* for fashion tips, which isn't a bad thing. I've had enough of tech bros and their sloppy clothes.

"Lily, hey," he says, opening his arms.

I transfer my wine from my right hand to my left, and extend my palm to his so I can head off a hug. He is not in the circle of trust.

He grins and takes my hand, then kisses my knuckles. "I see you've started early with wine. I'll need to catch up with you so we're both on the same page. Nice and buzzed. I might go with beer, though."

"Well, you're a beer guy, so that makes sense." I smile, tight lipped, feeling silly. Being alone in my spacious hotel suite upstairs seems like such a better option than this, and I'm regretting allowing Tanya to talk me into this "date."

I take a deep, fortifying breath as we're led to our table. This has all the hallmarks of being a long night.

◊

MAX

Lucas and I pull up to the team hotel in Vegas, exhausted after a long day of mountain biking. Whenever I'm having any sort of mental block—whether it's with my driving performance or a more personal matter—extreme physical exercise always sets me straight.

Every muscle in my body has a pleasurable ache. I didn't push myself to the very edge today, but the difficult trails in Zion National Park were challenging enough to give me hope that I'll get a good night's sleep. At the very least, the intense bike ride relaxed me a little after my fight with Lily.

I'm even thinking of stopping by her room to apologize. This morning, I was worried that Lily wanted me for sex and nothing else, but now that I've had the perspective of a day away from racing and her, I'm looking at things with a clearer mind and a heavy heart.

I was a dick. The stress of racing and the uncertainty of where I stand with Lily had gotten to me, and I snapped. Not cool.

The hired SUV stops at the valet, and we give the driver a giant tip and thank him. Lucas and I climb out, and I spot a flock of paparazzi on the sidewalk near the hotel. This isn't uncommon here in Vegas.

"Max. Max!" One photographer's screaming my name.

To get them off our backs, I give a wave, knowing that might be enough to make them go away. Often they only want one decent shot for the gossip sites.

Flashes pop and strobe. There's another shouted question, one that sends my pulse speeding.

"How do you feel about Lily Onassis going on a date tonight, Max?"

Lucas rolls his eyes. The doorman holds the big glass door open for us, and we walk in. People stare, but not because I'm a celebrity. It's because we're in our mountain bike clothes, covered in mud.

Our plan is to go to our respective rooms, shower, and meet up for dinner in the restaurant. As we walk to the elevator, I mutter, "What the hell was that question about?"

Lucas shakes his head. "It doesn't matter. They're trying to get under your skin. Don't let them."

"But what if—"

Before I can get another word out, I see two people walking toward me. One is Lily. The other is a guy who looks vaguely familiar, someone who was at a party in either Miami or Austin. It's difficult for me to keep track because I meet so many people.

Lily's wearing in a simple red dress. It's more revealing in the front than usual, and her hair is long and loose. She's in the heels from the other night, and along with the big diamonds glinting in her ears, the entire ensemble screams date night.

The guy has his hand on her lower back, which makes me bristle. So the paparazzi were correct.

Lucas spots them, too, then tries to steer me away. But the guy has already spotted me. His face is lit up and thank god, he's taken his hand off of Lily and is making a beeline toward me. A large family is standing between me and the elevator, so I'm trapped.

"Max. Hey, dude, imagine seeing you here," the guy booms. "I'm joking. Of course you're here, because you're going to win this coming weekend."

"Oh Christ," Lucas whispers.

The guy sticks out his hand. "Rob. My company's one of your sponsors."

"Motor oil?" I say in an arrogant tone, shaking his hand a touch more firmly than I normally do. I know exactly what company he works for. I simply feel like being annoying because he's with Lily.

"No, beer. We met at that party." He chuckles, and I do, too, but there's no humor in my tone.

"Ja, I remember now."

Lily's now joined us with an expression that tells me she wants to be anywhere but here.

"We were having dinner, Lily and me." He touches her back again. "Now we're headed to the hotel next door for a cocktail. We'd love to have you join us."

Lucas has wound his way around the family and is jabbing at the elevator button. Lily opens her mouth to say something, but I interject.

"I'd love to. But I need a shower." I sweep my hands down my body, which is caked with red dirt. "I'm a bit too dirty for polite company."

I make a point of staring at Lily while I say this, and she blushes. "You know, a late night isn't a good idea, Rob. Come to think of it, Max and I have an early meeting with a German magazine."

"Just one drink." Rob affects a pout.

"You kids have fun." I smirk at them as I walk away, but inside I'm pissed.

What kind of game is Lily playing with me? If that's what she's doing, I can play too. Tonight I'll sleep in my own suite.

CHAPTER TWENTY-NINE

LILY

Our SUV seems to be driving into the middle of the desert, an apt metaphor for how conversation is going between me and Max this morning. It's our day for the photo shoot, and instead of doing it in a studio or somewhere iconic on the Las Vegas Strip, we're going a half hour south of the city to someplace called Seven Magic Mountains.

From the tension inside this vehicle, it's more like Four Surly Adults and a Driver Who Plays the Worst Music Ever.

Tanya is sitting up front near the driver. Max and Lucas are in the second row of seats, and I'm by myself in the way back. Back at the hotel when we climbed in at five in the morning, Max tried to be chivalrous and take this seat, but I wouldn't let him.

That was the last thing we said to each other this morning. The ride has given me plenty of time to think about last night, when Rob and I ran into Max. Obviously, I didn't mean for that to happen. Tanya had told me to steer Rob to the bar next door so the paps could get some shots. After we had that drink, I'd told Rob I still had work to do (somewhat true) and had returned to my suite. I'd expected Max to text or call, and when he hadn't, I went to bed alone.

My sleep sucked. It looks like Max's did, too, because there are dark circles under his eyes.

Somehow, I can't get Max's wounded expression from last night out of my mind.

We turn down a road, and a tumbleweed rolls in front of our car.

"Okay, we're almost here," Tanya chirps. "Let me tell you a little about this place. It's a large-scale public art installation by Ugo Rondinone, who is from Switzerland. It's intended to be a splash of color in the Mojave Desert."

I have no idea what that means.

Tanya continues. "We have two hours for the shoot here, until eight. The magazine thought it was best to do this in the morning, when it's not so hot. There will be a trailer for changing and makeup, and the photos should be quick. I've told them that Max has to get back to the track for practice and we're on a tight timeline."

"Oh, look at that," Lucas cries.

I lean forward, trying to get a better look. I'm sitting behind Max, because if I sat in the other seat, I'd have to look at his profile. Still, it's torture, because I can smell his soap.

In the distance, out the windshield, I see what looks like stacked rocks painted in bright colors. Okay. I sit back and pretend to scroll through my phone.

The van comes to a stop and we're herded out by a chipper young woman with a blond ponytail. Behind her are seven stacks of boulders, each in neon hues, and all about the height of a four-story building.

Max squints at the rocks, and I can tell his analytical brain is having a difficult time interpreting them.

"Let's change and do a quick makeup. The photographer—his name is Legolas—wants to take advantage of this beautiful light."

Tanya and Lucas wander off to look at the giant rocks and Max and I make our way into one of two luxury RVs. This is a bigger budget photo shoot than I anticipated, but then again, it is *GQ Germany*.

Inside, a guy in skinny jeans whisks Max to one end of the RV, and the blond tells me to follow her into the back room, which is separated from the rest of the vehicle by a door.

"Okay, so we're thinking you would wear this." She turns to a free-standing clothing rack and plucks a silver minidress off a hanger.

I suck my teeth. Not only is the dress the opposite of anything I'd ever wear, but it looks like it might barely cover my butt.

Might being optimistic.

"Tell me something. My father was supposed to be in this photo shoot. What was he going to wear?"

"Oh, we were going to do that shoot on the track. When we found out you were taking over the team, we pivoted."

"Perhaps we should pivot to a different outfit." I cross my arms. "What's Max wearing?"

"Let me check." She turns to a clipboard and flips through a few pages. "He's wearing cowboy boots, jeans, and a T-shirt?"

I blink once, slowly. "You don't see a problem with me wearing that while he's in regular clothes?"

"Not really." She looks up from the clipboard.

"I'm not wearing that. I'm the team owner." At least temporarily. I go through the rest of the clothes on the rack until I find a black T-shirt with a cool retro print of some playing cards and the words *Sin City*.

"I'll wear this and the jeans I've got on," I declare. "Otherwise, count me out of this shoot."

I'm already wearing my kickass red cowboy boots from Austin.

She sighs. "Let me clear it with Legolas."

"You do that." When she leaves, I unbutton my blouse. As I'm taking it off, the door flings open.

It's Max.

"Excuse me," I say in a cross tone.

He ignores me. "What's this I hear about you not wanting to wear the outfit?"

I don't bother to put on the T-shirt. Instead, I stand there in my bra, jeans, and boots. It's not like he hasn't seen it all anyway. "She wanted me to wear this."

I point to the dress and Max grimaces. "I see."

His eyes drift to my breasts and he clears his throat. "I agree that's inappropriate. I'll talk with them."

He goes to walk out, but I stop him. "No. I've made my wishes clear. You don't need to fight my battles."

Max bites his lip, nods, and leaves the room.

The assistant slathers makeup on me, and I look okay, like a slightly vamped-up version of me. I'm not going to argue any more today.

Through an assistant, the one-named Legolas finally declares that it's okay for me to wear clothes that don't make me look like a show-girl, and we all troop out of the RV and into the desert, toward the rock columns.

Legolas, who looks similar to the assistant in skinny jeans but with a moustache, shakes my hand and looks me up and down. The blond assistant had knotted my T-shirt, so my boobs are accentuated. Then he scrutinizes Max, who is wearing a stony expression.

"Actually, I like this outfit better. Very retro."

He instructs us to stand near rocks painted in blue, white, and hot pink. Max folds his arms. I do, as well.

"Perfect. Now stand back to back, with those serious faces."

We do, and the heat of Max's body sends little tingles through my own. I try to focus on anything but him. The vast sky, the colorful, senseless rocks, the figures of Lucas and Tanya in the distance, looking like little ants.

"Sure is warm out here," he comments.

That it is. Even though it's barely seven o'clock, the sun is strong. I'm already lightly perspiring.

"Okay, Max, I want you to put your arm around Lily," Legolas shouts.

"Wait," I holler. "Why? This isn't an engagement announcement."

Legolas walks toward us. "Do you not want to touch him?"

I open my mouth, unsure of what to say.

"What Lily means is that she should project an image of power, not of one a traditional feminine role," Max says.

And now I love the man even more. "Exactly, thank you, Max."

Legolas considers this while biting his bottom lip. Finally, he says, "Then let's have Lily standing, with her arms folded, and Max leaning against the rocks."

We do this for a while, shifting into slightly different poses and expressions. As the sun climbs higher into the sky, I begin to overheat. Max isn't perspiring at all because he's used to the extreme temperatures of the cockpit of a race car.

Legolas points toward the other six rock columns. "One last pose. I want the two of you walking and laughing."

I fight the urge to curl my lip. Neither of us want to laugh right now.

Max and I glance at each other, then start walking side by side.

"Laugh," Legolas yells. "Look happy!"

"Do you remember the Acro-Cats, that roadside circus in Poland?" Max says.

This makes me laugh, for real. During the time we dated, after we'd finished a race in Austria we'd ended up traveling to Poland because we felt adventurous, and ran smack into a traveling big top that featured only house cats.

"I will never forget the Acro-Cats as long as I live," I say through giggles.

"Me neither. It was pure chaos. My favorite was the one who played the trumpet." Max makes a little *brr-brr* sound, like an off-key trumpet, and I am now chortling.

"I still have the photo we bought that night. Of us together, with the tabby cat."

"The one in the hat?" Max wipes the corner of his eye. He's either laughing so hard he's crying or is crying because the wind is kicking up the dust.

"That is perfect! You two are naturals. So gorgeous together," Legolas calls. "We're done."

Max and I walk silently back to the RV, our boots crunching the desert gravel underneath. We go inside and I'm about to turn to where my blouse is hanging when Max reaches for my arm.

"Can I have a word with you in private?"

"Sure." We walk into my dressing room and I shut the door.

"About last night," he begins. "I was . . ."

It's as if he's searching for a thought while he chews on his cheek. If I didn't know him, I'd assume it was because he was searching for the correct English word, but I know he's fluent in both languages.

"Uncomfortable. I was uncomfortable with seeing you with that man."

"Are you jealous?"

He stares at me with those ice blue eyes. "There's no sense in lying about it. Yes, I'm jealous. We had the most incredible night together in bed, and then hours later you go on a date with a beer salesman."

I'm a bit taken aback at how honest he is. The corner of my mouth quirks up. "He's a team sponsor, not a sales guy."

"Whatever." He curls his lip. "Wouldn't you be jealous under these circumstances?"

"Probably, yes. But it wasn't a date."

He lifts an eyebrow. "No? The two of you looked pretty cozy."

I lean toward him. "Tanya set it up so the paparazzi would take photos. She wanted to deflect attention away from us," I hiss. "That's why we had to leave the hotel to have a drink somewhere else. We paraded ourselves down the street for the cameras."

He scratches his neck. "I wish you'd told me."

"I might have, if you hadn't lost your shit in Austin."

"I don't lose my shit. I never lose my shit." His mouth affects a slight, adorable pout.

"Yeah, you did. You tore into me for no reason at all."

"I have a lot of anger over what happened between us. I'm trying to get over it. Lucas says I might need therapy to work out my feelings, but I've been trying to deal with it on my own. I'm sorry."

I bite my lip as my limbs suddenly feel too heavy for my body. My god, I feel like shit.

"I understand why you broke it off all those years ago. You were justified, Lily. This is a me thing. I need to make peace with it, or let you go for good."

This declaration steals the breath from my lungs. *Don't let me go,* I want to scream. *Never let me go.*

There's a sharp rap on the door. "Max?"

It's Lucas.

"Yeah," he calls, without taking his eyes off me. He reaches out and smooths a lock of hair from my face, and I want to cry because his touch is so tender.

"We need to get to the track. Practice starts in two hours."

"Coming." Max sighs. "Sorry for my attitude earlier. I had a shitty night's sleep."

"I did too," I whisper.

"Can I come to your room tonight?"

I nod.

He leans down and brushes a soft kiss on my cheek. "Let's get back."

He leaves the room and I change into my blouse, feeling warmer than before. I can't stand the feeling of elation going through me, because I know my heart's on the line, but I also can't wait until tonight.

CHAPTER THIRTY

MAX

As I expected because of my terrible night's sleep, practice was shit. That's okay, though, because I fully intend to make up for it tomorrow. In this circuit, drivers are allowed two full days of practice, unlike in other race circuits, so this is to my advantage. Today I got to know the track, drove in a mediocre way, and then the rest of the week I'll be untouchable.

At least, that's what I'm telling Lucas—and myself.

What are your plans for tonight? he texts me. *It's nine p.m. in Las Vegas. Want to drive up and down the Strip?*

Lucas loves seeing the sights at every race stop. He can't stop talking about that rock art installation earlier. Normally I'm up for some nighttime fun, but I have other ideas.

Going to hit the sack early. See you tomorrow.

He texts me a thumbs-up, and I suspect he knows I'm blowing him off for Lily. At least he's not lecturing me—that will come tomorrow if I don't get my shit together during practice.

I grab a pillow from the bed in my suite—it's got the perfect level of cushioning—and slip out of my room. Lily's suite is down the hallway, and I knock softly.

She opens the door, looking even more gorgeous than earlier. She's in a long-sleeved pink and white striped pajama top and matching shorts.

"Hey, I was doing some work, watching clips from last year's Vegas race. Also, I checked in on my parents. Papa's feeling better. He suggested we use a two-tire strategy for Vegas. Oh, and Mum claims she hasn't killed my plants." She walks away from me and I shut the door, suddenly feeling awkward.

She closes her laptop and stretches. There's her bare stomach again, and I ache, positively ache, looking at her.

"I'm tired after getting up so early," she says. "How about you?"

"Are you asking me to bed?" I grin.

She does, too, then stares at my mouth. "I guess I am."

Part of me expected that we'd talk more about our fight, or about how I was jealous of Rob. But it doesn't seem like she wants that, and who am I to argue?

I follow her into the bedroom, the sexual tension between us growing thicker. We each climb under the covers, the same sides we'd taken in Austin. She shuts off the light and flops on her side, with her back to me.

I spoon her, like we did before, and my muscles instantly relax. It's as if our bodies are made for one another. Who needs talking when we have this?

She snuggles into me, winding her leg between mine. I wrap my arm around her, capturing her fingers, but she instead puts her hand on top, and moves my palm to her stomach, underneath her pajama top. The feeling of her soft skin sends a sharp current of desire through me, then when she wiggles her butt against my hips, my dick springs to life.

I kiss her neck, and the next thing I know, she's sliding my hand to her breast.

I groan a little as I play with her taut nipple, then can't take any more. Another wiggle of her butt and I'm done.

Roughly, I flip her onto her back and capture her mouth in mine. Within a minute, we're both naked and needy, and I don't hesitate to reach for a condom, because all I want is to bury myself inside her.

CHAPTER THIRTY-ONE

LILY

Max has an incredible week. After our night together, he is perfect during the second practice, takes pole during qualifying, and is first on the podium on Sunday. Every night we sleep together, but we stop having sex the night before the race.

After the race, however, we're both ravenous for each other. We have a quickie at the hotel between the end of the race and the celebratory party, then we spend all Sunday night in bed.

We're still in bed Monday, and I'm hoping we won't have another fight.

"We have few days off between races, until we have to get to Montreal on Tuesday night. Let's go somewhere." He says this while we're burrowed under the covers. Like when we first met, we share a love of a subzero air conditioning while buried under a thick down duvet. We're probably generating enough heat under the blanket to power the Las Vegas Strip.

The curtains are open, sending sunlight pouring into the room. My stomach rumbles, and I remember that I'll need to eat at some point. That I can't feast only on Max. I'm almost giddy that we put our fight behind us, although I know nothing's truly resolved.

Maybe it never will be, and I need to enjoy whatever moments I can steal with him.

"Where should we go? Won't Lucas be upset?" I roll onto my side, folding myself into his body. My lips feel kiss stung and swollen, and my entire body aches in a satisfying way. I've lost count of how many orgasms I've had, and my brain feels pleasantly fuzzy, as if I'm a little drunk on champagne.

"Hm. Somewhere private. And no, why would you say that about Lucas?"

Somewhere where we can get each other out of our systems. "He's been a little frosty, and I get the impression he's not okay with the two of us being together."

Max kisses my fingers. "He doesn't want me to be depressed again. Like I was."

"I see." There's a pause, and I'm hoping this conversation doesn't go south. So I change the subject quickly. "The Caribbean?"

I trail a finger down his chest. He's grown a sprinkling of chest hair since we were first together. I like it. A lot.

"Perhaps. Or how about this? One of the other drivers was talking about a place north of Montreal. It's a resort town, in the woods, secluded cabins and such."

I lift my head. The idea of being in the cool forest after all this desert heat sounds incredibly appealing and cozy. "You know, I've never been up that way."

"There's a lake and we could swim. You in a bikini."

"Oh yeah, that's a real treat," I say sarcastically.

"You really haven't changed, have you?" He stares at me, his blue gaze unwavering.

"What do you mean?"

"You still don't think you're gorgeous."

"Max." I kiss his nose. "I appreciate that you think I'm pretty, but objectively, and I say this without emotion, I'm an average-looking human. Especially around you and Anh and all of the beautiful people in this sport."

"I don't think that at all. I've never thought that."

"Thank you. But you surely know what gorgeous women look like."

"Seriously." He traces my jawline. "I always looked at you like a slot machine jackpot."

A look of horror crosses my face. "What?"

"Let me explain."

"Please, because this sounds really weird and borderline offensive."

He kisses my cheek. "Hear me out. Remember the time we were in Monaco at the casino and no one recognized me because I was new and we played all those slot machines?"

"Yep. Sure do." It was one of my fondest memories, a time when we'd flown away together for a weekend, before he was superfamous. Before I got freaked out and before my father got angry.

"You know how you win some money if you get like, two cherries, or three oranges, on the machine?" He rotates his finger to mimic the spinning icons of the slot.

I nod.

"But those prizes aren't the jackpot. I consider other women like the cherries or the oranges. I was happy with the result. I had fun playing. But I was chasing the jackpot. The row of sevens."

"I see." I'm not sure I do, but I want him to continue.

"You're the sevens. You're the jackpot. I don't know why you are that for me, but you are. It's a combination of your humor and your mind and your looks and everything about you. I've been chasing the jackpot of you for years."

Now I'm stunned into silence. We lie there for a while, snuggling. I'm trying to come up with a witty retort and I can't.

"You know, I like this idea of the cabin more and more," he says, changing the subject. "I'll have my assistant book a villa and a plane." He lets out a laugh.

"What?" I ask, still reeling from his words.

"I remember when we were together before. I never dreamed I'd reach private jet levels of success."

"Well, I always believed you would." And that's precisely why I'd ended our relationship. Because I knew he'd be a superstar, and that wasn't a life I wanted to lead.

Yet here I am. In bed. In the middle of the maelstrom that comes with Formula World. I'm trying desperately to hang on to my normal life, and yet I'm planning on flying to Canada with him so I can soak up more time in his presence.

Because who knows how long this, us, will last. It's a question I don't want to ask myself, much less ask him. It sure seems like he's interested, though, and that fact makes my heart soar. Best to take this slow, though.

I reach for my phone. "Probably I'll fly separately, because I should go to Miami to check on my father."

"Ohh, Mausbär. We can stop in Miami. Let's fly together."

"You're sure?"

He kisses my nose. "Very sure."

CHAPTER THIRTY-TWO

LILY

We manage to get out of the hotel (separately) and to the private airport (in different cars) without being seen. Max is now swarmed with a new crop of press wherever he goes because of his record-breaking race times in Austin.

This means we've got to take extra precautions about being spotted together. I'm still able to move around without much notice, probably because I'm able to throw on a pair of shorts, a T-shirt, and a ball cap and look like any other thirtysomething woman. I don't have the luxe look about me, never have.

I'd prefer to think of it as blending in, which is exactly what I want right now. I board the private jet a half hour after Max. Even on board we keep our hands to ourselves and act professional, each tapping on our laptops from opposite sides of the aircraft—who knows if the gossip press is paying the flight attendants to keep tabs on Max.

When we land in Miami, I murmur a discreet good-bye to Max and climb into a chauffeured car to go to the hospital in downtown Miami, where my father's still recovering from his surgery. Max has arranged to do a meet and greet with a Down syndrome group, so he's in a separate SUV.

At the hospital I find Papa and Mum doing what they do best: bickering.

"I will not leave this hospital and get you a milk shake. Absolutely not. Drink your green juice, Adrian." Mum pushes a bottle of something that looks like liquid grass toward him.

"Hey, kids," I say, leaning down to kiss my father on the forehead.

"Thank god you're here. Your mother's trying to kill me."

"He's impossible, Lily. Look at him." My mother, who is wearing some sort of pink gauzy duster over an all-white getup of leggings and a tank top, gestures with an arm adorned with bangles.

"Good to see you two getting along as usual."

"We're fine," Mum says, brushing me off as she always does.

Papa grabs my hand and I study his face. "You look like a whole new man. When do you get to leave? Have you reconsidered going home to New York?"

"The doctors say soon. Your mother and I are still planning on staying at your place."

"Okay. Don't let Mum kill the plants. The last time she stayed in my place she massacred two *Monstera* plants."

A pang of homesickness goes through me, thinking about all of my green friends at home. I'd been trying to cultivate a peaceful life out of the spotlight after I was fired from my job. Now I'm sneaking around the world with Max and letting my little plant babies fend for themselves.

"Lily? Lily!" Mum waves her arm, the bangles jingling.

She startles me out of my thoughts, and I shake my head. "Sorry. I'm a bit exhausted from—"

From getting railed by our team's star driver all night. "—from all the excitement of our recent win."

Papa's eyes twinkle. We talk about the race for a while, and when his nurse comes in for a round of checks, he introduces me as his protégé.

"She's the reason the team won in Las Vegas," he says.

"No, not really," I say, but I'm inwardly glowing at all his praise. It feels like it's the first time someone has acknowledged that I've done a good job at anything in years; back when I was in tech, it seemed that nothing I did was ever good enough.

"I'm going to need to borrow your father for a few final tests," the nurse says.

"No worries," Mum chirps. "My daughter and I will grab lunch."

Papa looks at her, pleading.

"No milk shakes for you, mister." She taps him on the nose like he's a dog, and I shake my head. Sometimes they're adorable, sometimes they're annoying. Today's one of the adorable days, at least right now.

Mum and I wander out of the room and head to the cafeteria. After the intense crush of press in Austin, it's a relief to be back in the real world. We grab salads—and fries—and head to a table. It's next to a window overlooking a courtyard bursting with tropical foliage, and this makes me miss my condo all the more.

How I wish Max and I could hole up at my place for a few days.

"Did you change your skincare routine?" Mum stares at me.

"No. I don't have a skincare routine." I know what she's getting at, and I'm playing along by being coy. I swipe a fry and chew, pretending not to pay attention to her.

She makes a *tsk* sound with her tongue. "Then what is it? You look luminous. Oh wait. Lily." Her hand flies to her chest. "It's Max, isn't it?"

"Mum," I whine, suddenly morphing into a hormonal sixteen-year-old. She leans in and I lower my voice. Although I'm not sure why because no one is paying attention to us and the din of the cafeteria is a dull roar. "We spent the night together last night. Well, the past several nights, actually. Since Austin. And we had a fight but made up. I don't know what I'm doing."

She tilts her head and a little smile tugs at the corners of her mouth. I expect her to say something, but she doesn't.

"What?"

"Nothing." She sips her water, holding the glass daintily with both hands.

"You want to say something. I can tell."

"You two would make such beautiful babies. I've always thought that."

I allow my head to fall back and press the heels of my hands against my temples. "That's your takeaway from all this? That we'd have cute babies together?"

"Not cute. Beautiful."

"Mum, I'm not even sure I want children. I don't know if he does either." I stuff two fries into my mouth.

"Well, I'm not going to pressure you."

"Uh, you already are. Don't you think it's pretty bad that I'm sleeping with the driver?"

"Not the most scandalous thing I've heard in Formula World. Remember that one driver who used to be on our team, what was his name? The man from New Zealand? It was back when you were about twelve."

I mention a name, curious. I recalled that he was an excellent driver but never good enough to win a championship. "What about him?"

"We had an affair."

"What?" My voice comes out in a screech, and people at nearby tables pause their eating to look at us.

Mum seems unfazed. "Well, it wasn't actually an affair. It was during the first separation with your father. Papa had owned the team about seven years at that point, and was spending all of his time on the road. We separated and then I ran into the driver one day at a private airport lounge. One thing led to another, and . . ." She lifts a shoulder into a shrug.

I calculate the years in my mind. I recall being sent off to summer camp that year and my parents being extremely frosty to one another. Then they'd separated but had gotten back together by the time the next summer rolled around. "Does Papa know?"

"Of course he knows."

I look at her in horror. "You two have the most messed-up relationship, you know that, right?"

Mum opens her eyes wide and blinks. "We love each other very much. But we don't see eye to eye on some things."

"Mum, you drive each other crazy. You slept with someone else."

"So did he, two years later," she retorts. This I knew about, because my parents had argued over it for years. "But we worked it out in therapy."

"Oh god, you two. This is part of the reason why I'm so reluctant to get into a relationship with Max. Or anyone. I don't want to end up in a—" I gesture wildly with a fry in my hand. "A strange situation like yours. I don't want to be cheated on. I don't want to cheat."

"My dear, your father and I have an unconventional relationship. But we adore each other."

"But you sleep with other people. You keep secrets."

She frowns. "Not anymore."

I can't control the snort that comes out of my mouth. "Whatever."

"You're my daughter. He knows that my bond with you comes first.

That's what makes your father so special. He's not jealous. So don't knock it. And don't be afraid of commitment."

"How can I not when the two of you are out in the word, being weirdos?" I pause. "And, anyway, I'm technically Max's boss right now. If it got out that we're together, it would be a huge scandal. Papa would be pissed."

"It would be a scandal, but I'm not sure he would be upset. Not at you, at least. Or maybe he would, for distracting his star driver. Anyway, your father's planning on returning in a race or two."

"Is his doctor aware of this?"

"He is. He says Adrian's recovering nicely after his surgery and should be cleared to work in a couple of weeks."

I scrunch up my face, unsure of how to feel about this. Not only do I not want to give up Max so soon, but I also don't want my father pushed over the edge. "The doctor's aware of Papa's line of work? His isn't a desk job."

Mum stares at me. "Do you think your father can go five minutes without mentioning his team? Hell, Lily, he gave the doctor VIP tickets for the Mexico City race."

I blow out a sigh.

"Honey, I don't want you to worry. Where's Max now?"

"He's at a charity autograph event here in Miami. We flew in together and we're planning on spending a couple of days in Quebec together before we go to Montreal. He's arranged a cabin in the woods."

"Ooh, fun. Let me know where, because I probably know of a good yoga teacher. I've been several times."

"Mum, we won't be doing yoga."

Mum giggles and I stab at a tomato sitting atop my salad. "I really, really like Max. More than like. But all these issues are keeping us apart."

"Doesn't sound like you're apart if you're going on vacation together."

"Keeping us from being anything but friends with benefits, I mean. And we're not vacationing. We're spending a couple of nights in a cabin."

She purses her lips, obviously trying not to laugh. Mum can see right through my crap. "Other than the team issue, which will be resolved soon, what's keeping you apart?"

I snort, as if the answer's obvious. "His career. His fame. The never-ending spotlight of Formula World. I don't want that life. This past week has been a lot. I'm doing it for Papa, but I don't want to live the life of a race-car driver's wife. Max is nowhere near retirement. He's at the top of his game."

"Being a driver's wife isn't so bad, honey. Try being a team owner's wife."

"Is there any difference? Also, you're an extreme extrovert, and you parlayed it into something you love. I also want to do something I love, but more low-key. Ideally a job similar to what I had, but with less sexual harassment."

"Max won't be a driver forever."

"True," I grumble.

"So why don't you ask him what he has planned for the future? And if it includes you?"

That's one conversation I haven't thought of, partially because I fear that he only wants me temporarily, like all the other women he's slept with since me. "That's the other thing. We haven't been back together long. I don't know if he wants anything permanent. Given his track record, I'm guessing not."

"It's not like you've been celibate since him."

"True," I muttered.

"Didn't you say you and Max slept together several nights?" She looks at me suspiciously, as if my story isn't holding water.

"Several nights together. We haven't had sex *every* night. Jeez."

Her eyebrow quirks up, and I add, "It's a long story. But we've only been together-together a few nights."

"You two are adults, doing adult things in bed, so have an adult conversation. Simple as that." She tucks into her salad and glances around the room, indicating that she's finished with the conversation. "Or maybe it's not so simple, because you still haven't figured out if you can handle life on the track. That's up to you to figure out."

I eat in silence and wonder. Mum's right, of course. I hate when she is. But she's crystallized the real dilemma: Is my desire for Max greater than my dislike for the Formula World life?

CHAPTER THIRTY-THREE

LILY

After Mum and I eat, we head back upstairs so I can say good-bye to Papa. He wants to know if I'm headed immediately to Montreal, and I hedge.

"I've been invited to a cabin in Quebec for a couple of days."

"So cryptic." He frowns. "Is it with a man?"

I clear my throat. "It's a chance for a little rest and relaxation before the race. Don't worry, I'll be doing lots of work while I'm there. And it's only a couple of hours from the track in case I need to get there quickly before practice."

"How is everyone on the team treating you?" my father asks.

"Good," I say slowly, and when he eyes me suspiciously, I quickly follow with, "Excellent, actually. No problems so far."

"Esteban looked solid. And Max was superb as always."

"Yes, he was." I can't meet my mother's gaze because I'm worried I'll reveal too much. "Oh, look at the time. I have a plane to catch."

I kiss my parents good-bye, once again beg my mother not to kill my plants while staying at my condo, and leave the hospital. As arranged, Max is already at the executive airport on the plane by the time I arrive, and we take off without any contact with the media. Max's presence at the charity event seems to have appeased them.

Once again, on the flight and the ride from the private airport in Canada to the cabin, we barely talk with each other beyond a few race details. I work on my laptop and he's on his phone. But there are long, lingering looks, and every time I glance over at him, he's staring at me with a half smile that cuts into my heart like a blade. Every minute we spend together the air between us crackles and sparks like an electrical storm. Getting each other out of our systems is the best idea we've ever had.

Somehow, not acknowledging each other's presence beyond business makes me even hotter, and the minute we get inside the cabin, we collide. I wrap him in a giant hug, and he lifts me off the floor, twirling me around.

"Don't you want to look around the cabin?" he asks. As he puts me on my feet, I slide slowly down his body.

I swivel my head and take in the new surroundings. It's a log cabin, decorated with a few tasteful moose knickknacks. Very Canadian. The furniture screams of luxury and pine, and the open floor plan with the living room–kitchen combo is pleasantly benign.

"I'd rather look around the bedroom."

He laughs and grabs my hand. "Let's go exploring, then."

It doesn't take long for us to find the main bedroom, or for me to wrap my arms around him and press my lips against his neck.

Max and I move together toward the bed as we kiss, a fierce, quick dance that ends when the backs of my knees hit the bed. He presses me back and cages my body with his hands. We're still kissing, and the reality of what we're doing makes everything a little off kilter, as if the world is tilting off its axis because of our intensity together.

I tug at the hem of his T-shirt and he impatiently strips it away so my fingers can stroke his sinewy, powerful chest. He abruptly stands, just out of my grasp, and I'm about to protest when he undoes his jeans and lowers them, and his underwear, to the floor, kicking off his shoes.

He laughs a little when he sees me staring at his erection. He's heartbreakingly beautiful, too handsome for me. The sun has made his skin a light tan, his hair golden, and his eyes a crystal blue.

"I like," I murmur, reaching for him.

We move into the middle of the bed.

"Your turn," he says, slowly skimming his hand under my shirt. I wriggle out of my shirt and he traces the lace on my bra, the spot above my nipple.

"This is a very pretty piece of lingerie."

"I have matching panties."

"Let me see."

I raise my hips and slide off my skirt, revealing the matching black lace panties. He sucks in a breath as he studies me.

"I love looking at you," he finally says. "It's my favorite thing in the world."

His fingertips slowly skim down my stomach and lower. I open my legs a little and he traces the edge of my panties. He starts with the elastic band below my belly button, then trails his fingers to the band circling my right leg. His touch teases, and I'm getting wetter by the second.

If only he'd move a few inches.

I shift impatiently and whimper a little, hoping his fingers will touch the most desperate, needy part of me. He chuckles and strokes my leg, sending another electric current right to my clit.

With an even slower journey, he traces the inside of my thigh, all the way up to my pussy. And that's when he makes tantalizing, maddening circles right over my clit.

"So wet," he whispers. His eyes are half lidded, lazily going from my face to my body.

"Max," I murmur.

"Yes, Lily?"

"I want . . ." My voice dies as his circling becomes more insistent. I could almost come like this, but almost isn't going to cut it. I need his fingers on me. In me.

"What do you want?"

"You know."

"I need to hear it." He dips his head to kiss me. "Do you want my tongue down there?"

"No," I whimper.

"Then what?" His fingertips stroke my labia, driving me almost out of my mind with need.

"Touch me."

"I am touching you."

Dammit, he knows he's teasing. He knows what he's doing to me.

"My clit. Please?"

"Your clit? Hmm. Let's see. Do I remember where your clit is?"

"Hush. This is no time to joke," I hiss.

His hand dips under my panties and I exhale a *yeah*.

An open-mouthed smile forms on his face when his fingers slide through my folds. Somehow, he manages avoid my clit. "You are soaked."

"Please?" I'm not above begging.

He slides a finger inside me. "Please what?"

"You know."

He slowly plunges into me, dipping two fingers in and out. "I don't know if I do. Maybe I've forgotten."

Damn him and his teasing. "Make me come. Please? Touch me until I come."

His lips are against my ear. "I've always loved when you beg me."

I whisper a plaintive *please* again and he eases his fingers out, sliding them inch by agonizing inch up to my clitoris.

"Here?" He's finally found it.

"Yes. There. Please, please?"

"Like this?" He circles slowly and I feel like a ripe fruit about to burst. I shut my eyes, wanting to concentrate only on the sensation.

"Just like that."

"You're going to come for me, aren't you?"

I can't speak, can't form the word *yes*, because I can only moan. He circles faster, using a little more pressure, and a wave of pleasure hits my core.

"Oh," I finally cry out, a jolt of release striking my bundle of nerves. I chant his name and arch my back into the air, feeling a jolt of pleasure shake through me. I thrust my hips into his hand and he maintains the same fast, furious pace until I fall over the edge.

I clutch the duvet in one hand and gasp aloud. Probably the body-guards staying in the cabin next door can hear me, but I don't care because this is the best orgasm I've had in years. Like a body rocking, soul shattering, life draining release.

Max wrings out a few more pulsing, throbbing remnants of my orgasm with his fingers. He knows that my orgasms last a while—at least they do with him—and a second shock rips down my spine and leaves me shuddering. He keeps moving his hand, slowly undulating, circling, and soothing, and I let go once again.

Finally, I'm finished, and I slowly float back to earth and am finally relaxed. My muscles feel like jelly.

He nuzzles my cheek and I can feel his smile against my skin. I'm acutely cognizant that my face is bathed in sweat, that my pussy is coated in my own wetness.

I'm also hyperaware that Max's arousal is pressing against my hip, a reminder that this is nowhere near over, and that I get to enjoy him for two whole, glorious, uninterrupted days.

"Was that adequate?" he asks in an amused voice.

I sit up and unhook my bra while grinning. "You know it was much more than adequate. You know exactly what you do to me."

"I've never forgotten." He reaches for my breasts but I squirm out of his touch so I can take off my panties. It's an interesting statement, but I don't dwell on it because I have more carnal needs right now.

"Where are the condoms?" I ask, wanting more.

Wanting it all, from him. He takes me hard, and fast, and his orgasm rips through his body.

When we're finished, I grow drowsy in his arms. The bedroom has a large, floor-to ceiling bank of windows overlooking a vista of green, rolling mountains. The sun's about to set, and everything feels like a dream.

"I could stay here forever," I murmur.

Max kisses my forehead. "Me too."

I remember what Mum said earlier, about asking Max what he has planned for the future. Now would be a good time, but I'd rather not ruin this perfect moment. Long ago, Mum had taught me something else.

Never ask a question that you don't want the answer to.

CHAPTER THIRTY-FOUR

MAX

I pull a quilt over Lily's body, then kiss her temple and slowly slide out of bed. Once I've located my boxer briefs and a T-shirt, I throw them on. Even though it's early evening in July, it's far enough north to have a slight chill in the air—which is totally welcome considering we've been in Florida and Texas in recent weeks.

"Max? Where are you going?" Her voice is gravelly from sleep.

"To make dinner for us."

She frowns and makes a cute little squeak. "Oh. I didn't even ask. Do we have food or do we have to order some? Or are we going out?"

I've always loved the way she looks when she's sleepy, all sensual and soft. She sits up halfway. "I can help."

"No, babe. The rental company stocked the fridge. We never have to leave the bed if we don't want to. I'll make dinner. I was thinking about apple pancakes." Not the most conventional of dinners, but for some reason, I've been craving my mom's recipe—and I know that Lily, with her sweet tooth, will love them.

"Mmmm. That sounds amazing." She flops back down and closes her eyes, her lashes almost touching the tops of her cheeks. Her breathing becomes deeper.

For a solid minute, I sit on the side of the bed, watching her sleep. She's so gorgeous that I almost ache a little inside, but part of me is wondering where this is going, and what I'm doing.

There's no question that sleeping with her—my team owner's daughter, who is currently in charge of the team—is poor judgment. But the feelings I've harbored for her all these years have come rushing back in full force.

Giving her up again will be impossible.

I pad into the kitchen and quickly text Lucas. He knows where I am, and doesn't approve. But he also knows me well enough to know that when my mind is made up I can't be talked into changing it. I assemble my ingredients. Like racing, I'm precise when I do anything, whether it's working out or cooking. Before we arrived here I made sure that we had only the best, freshest organic ingredients delivered, and I'm not disappointed.

Mostly, I want to show Lily that I'm now capable in the kitchen. Back when we were together, I was a totally different man, one who loved the newfound trappings of wealth and fame. A private chef and exclusive meals at top restaurants were my staples. Now, I try to cook whenever I get a chance.

I'd love to learn to truly cook, and if I left the sport, it's one more thing I could explore. The offer of consulting for the electric car race circuit weighs on my mind as I begin peeling the apples for the pancake. The owner of the circuit emailed me again today, and I spent most of the flight to Canada trying to decide what to respond. Part of me wants to tell Lucas, knows I need to, sooner or later. He's been by my side for a decade. But I don't want to say anything until I decide.

In the end, I consulted with my agent. We decided to hedge yet again, saying I wanted to get through the next couple of races before making any concrete decisions. My agent thinks it's a once in a life-time opportunity to change an industry.

I'm not sure what to believe.

It would be interesting to hear what Lily has to say about the offer. I value her opinion. But she is the team owner and telling a team owner about a rival offer midseason is a career death sentence. If I reveal that I'm considering retirement, every dynamic between us will shift.

And I'm so damned happy in her presence that I don't want to risk doing anything that will jeopardize what we have right now. For the next forty-eight hours, I want to worship her in the all the ways I should have seven years ago, when I wasn't enough of a man to rec-ognize what I had. Perhaps neither of us did, and that's why we didn't fight for the relationship. We know better now.

There are footsteps on the wood floor, and I look up from the apples. Lily's in a white robe, coming toward me.

"I probably shouldn't be sleeping at this hour. I'll never be able to get to bed later."

She comes over and wraps her arms around me, surveying the kitchen island counter, which is covered in every ingredient for the skillet pancake. "What exactly are you making?"

"It's a bit of a mess right now, but I'm working through it. It's an *apfelpfannkuchen*. It's a fluffy apple pancake."

She laughs and kisses my neck. "Fluffy apple anything sounds amazing. You sure you don't want help?"

"Nope. You relax."

Her gaze goes to the small bottle of rye whiskey, and she untangles her arms from my body and picks up the liquor. "What's this for?"

"That's part of the recipe. It's the secret ingredient, according to my mother. She used to make this at Christmas usually. Would you like a little glass? I won't need all of it."

She says yes, and I pour both of us small glasses of whiskey over ice. We toast and sip, and I return to the apples. Lily slides onto a stool.

"This is a Christmas dish?" She reaches into the bowl and swipes an apple. "But it's July."

"It feels like Christmas, doesn't it?" I slice the final apple and hold it out for her.

"It does." Her voice is soft. She bites a chunk off, and I pop the rest in my mouth, then arrange the rest of the apples in the cast iron skillet and carefully pour the batter over them.

While I'm leaning sideways to check the gas flame on the burner, Lily says my name.

It's a warning tone, a definitive we need to talk statement, all wrapped up in the way she says my name. I know her well enough to recognize this.

I straighten my spine. "Yeah?"

"We need to talk. About this. About us."

I glance down at the cake, then back at her. "Okay. Could we do it after I've made us the pancakes?"

"Definitely."

She gets down from the stool and wanders into the living room, settling onto the sofa with her whiskey. I'm left alone in the kitchen, wondering how tonight will unfold. The last time we had an intense discussion about our relationship it led to a fight, then our breakup.

By the time I'm done with both plate-sized pancakes my heart is thundering against my chest—no small thing for a person who is so athletically conditioned that his heart beats at a cool fifty beats per minute when at rest.

"Powdered sugar or maple syrup?" I call over.

She sits up and peers at me, her eyes wide with excitement. "Both?"

This makes me chuckle, and I happily add both to her pancake, then bring her the plate, utensils, and a napkin.

For the next ten minutes, the only sound is us devouring the pancakes and her satisfied moans.

"Oh my god, Max. This is incredible. It's like an orgasm in my mouth." She pops the last bite into her mouth.

"Do you want me to make more?"

"Perhaps. It even goes well with the whiskey." She takes a little sip. "Maybe after your Formula World career you should think about opening an apple pancake restaurant."

She leans in to kiss me, and she tastes like apples and cinnamon, whiskey, and maple. I want to take her back to bed and feast more on her body, but instead, I clear the plates away and put them in the kitchen, then return to the sofa.

"Okay, let's talk." I suddenly feel oddly formal.

She holds the whiskey glass in both hands. "Us. This. It's a shock, honestly, especially after our past. I thought we should be adults and talk. You're twenty-eight, and I'm thirty-one, and well, I kind of want to know if this is a temporary fling or what."

She can't look me in the eye when she talks, and I'm torn over whether I should get on my knees and pour out the contents of my heart, or if I should show her how I feel with sex.

Why can't I tell her how I feel? I'm going to have to try, even if emotions don't come easy to me. This is too important to screw up. "What do you want this to be?"

I don't like the way she licks her lips nervously and hesitates to answer the question.

CHAPTER THIRTY-FIVE

LILY

His question hangs in the air.

"I don't know." I draw out my words.

A shadow crosses his face.

"I feel bad about how we ended." It's difficult for me to admit that.

Another nod, and a glance up at the ceiling. Oh great. The uncommunicative Max has taken over. The Iceman.

"I feel the same way," he finally says.

"I panicked, and I ran. I shouldn't have. I regret it." This is the first time I've said that aloud to anyone but my mother, and Max is staring at me, unblinking.

"Although I love the sport itself, I don't like a lot of the lifestyle. The incessant travel, the showiness, the parties. It's torture for me. Don't like the spotlight. Hate the media attention. Still do. But I really,

really, really loved having you in my life. Being with you these past several days have made me want more of you, and maybe I shouldn't say this, but I miss you. Now that I'm older and more secure"—I pause here, because I'm still not sure I'm more secure, but I'm already well into my monologue—"I think I can handle the rest because I know it comes with the goodness of you."

He's still not blinking, just staring at me from the other end of the sofa. The luxurious log cabin now seems altogether too airy and spacious, and the only sound is the tick of a rustic cuckoo clock on the wall.

Tick. Tick. Tick.

Ten ticks go by, an interminable amount of time.

I've said the wrong thing. I've opened myself up to a man who only wants sex. Max is no longer the man I once knew, the guy I fell for. He's changed. The years of Formula World and easy sex and women available at the snap of a finger have changed him irreparably.

"You don't feel the same, do you?" I whisper. Humiliation burns in my stomach, mixing with the sweetness of the apple pancake and the bitterness of the whiskey.

"Lily," he says, his voice cracking. "I—"

"I'm sorry. Sorry to have brought this up. It's too soon, too fast." I start to rise and he grabs my wrist.

"Sit," he commands, while gently tugging me next to him.

I'm on the verge of tears. I revealed too much, took too much of a chance. He releases his grip on my wrist and leans forward, his palms against his cheeks. This is going far worse than I expected, and I can barely breathe.

"Forget I said anything, okay?" My mind is already spinning to tomorrow morning. I'll get a car and head to the team hotel. Maybe I still could tonight, since it's not that late . . .

"Lily."

"Seriously, ignore me. I'm in a mood. I shouldn't burden you with my emotions. I'm all over the place because of my father and all the travel and my recent job situation and—"

"Lily." His tone is sharper than I've ever heard, but my mind is racing a million miles a second. "I love you. I've always loved you. It's time I tell you that. I never did before, and I might not get another chance to say the words."

"And I don't know what I'm doing with my life and . . . wait, what?" His words begin to sink in, dissolving the humiliation and fear.

"I love you." He's now sitting up, his back against the sofa, staring at the massive stone fireplace that's the focal point of the room. It's as if his eyes can't tear themselves from the damned fireplace.

I can barely breathe. "Why aren't you looking at me?"

He swallows. "Because I'm kind of freaked out. I've never said that, to anyone. But that's the way I feel."

Now I'm frozen on the sofa, staring at him. We're two bundles of awkward. "You do?"

He finally turns to look at me. I expect him to grab me in a clench, like in a romance novel or a romantic movie. Instead, his pinkie finger finds mine while we stare into each other's eyes.

"I was miserable when we broke up."

"Not too miserable to sleep around, though."

The side of his mouth quirks up. "I thought you weren't jealous."

"I'm not. Just making an observation."

His pinkie hooks into mine. "I had some pretty wild times starting about six months after we broke up. I won't deny it. I was looking for what we had. I didn't find it, because there's only one you, one us. I love being with you. Talking to you. Laughing with you. I feel comfortable around you. Like you're my family, but better, because I'm also so attracted to you. It's always been you, Lily. No one else."

I lick my lips, unsure of how to feel about this. Part of me is soaring, thrilled that he's finally expressed his feelings. Another part of me is scared as hell. I think about his weird slot machine metaphor and the tattoo on his thigh and it all makes sense now.

"I got caught up in the scene, the Formula World party circuit crap. That's also why I slept around. Because I could. Because I was trying to block out the loneliness I felt. I'm not blaming you at all, it's on me."

"You think you're over that, ah, phase?"

Now his entire hand covers mine. "I know I'm over it. I've been over it for the past couple of years. Ask anyone. I haven't even been in the tabloids for anything more than racing. I haven't had sex with anyone for months, until you."

The part about the tabloids was true, even if I hadn't wanted to admit it to myself. "I figured that you got better at hiding your activities from the press."

"No. I've changed. Matured. Whatever you want to call it."

It's difficult to believe this is happening. Hard to fathom that he loves me, and I think I should say it back. I gulp in a deep breath, then another, then a third, and when it seems like I'm on the verge of hyperventilating, I feel Max's strong arms around me.

"What are we going to do?" I murmur into his neck as we collapse together on the sofa. We end up lying down, with me half on top of him.

"What do you mean?" He brushes my hair back from my face.

"With the team. Me being in charge."

"That's not for long, you said so yourself. Your dad plans to return soon, you said."

"Yes, but eventually we'll have to go public, and that will raise so many eyebrows and cause scandal and . . ." I heave a sigh.

"Mausbär, we can get through this. There are ways. We'll keep things quiet for the rest of the season, then once your father's back I'll talk to him."

I lift my head. "Why? What do you mean?"

"I want to tell Adrian, man-to-man. He should hear my feelings and my intentions from me."

"What are your intentions, anyway?"

He hums and slides his hands under my white fuzzy robe, cupping my ass. "My intentions right now are to get you naked again."

I'm laughing as I sit up and shrug off my robe, but my laughter dissolves as he flips me onto my back and parts my legs. He kisses his way down my body, pausing to nibble at the crease of my thigh.

Then all at once he dives in with his mouth and his fingers, simultaneously filling me and tasting me. It's like the man's sole mission is to worship me, something I'm not used to with the men I've been with.

"You're way more delicious than the apple cake," he mutters against my skin.

So are you, Max. So are you.

We spend the rest of the night and the next day in bed, getting properly reacquainted with one another's bodies. I recall that Max still enjoys breathy moans in his ear while he enters me, and he remembers that I love having my hair pulled.

Most of all, though, we talk. It's not like we can have sex every waking moment. We bring each other up to speed about our past seven years, and I tell him about my dreams of someday finding a job that involves motorsports yet without the entrenched bro culture of the tech gaming world.

"Why don't you work with your dad?" he asks, staring at me with serious blue eyes. We're propped up in bed, him shirtless, me wearing his Team Onassis T-shirt, which smells like him.

"While sleeping with you?"

He lifts a shoulder. "You never know. Things could change, and if you weren't the boss, it wouldn't be so bad, would it? Stranger things have happened before on a team. Remember Savannah and Dante? They hated each other when they first met, and the only reason they started to date was because the team owner wanted good PR."

I stare at him, horrified. "No."

"Yeah. I was there. It was my first year on the team, that season after we broke up."

"Wow." That was my first year at the game company, and I was trying not to read anything about Max's new team. "I must've missed that scandal. I thought they fell head over heels instantly."

He huffs out a chuckle. "Hell no. Dante, being the arrogant SOB he is—or was—didn't even want her on the team. Then Brock Bronson, the owner, proposed a whole fake relationship scenario. He claimed it was because I was under investigation by the FIA, along with my engineer and Lucas."

I groan aloud. "I remember that. What a mess that was."

Max's old engineer eventually retired from the sport.

"Yeah, between that and our breakup, I wasn't sure if I'd even continue in the sport."

There's a touch of bitterness in his tone, and I run my fingers through his golden hair. "I'm sorry."

He shakes his head. "There's no need to apologize. I'm not proud of some of the things that engineer did back then, or of some of my personal antics. Eventually I had to make it all right, though. I had to be right with myself."

He pauses to kiss my lips. "I think that's why I'm able to be so open and honest with you. I know what I want now."

His disarming, matter-of-fact words are enough to silence me.

I can't stop thinking about how I want to tell Max those three little words: I love you.

Somehow, because I'm his boss, because I'm running the team he works for, I feel like it's a line I can't cross.

Even though in my heart I've already crossed that line, sped past it, and left it far in my rearview mirror.

CHAPTER THIRTY-SIX

LILY

The next morning, after Max wakes me up with kisses that end with me on all fours and him absolutely pounding into me from behind—and another soul-draining orgasm—we shower and throw on T-shirts, shorts, sneakers, and matching Team Onassis ball caps.

Never in my life have I been the kind of person to wear matching clothes with a guy, but here I am. We look so adorable in the hats that I insist on taking a selfie.

"We should put that on the team's Instagram account," he says.

"Yeah, right. My father would lose his shit." I'm already feeling guilty enough about my relationship with Max and going behind Papa's back. That's a problem for a future me, though, because as far as I'm concerned, Max and I can keep this thing on the down-low for months.

I'm wearing my bathing suit underneath my clothes. Max puts a couple of towels, two water bottles, and some granola bars in a backpack and we inform the security—who are staying in a small cabin next door—that we're leaving. We head outside alone, freed from the shackles of 24/7 monitoring because we're so secluded and safe here.

According to the photocopied, dog-eared guest guide left in our cabin, there's a path in the backyard that leads to a small pond. We find it easily and begin to walk. The cool morning air, damp with dew, mingles with the hush of the forest. I breathe in deeply, relishing the freshness against my throat. The sun is beginning to rise and the path is illuminated in soft light and warmth. For the first time in a while, I'm totally relaxed.

Max makes me walk ahead of him, and we're mostly silent as we make the two-mile trek to the pond. It's a comfortable silence, and I easily slip into a fantasy.

This is how our lives could be.

He'd retire and we'd travel the world, having adventures together. Maybe learn to mountain climb—Max has always been intrigued by extreme sports, and I like the idea of roughing it, backpacking, being in the middle of nowhere with only him.

As I'm about to ask him if he's ever thought of going to Nepal, I spot a rustling in the brush up ahead and slow my gait to a stop.

"What is it?" Max whispers. He comes up behind me and wraps his arms around my midsection while planting a kiss on my neck.

"I don't know." I point in the direction of where I saw the movement.

"Oh! Look, look, look," he whispers in my ear.

There, on the trail ahead of us, is a giant deer. The kind with horns. It's about twenty yards away, but we're close enough to make eye contact. I haven't seen wildlife in years, since I've been living in cities, and I feel as if I could reach out and touch its sleek brown coat, which glows in the morning sun. I see its enormous eyes watching us, cautious and thoughtful.

"Wow," Max breathes.

The buck surveys us for a long moment, then darts off, into the woods.

"That was really cool," he says, then starts talking excitedly about deer in Germany near his family's home. "Hopefully you'll see them when we go visit."

Although I met his family years ago at various races, I've never been to Germany. Years together stretch out in my mind. Adventures, possibly a family of our own. Max would be a great dad, involved and caring. Although he'd probably want his child to be involved in racing.

We stroll and talk all the way to the water. When we reach the pond, I realize it's more of a lake, ringed with deep-green pine trees and a small patch of sandy beach. It's the opposite of the frenzy we'll experience in a few days in Montreal, and I couldn't be happier.

"It feels like we're the only ones here." My voice seems tiny against the vastness of the landscape.

"That's a blessing." Max strips off his T-shirt, revealing his lithe, fit body. "I'm going in. You?"

Since I'm hot from the sun and exertion, he doesn't have to ask me twice. I strip down to my bikini and chase him into the cold water, screaming at the sensation against my skin.

We splash each other and scream, and at one point, I try to swim away so he'll chase me. Being so athletic, he catches me easily by the ankle and pulls me into his body. My heart pounds as I wrap my legs around his waist and arms around his neck, mesmerized by the way the sunlight reflects on the water droplets clinging to his eyelashes.

We kiss, slowly and deeply. This is probably the time to tell him I love him, but I also don't want to ruin the moment with words.

I rest my forehead against his, and close my eyes, trying to hold on to this moment in the cool water that's caressing our skin.

When we pull away, each of us looks surprised by the intensity of what's passing between us. A smile is plastered on my face so big that it hurts.

"I'm glad we're here together," is all I manage to say before we start kissing again.

We're practically inhaling each other here in the lake, and when he begins to slide a hand under my bikini top, I break away.

"Let's go back."

"You don't want to—"

"Here?" I interrupt, with an incredulous laugh. "No."

Even though there doesn't seem to be anyone around, I'm not quite comfortable enough to have sex out in the open.

"Okay, okay. But what if I buy us a private lake in Germany?"

I kiss his nose. "Is that your fantasy, to fuck in nature?"

He squeezes my ass, hard. "Maybe."

Giggling, I swim away, back to shore. We loll on the little beach for a while, drying off and eating the granola bars. He glances at his watch.

"Crap, I have a call with my agent in an hour. We'd better get back."

It's probably for the best because I'm certain I have a mountain of emails as well. We power off, neither of us wanting the morning to end.

The sun's rays caress my damp face. The smell of pine permeates the air and I take a deep breath, closing my eyes and memorizing the scent for a few steps. Although I think my balance is impeccable from my occasional yoga classes, it's obviously not, because I lose my footing, stumbling and toppling over.

I land, laughing, in a thicket of verdant foliage. Max rushes over, asking if I'm okay.

"I'm fine, I closed my eyes and lost my balance."

He holds out his hand and I grasp it so he can hoist me up. "Sometimes I'm kind of uncoordinated," I say with a laugh. "Unlike you."

"I've got enough coordination for both of us," he says, kissing me on the cheek.

I brush myself off and continue walking. About fifteen minutes later, as we're nearing the end of the trail, I feel a deep burning sensation on my bare legs. I stop to inspect my calf and itch furiously.

"Did something bite you?" He kneels to inspect my leg. "It looks pretty irritated, so don't scratch anymore. Oh, the other one does too."

"Weird." But telling me not to scratch is like telling a fish not to swim. I can't keep my nails off my legs. "I'll be okay."

"I saw a first aid kit inside. Maybe there will be some cream." His face is pinched with worry.

By the time we're back at the cabin, both calves are an angry red and I feel like jumping out of my skin. My legs not only feel like they're on fire, but they're an alarming, hot temperature as well. I kick off my shoes and socks, whimpering.

Max finds the kit and unscrews the cap from a tube of calamine lotion. "It's expired," he says with a wince.

"Let's try it anyway."

He squeezes a thick dab into his hands.

"Wait," I say, a little too loudly.

He looks up.

"If I have plant poison or sap or whatever, on me, you might get it on your hands. Don't touch me."

"Ooh, right."

I scoop the lotion off his palm and rub it into my legs.

"Better?" He's standing over me, hands on hips, gnawing on his bottom lip.

"Maybe a little? You need to get on your call."

"Right, right. I'm worried about you, though. You might've come in contact with some poison ivy. Do they have that here in Canada?"

"Eww. I dunno. Let me find out." I head to my laptop and Max goes into the other room, where his phone is, to make his call.

While I overhear snippets of conversation about autograph sessions, interview requests, and the offer of a biography, I try and fail to keep my hands off my legs. A quick Google search reveals that indeed, poison ivy is everywhere in Quebec, and a brief peek at my calves proves that the expired calamine lotion isn't doing squat.

Holy crap, is my skin blistering near my ankle? I twist my leg and contort my body so I can peer at the spot near my Achilles tendon. It is, indeed, puffing into a blister.

"Gross," I whisper.

Max appears in the room while I'm twisted like a pretzel. "That looks awful. I think we should take you to the hospital."

"No, no," I wave him off, biting back the discomfort crawling across my legs. "I'll be okay."

"We should try a cold bath with baking soda or maybe oatmeal."

By the time he fills a tub, I'm almost crying from the throbbing, fiery sensation. It's like a million stinging ants.

There's some temporary relief when I step into the tub, which Max has filled with cold water and white, pasty baking soda. I yelp because the water's colder than the lake. I haven't even bothered to take off my shorts or bikini bottom, because I'm that distracted by the pain.

"I know, it's not going to feel good. But you need to bring down the inflammation." He holds my hand and elbow as I sink down, the cold water numbing the irritation.

"How do you know what to do?"

"We had to take a first aid course when I was younger and getting into go-karts."

"And they gave you a lesson on poison ivy?"

He grins, the worry smoothing from his face. "They did, actually. They're very thorough in Germany."

"Thank god for that." I blow out a breath.

"Is that better?"

I ponder this for a second, then screw up my face. The pain is so intense that tears are streaming from my eyes. "No," I wail. "It still feels like it's burning my skin off."

"Okay, that's it, we're going to the hospital."

The next hour is both quick and excruciatingly slow. Max alerts the bodyguards and the driver, and they pull the SUV around to the front of the cabin. Then Max hoists me into his arms while I protest that he's going to get poison on him.

"I don't care," he growls.

We end up in the backseat, and because we're so secluded, we must drive for a solid thirty minutes to get to the hospital. Once there, a doctor recognizes Max and I'm whisked into a private room.

By this time, the back of one leg has formed multiple blisters. It's so disgusting that I can't even look at it. I'm unable to form words anyway, and communicate only in whimpers. Thank goodness Max is there to talk with the doctor.

Good lord. This is the second hospital I've been inside this month. What is my life?

I'm given an industrial-strength steroid, some antibiotics, and a painkiller. I feel almost instantly better, but a little inebriated. Maybe I'm drooling a little, but I don't care. It's better than feeling like my legs are on fire.

By the time that's all happened, Max and the entire hospital staff are old friends, and I woozily invite the doctor to the race on Sunday.

"Oh god, the race," I mumble, as Max pushes me out of the hospital in a wheelchair. "I need to call Papa. Or Jack. I'll be okay to go to Montreal tomorrow."

"We'll see, babe. Let's get you back to the cabin so you can sleep all this off."

He pushes me outside, where the SUV is waiting. So are two photographers and what look to be three or four reporters. In my slightly altered state, I can't really tell the media from the people gawking at us outside of the hospital. It's not every day that a Formula World driver pushes a drooling woman in a wheelchair out of a medical facility.

This thought makes me giggle, then hiccup.

"Oh, shitballs, it's the paparazzi," I slur.

CHAPTER THIRTY-SEVEN

MAX

If there's a constant in life, it's the media. They're everywhere and unavoidable. Over my years in Formula World, I've learned to ignore them. Focused on blocking out their noise and static.

I'd learned by jumping immediately into the fire; my first couple of years in the sport were marred by scandal due to my former engineer and his shady method of getting information on other teams' cars.

After dealing with that, I developed an iron-clad ability to ignore the press. But now that I'm pushing a wheelchair carrying an obviously drugged Lily in front of a rural Quebec hospital, I'm rethinking my apathy.

I push her toward the SUV while one of the bodyguards attempts to block a photographer from snapping photos at close range.

The other bodyguard dashes ahead to open the car door, and when we're about a foot away, Lily stands and wobbles. The doctors gave her quite a heavy sedative.

"Watch your step, Ms. Onassis," the bodyguard says, almost catching her as her knees wobble. He helps her into the car.

Meanwhile, the small cluster of reporters are shouting questions at me, things like, "What happened to Lily Onassis?" and "Did she overdose?"

That last question annoys the shit out of me, so once I see Lily is safely buckled into the backseat, I stand between the open door and the reporters.

I inhale a fortifying breath and keep my gaze on the sliding hospital doors. This way I don't have to look any of the journalists in the eye. "I brought Lily Onassis to hospital today because she had a terrible reaction to poison ivy on her legs while hiking. She was given a mild sedative due to the discomfort. She will be present at the race in Montreal later this week. Thank you."

That's all I'm going to say, but it doesn't stop the reporters from yelling more questions as I slide into the seat next to Lily. The final question before the bodyguard slams the door echoes in my brain.

"Why were you the one to bring Ms. Onassis to the hospital, Max?"

The SUV pulls away, almost clipping one photographer who is pressing his lens against the window. Unfortunately, it's right when Lily topples over, practically collapsing in my lap.

"Max, baby, thank you for bringing me there. I feel so much better now. But sleepy."

She lifts her head and smiles, and even though she's drowsy and sedated, I can't help but grin back.

"Come here," I say, pulling her upright so my arm is around her shoulders.

That's when I realize that I don't care if anyone sees us together. I don't care about the public scrutiny, or Lily's father, or the media.

I'm one of the biggest racing athletes in the world. I'm unstoppable, especially with Lily at my side.

"What's the worst that can happen?" I murmur as I kiss Lily's hair, which smells like hospital.

"Blergh," she responds.

She drifts off to sleep in my arms on the long ride back to the cabin. Once we're there—and determine that we haven't been followed by paparazzi—I carry her inside and to the bedroom.

Her eyes flutter open as I lay her on the bed. "I'm feeling better."

"I'm glad. You should rest, okay?"

"I'm sorry to ruin our time together."

I peel the sheet back and she crawls underneath, making adorable little grunting noises.

"Why are you apologizing?"

"I wanted this time to be perfect. For us. You said we had a lot of time to make up for."

Her words put a little crack in my heart and I stretch out next to her. "We've got all the time in the world, babe. But right now, you should sleep."

"Do we have all the time, though? We have to get to the race tomorrow."

With a sigh, I pull her close. Maybe someday there will be a time where we have no place to be, and no races to win. Until then, I need to get my head on straight and focus on Montreal.

LILY

"Everything would be great if it wasn't for the oozing on my right calf. At least it doesn't feel like I'm on fire anymore, so that's a big plus."

I'm on the second-floor balcony of the cabin, video chatting with Mum. It's early Wednesday morning and I'm telling her about my brush with poison ivy and getting an update on my father.

He's doing great, according to her and an email I'd gotten from his doctor.

My legs still itch a little, but the steroid shot is working wonders on my skin. I hope it holds through the week and the race.

If it doesn't, I suppose I can visit the team doctor. "That sedative knocked me out, though. I slept for a solid twelve hours."

"You've always been sensitive to pharmaceuticals. Can I see the blisters?" Mum peers into the phone, looking entirely too eager. She's one of those people who has a grim fascination with pimple popping videos, so this doesn't surprise me.

She's sitting on my sofa and I'm trying to figure out if the plant next to her is dying or merely in a bad light.

"No. Max bandaged it an hour ago. Did you overwater the *Monstera* plant?"

She glances over. "Oh, I've watered it a couple of times."

"Mum! Stop watering. You're going to kill it." I imagine all of my plants, withered and brown, and sigh. I'm about to tell her about an app that pings with an alert when it's time to water, but my father's voice booms in the background, and I wince.

"Uh-oh. I thought you said he was in the bedroom?" I ask.

"He was." Mum looks away from the cell camera. "Adrian, do you need something?"

"Is that Lily?" Papa roars.

"Oh no, what now?" I whisper, taking a sip of my coffee.

"Here, talk to her. Don't yell in the background." I almost get woozy as the video on the cell screen jostles and shifts away from Mum.

My father's face fills the screen.

"Your color looks so good! You're not gray anymore."

"Stop saying that! Jesus. I don't want to talk about my health anymore. What's going on up there in Canada?" my father says in a demanding voice.

Eeek. I don't like his tone at all.

"You seem to be quite alert. How are you feeling, Papa?" I use my most soothing voice.

"I'm fine. Sick of staying in bed all the damned day," he barks. "I want to know what happened to you. I saw something in the *Daily Mirror*. A photograph. You were in a hospital?"

Oh crap. This is bad. I remember the media at the hospital, but in my fuzzy mind I thought it was only one reporter, and was secretly hoping it was someone from a local paper. Apparently, my sedative-addled mind didn't take in the full scene.

Funny, Max didn't say anything about a photographer this morning when we woke up.

I pause for a fraction of a second to collect my thoughts. Finally, I decide on telling him the truth. "I was hiking and fell into some poison ivy and had to go to the hospital because my legs felt like they had been dipped in lava. I have blisters. It felt like I was going to lose a limb."

"Uh-huh. And why did Max bring you to the hospital?"

Somehow Papa's glossed over the blistering skin part of my story and has honed in on the part that I wanted to avoid.

My eyes shift to my coffee, to the rolling green vista of the Laurentian Mountains. "We were hiking together. There's a lake here."

Papa runs his tongue across his teeth, a sure sign he's getting worked up. "Why were you hiking together?"

Because we needed to do something other than have sex, I want to yell.

"We were talking. About racing. And the team." I know I sound ridiculous. "And we both needed some exercise."

That's probably the silliest thing I've ever said in my life. Max has world-class personal trainers at his disposal and a physical fitness routine. Going on a little hike for him is nothing.

"Kamari mou, I think now is the time to come clean about your relationship with Max."

"Okay?" I should tell him what's going on between Max and me. Spill my guts now and get it over with. Part of me wishes Max was here with me to share in this dubious moment. But I'd told him I was calling my parents and asked him to stay downstairs. I hold my breath, waiting to hear what my father says next. "What do you want to know?"

"How long has this been going on between the two of you? Tell me the truth, Lily. What is your relationship with Max?"

"We're . . . friends."

"Friends." His brow furrows into a deep scowl. The lines between his eyebrows are the Grand Canyon of face wrinkles.

"Yes."

"There are going to be rumors, with this photo of him pushing you out of the hospital in the wheelchair. Why couldn't you walk on your own?"

"I guess you didn't hear me when I said it felt like my legs were dipped into lava," I snark.

"Don't sass me, missy." Papa hasn't used this tone of voice with me since I was sixteen and threatened to leave boarding school to follow the Dave Matthews Band around the country.

Mum's face comes into view. "I saw the photo, Lily. Your mouth looks weird and slack, like you're drooling. Poor baby. If I wasn't taking care of your father, I'd fly to see you. Well, and you know how much I love Quebec. You should put some apple cider vinegar on your skin."

"Mum," I warn through gritted teeth, "I'm at a vacation cabin. I don't carry around apple cider vinegar."

"Where is Max now? Is he with you in the cabin?" Papa's voice is a low growl. He's not a stupid man. He knows something's up. "Maybe I should call him."

"This really isn't a good time to talk. I need to get to Montreal, and my cell reception is terrible here in the cabin. Can we chat later? I'll call you once I check into the hotel, and I need to call the doctor and let him know my legs are doing better. They were so lovely at the hospital." I babble on for a few seconds about the excellent health care.

My father's nostrils flare. "Fine. But I'm begging you to not embarrass me or the team this weekend. I should be back in a race or two."

"I won't, Papa, I promise. And please don't rush back on my account. I've been trying to hold it together for you."

"I know, and from what Jack told me, you're doing a good job. But we don't need any scandals."

The subtext: a team owner sleeping with the star driver would be the scandal of the century in this sport.

"Okay, gotta run, love you both!"

I blow my parents kisses good-bye, feeling deeply guilty that I've already broken my promise.

CHAPTER THIRTY-EIGHT

LILY

Since we're about two hours from Montreal and because we probably shouldn't be seen arriving at the track together, Max takes a helicopter to the city, while I ride in the back of the SUV. He has far more obligations than I do, a never-ending schedule of autographs, appearances, and training sessions.

I'm merely a figurehead, I've come to realize; someone who approves memos and listens to reports. And, good god, there are reports. Everything from the possible tire strategies of the race to the cost of lug nuts to whether the team needs to hire additional people for the catering at an upcoming race in Italy.

The team principal—in our case, Jack—handles the leadership, racing, and day-to-day decisions.

The team owner does none of that. It's all fine with me because I'm used to the corporate world. Unlike the Formula World teams owned by car manufacturers, Onassis is a relatively small team, with only a few hundred employees. It's much smaller than the gaming company I worked for, and much more manageable, as far as I can tell.

I'm in the car, in Montreal traffic, on my laptop reading a report about the weather for the rest of the week—we contract with a local meteorologist before every race so we can determine which tires to use—when Tanya calls.

I tap on the Bluetooth headset attached to my ear. "Hey, there! How are you?" Goodness, I sound more bubbly than usual.

"Lily? You okay?"

"Yeah, I'm better. Steroids are miracle drugs. I assume you saw the hospital photos."

"I did." She pauses, and I have the uncomfortable feeling she's about to say something else.

"And?"

"Have you seen *Drive Dirty* today?"

"No. I've been reading the weather report. Looks like it's going to rain hard this weekend."

"Yeah, uh, I think you need to check it out."

"Why?" My stomach suddenly feels like it's plummeting to my knees.

"There are some photos. Now, mind you, they're not superclear, so it's difficult to tell if they're authentic, or even if—"

"What photos?" I interrupt.

"They're taken with a long lens, or maybe a decent cell camera but zoomed in, and they're quite fuzzy. I think we should deny everything."

I swear out loud and type the *Drive Dirty* address into the website bar. "What. Photos. Are. You. Talking. About," I growl.

The website pops up, and I gasp.

MAX BECKER TAKES A STEAMY SWIM WITH TEAM OWNER LILY ONASSIS.

There, in full color, is a grainy photo of me and Max, inhaling each other's faces while swimming in the lake. Our faces are obscured and we look like gray blobs, but it's also easy to tell it's Max due to his muscular shoulders and distinct nose. I'm out of focus, but I know it's me.

But will the world recognize me? That's the million-dollar question.

"Gah," I say aloud, then let out a muffled groan.

"So here's the good news," Tanya says.

"There's good news?"

"It's not a clear photo. You can't really tell it's the two of you. I think because your hair is wet, it looks more like two Loch Ness Monsters. Well, if one monster had boobs."

"Do you think this is funny?" I'm furious now. At Tanya and at myself, for being so weak willed. For needing Max so much that I'd put us—and my father's team—in this position.

"No, I don't. But I don't want you to panic. We're going to say it's not the two of you."

"But it's easy to piece together. Hours after this photo was taken Max and I were spotted coming out of a hospital together."

"Well, this is true. I think we need to play up your poison ivy issue. Say that you're extremely allergic and almost died."

"That seems extreme. How is that going to help anything? No one's going to focus on that because there's actual evidence that Max and I were sucking face in a lake." I'm shrieking now, and look up to see the driver wince into the rearview mirror.

This day is getting better and better.

"Look, let's discuss once I get to the track, okay? Come up with a strategy."

"Good deal. Don't worry, Lily. This isn't the worst scandal I've ever managed."

I end the call. Almost immediately I receive another, this time from Papa. Fear stabs me in the heart, and I don't have the courage to answer it.

I let it go to voice mail and stare out the window all the way to the track, wondering if Max has seen the photo. An idea flashes in my head, and I take out my phone, my thumbs flying across the screen.

Mumsy, please tell Papa that I'll call him later. I'm superbusy this morning.

She sends me a thumbs-up and, inexplicably, a flip-flop emoji. "What's that supposed to mean?" I mutter aloud.

As I stare at the screen, another text from Mum pops up. It's of a beach umbrella, the sun, and a blue wave. *Can you guess where we are today?*

I let out an exhale. The beach is the perfect place for them. Maybe she's even distracting him from the headlines about me and Max. One can only hope. Despite all of her flaws and lack of physical attention, she is in my corner.

My car maneuvers through various checkpoints and security booths on our way into the track, then parks near the team's compound. I thank the driver-slash-bodyguard, a guy who is employed by Max.

When the guy, whose name is Donnie, takes a few steps alongside me on my way inside the team's makeshift office, I turn and stare up at him as we walk. He's like a giant fire hydrant with legs, he's so muscular and large. That's odd. Why is he sticking close to me?

"I think Max will be in the garage. That's over to the right. I'm headed to the office, that way, so thanks again."

"Max told me to walk in with you," Donnie says.

"He did? Why? I'm only going a few hundred feet into the—" My voice dies when I make eye contact with one reporter a few feet away. He speeds over to me, and as if he's the first of many swarms of insects, is joined by a group of journalists with cameras, notebooks, and video equipment.

Dammit, this entire area is open to anyone with a pit pass or a press badge.

"This was why," Donnie replies gruffly.

He tries to block them from my path but there are too many. I shake my head, trying not to make eye contact, trying not to listen to any of the individual questions because I know they'll be too upsetting. But it's impossible.

They know. They know about me and Max.

"No questions," Donnie shouts, and I wonder if Max told him to say that. Probably I should be grateful, but all I feel is ashamed.

They don't stop screaming into my face, and by the time we run inside, my nerves are frayed and I feel raw, violated, even. I slip into the little office alone and shut the door, gasping for breath. The echo of the probing questions ring in my brain, and it's as if I can't get the looping sounds to stop.

When did you and Max Becker start sleeping together?

Does your father approve of your sexual relationship with Max, his driver?

Doesn't Max have a potential sexual harassment claim against you because you're his boss?

CHAPTER THIRTY-NINE

MAX

Days before every Formula World race, drivers and engineers from each team participate in a time-honored ritual.

The track walk.

Sometimes this happens on Wednesday, the day before practice. Other races, like this one in Montreal, the track walk happens on Thursday morning, prior to practice. For the seasoned drivers like me, it's optional, but for the younger drivers, it's essential.

Walking the track is a way to get to know the circuit. See if anything's changed since last year. Look at the curbs and judge in our minds how our cars—and our driving—will fare. It's also a chance for the team social media crew to get photos and videos of us scrutinizing every millimeter of the track, and fans believe that we're doing this to look for any possible advantage on race day, however small.

Mostly, though, the track walk is tradition. For me, it's superstition. I could shrug off, having won here in Montreal four times in my career. God knows I have a ton to do, from charity appearances here in the city, to autographs, to a session with my physical therapist.

But I enjoy the walk, and today with Esteban, Jack, and a few other engineers, is no different. We're gathered to walk around the 4.361 kilometer circuit—that's just over 2.7 miles—in drizzly, cool weather. Lucas stays behind because he's not part of the technical team.

The four of us are bundled in black Team Onassis windbreakers, and Esteban and I are wearing knit caps. It's that chilly out here, and neither of us want to risk getting a cold.

As we leave the garage our group of engineers protectively form a circle around Esteban and me—this is also the day when fans with weeklong, VIP tickets can stroll around pit lane. We don't need to be distracted or delayed by people seeking photos or autographs.

A few people slip through, though, so Esteban and I pause to accommodate them. Both of us are big softies when it comes to that, never turning down a request if we don't have to.

Finally, we're out on the asphalt of the track, walking briskly. The Circuit Gilles Villeneuve is one of my favorite tracks in the world, actually. While I love Monaco for the glamour and street racing, and Singapore for the night circuit, the Montreal track is unique because it's set in an actual park, one that's normally open to the public, except on race week. It's situated on an actual island in the St. Lawrence River, but also a quick subway ride to the heart of downtown.

We set out in the soft rain. Jack and I spread out from the others, and several hundred yards ahead I see another team doing the same thing we are.

I couldn't get enough of this track. I wanted to soak it all in. That was the joy of the track walk, seeing the course in its pristine state, without fans, without engines. It's me and the asphalt, and it always feels like I'm soaking up the energy of the track with every step I take.

"How were your few days off?" Jack interrupts my reverie with a hesitant tone, then clears his throat. "I saw the photos of Lily at the hospital."

I keep walking, my hands stuffed in the pockets of my jeans.

"She's doing much better. The doctor said she's got quite an allergy to those plants," I say in a clipped tone, hoping he won't ask more questions.

"Mate, let me give you a piece of advice," he says.

I glower at him. He's going to warn me about Lily's father, the man who signs my paycheck. Surely Jack understands that since I'm at the peak of my career, I'm practically untouchable.

"No woman is worth your career. You've still got years ahead of you in this sport."

I remain silent, mulling this advice over. Do I have years left? At twenty-eight I'm nearing the twilight of my racing career. Sure, other guys have stayed in until their midthirties and early forties. But the reality is, this is a young man's sport, and the injuries I've sustained are bound to slow me down at some point.

As we walk, I think about all the times I've raced on this track. It's always been good to me—great, actually. I've won four of the seven races I've been in here. The first, when I was only twenty-two, was my first podium. I'd come in third, and that was when I was dating Lily.

I'd stood on that stage after the race, spraying champagne into the crowd. All I could think of was celebrating with her. Taking her in my arms and kissing her. Holding her tight, and never letting go.

I don't care what Jack, Lucas, or the world says. I've wanted Lily for years, and pride and a sense of decency kept me from contacting her. Now that she wants me, I'm not letting her go again. Even thinking about her being back in my life gives me a new energy about this weekend's race, as if everything I'm seeing and experiencing is fresh again.

About a kilometer into our walk, the sun peeks through the thick foliage of pine trees, and I take a deep breath. The scent of rain and fresh-cut grass tickles my nose.

We're now at turn six, and Jack stops on the steep embankment, waving me over.

"They've redone the curbs here," he says, pointing to the embankment. "It feels steeper than last year."

Doesn't everything feel steeper than last year, more difficult, more fraught with potential roadblocks?

This is what I'm best at, though. Overcoming obstacles. Winning when it's impossible, like when I started from the back of the pack three years ago here in Montreal and ended up third on the podium, keeping me in play for the championship. All the racing analysts on TV said I couldn't do it, but I did.

I look at the curb and nod, taking it in. Unlike what the race fans see on television, embankments are often steeper than they look—and they can be pitfalls for the drivers. Deadly ones, in some cases.

We continue walking, chatting about various adjustments I need to make at certain corners. Our little group pauses at a new speed bump, which was installed at a chicane to keep drivers from cutting the corner. We all stand on the bump and jump up and down a little, talking about how we'll handle this in the cars.

Then we round the hairpin and saunter down the straightaway. The rain picks up, pelting us with cool, steady pinpricks. As the pits come into view, my phone buzzes in my pocket. It's a text from Tanya, and I have to hold my hand over the screen to shield it from the rain.

Please meet me ASAP in the conference room after your track walk.

CHAPTER FORTY

MAX

Fifteen minutes later I open the door to the conference room to find Tanya and Lily sitting there, stone faced. An open laptop is in the middle of the table, and the air in the small room is thick with tension.

"Hallo, ladies," I say, shaking out my wet hair. "It's raining cats and dogs out there."

The two women look up.

"Have a seat," Tanya says, all business.

I sink into a hard, plastic chair, unable to see what's on the screen. For some reason, Lily's not meeting my gaze. This can't be good.

"What's up?"

She turns and slides the laptop toward me. There, on the screen, is a giant photo of Lily and me kissing in the lake. I'm unable to contain my shock, and my jaw drops.

"What the hell?"

Lily's elbow is propped on the table, her hand cradling her forehead.

"Has your father seen this?" I ask her.

She shakes her head. "No. Yes. I don't know. He's been calling me nonstop but I haven't had the guts to answer."

"Okay, we could do one of two things," Tanya says, ever the chipper public relations person. "We could deny that's you. After all, the photo is grainy. You can't see your faces. It might be difficult to actually prove it's you, or it could take a few days to confirm it's the two of you."

"I have a pretty distinctive nose," I say, touching the tip.

Lily narrows her eyes at me. "Do you think this is a joke?"

"No," I growl. "But our private life is our private life. Don't we get to enjoy a moment together?"

"Not when you're one of the world's best paid race-car drivers making out with the team owner," Lily spits.

Tanya interrupts by putting her hand on Lily's forearm, a move that I'm sure makes her skin crawl. "We could also embrace it."

"Embrace what?" Lily says in an icy tone.

"Your relationship."

I look at Lily, then at Tanya, who looks at Lily. She's staring at the ceiling. "Holy crap, I can't believe this is happening," she whispers.

Her bottom lip trembles and her eyes look glassy, like she's about to cry. A panicky feeling wells in my chest and out of instinct, I reach for her hand across the table.

She snatches it away while glaring at me. "Tanya, can Max and I have a moment to talk in private, please?"

"Sure. I have to use the ladies' room anyway." She scrambles out, leaving the open laptop and that damned photo behind.

When the flimsy door clicks behind Tanya, Lily stands up and cries, "Max, what the hell are we doing?"

I throw my hands in the air. "I thought we were trying to have a relationship again."

"Is that what you want? Do you really want to ruin your career, and further ruin my reputation, for this?"

I'm shocked she's so angry, and my mouth hangs open.

She slumps into a seat. "I found out about this photo on my way here when I was in the car. Then I was swamped with media shouting awful questions at me. And I can't bear to call my father back. I wonder if . . ."

Her voice trails off.

"You wonder what?"

Her face looks so anguished, so conflicted, I feel like she's going to break my heart all over again.

LILY

Was this a mistake?

Those are the words I can't say aloud. I'm still shaken by the barrage of questions, the pointed barbs, the shouts and shoving, the reporters' bodies brushing into me.

"Babe," Max says softly. "Take a breath."

My instinct tells me to rage, to be angry, to blame him. He's not to blame, though. If anything, I am. But I follow his directions, close my eyes, and inhale. Twice. I detect notes of sawdust and paint in the air, because everything in this prefabricated office smells like it recently came out of a furniture-store box. Max's aftershave is also a faint scent, and if we weren't here in the office I'd crawl in his lap and bury my nose in his neck so I could breathe in his essence.

"Can I hold your hand?" he asks.

I open my eyes and nod. He reaches for my hand and covers it with his.

"I'm not going to lie. This won't be easy. This weekend will be a circus. We're going to get a lot of questions. But we'll get through this, I promise."

"Easy for you to say. You're the Iceman," I retort in a too-sarcastic voice.

"You don't think some of these questions hurt? They do. But I've learned to block it out. That's what you need to do. That's not reality." He points to the door with his free hand. "This is reality. Me and you. We're all that matters."

His certainty is reassuring, but only to a point. There's the issue of my father. "I don't know."

"I do. I've been in the press a lot. Involved in a lot of scandals, some big, some small. It comes with the territory. Eventually they'll move on to something and someone else."

"I'm aware of that. It's that—" My frustration steals the words from my mouth. I hate how I'm crying and a mess when he's so calm and collected.

"Talk to me." His voice is soft and encouraging.

I shake my head. "Don't you have practice?"

"Not for an hour and a half."

"This isn't the time." I shove my fingers under my glasses, wiping away the tears.

"It is the time."

"Max, here's the thing. When a man's involved with a public sex scandal, he comes through unscathed. Or better than he was before. Women in sex scandals never fare that well. We become the sluts, the messy ones, the crazy ones. I know that firsthand."

Memories of tweets during my scandal at the game company come wafting through my brain. I was called a bitch, a company wrecker, and a shrew. And those were the nice comments.

Max sighs. "I know. It's unfair. But if you want this, us, to work, we've got to go public at some time. We can't hide forever."

"So you're saying either rip the bandage off now, or later?"

He squeezes my hand. "Pretty much."

I know he's right. But I'm not sure I can handle such intense scrutiny right now, especially after my firing two months ago, Papa's heart attack, and running this team. I don't have the heart to explain this to Max. Definitely not before he's about to practice a few laps on the track.

I snortle in and muster a giant smile. "Okay. I'm going to think about all this. You go practice, and I'll keep talking to Tanya. I think for now we shouldn't say anything, okay? We need the attention on your driving, not your sex life."

A playful grin creeps on his lips. "I adore you. I didn't tell you that enough when we were together before. I should have."

I open my mouth, then close it. His declarations of affection throw me off balance every time he says them. It's as if I almost don't believe him, or don't think I deserve his love.

There's no time to unpack those thoughts now, though, so I stand and brush a kiss on his cheek, then call Tanya back into the room so we can come up with a strategy for the weekend.

Deny, deny, deny. That's my new motto.

CHAPTER FORTY-ONE

LILY

When Max goes to the noisy garage to prepare for his practice laps, I remain ensconced inside the silent, sterile office.

Not because I'm worried about the media; they don't have access to the garage or the control center area where the engineers watch Max's driving on monitors, while his car is hooked up to computers. I could hang out in there and the team wouldn't dare say anything to me about the rumors.

No, I've stayed behind because I must do something even more important.

Call my father.

I check my watch. It's been a few hours since Mum sent her emoji-filled text, so perhaps they're back in my condo. My hand goes to the back of my leg, which is again pulsing and prickling.

Eep. Can't do that. The doctor specifically wrote on my discharge instructions to not scratch. I straighten my skirt and rub my hands over my thighs instead, then reach for my phone.

My leg jiggles violently as I wait for my father to pick up.

"Lily." He doesn't say hello, doesn't call me kamari mou, doesn't have a warm tone at all.

"Hi, Papa."

There's a pause, a terrible, scary silence. An empty feeling settles in the pit of my stomach. If only I could tear out of this little, closet-like space and run far away, back to my cozy, light-filled condo, where I can hide from the world.

"I need to tell you something." The words tumble out of me. "Max and I are, are . . ."

Are what? In love? Together? Having sex? I struggle to find the best explanation for our relationship and wish I would've rehearsed.

"We were together seven years ago and then I broke up with him. But you know all that. Now we're back together," I say, acutely aware that it probably sounded like all one word. "I'm hoping you don't get as upset as you did before."

While waiting for him to say something, anything, I feel like vomiting. "I, I love him," I manage to get out.

There's another awful few seconds of silence. "Papa, please say something."

"I know, kamari mou. I just want you to be happy. If this is what's going to make you happy . . ." The cell connection fades into static for a moment.

"What?" I shout. "I can't hear you."

There's a jostling and my father swears aloud. "Eileen, I'm going to FaceTime. I need to see Lily," he says crossly.

"Papa?" I move the phone from my ear in time to see the video flicker on, a closeup of his ear.

"Like this, Adrian." Mum comes into the frame sideways. "Here. Prop it up like this."

The video rights itself and my father's head and shoulders come into view. He looks incredibly scowly with his bushy salt-and-pepper eyebrows knitted together. He's so close to the camera I can see his nose hair.

"There we go," I say. "What were you saying?"

"I want you to be happy, and if Max makes you happy, I'm not going to stand in your way. Not this time. All those years ago, I didn't like that you and Max were together, mostly because I thought you were both too young and he was working for the competition. You were my baby. I was worried he was using you for information. Or worse. Using you for sex."

I grimace. This is not the direction I want this conversation to go. "He wasn't using me. And I was well over twenty-one at the time."

"You're always my baby."

"Always *our* baby," Mum hollers in the background.

He shakes his head. "Men in Formula World, well, their first few years can be unpredictable in the sport. They usually sleep around, and I didn't want you to get hurt. Then when you left to take the gaming job, I figured it was over. I watched over the years as Max grew and changed into the man he is today."

"You're not angry?" I have to rest my hand on the desk because everything seems so unreal.

"Angry?" He sighs. "No. It's not an optimal situation, with the two of you, but we'll handle it. God knows we can't deny our desires. If we could, I would've left your mother a long time ago. But when you find your person, there's no letting go."

"Yeah." I sigh.

"I actually blame myself."

Oh god. Way to make me feel even more guilty. "What? Why? About me and Max?"

"No, no. If I never had this damn heart attack, we wouldn't be in this position." He runs a hand through his thick silver hair.

"I'm sorry," I mutter.

"No, I'm sorry. I wish I could be there. Hopefully in a few races." The disappointment is heavy in his voice, and I can tell he's not happy from the way his lips are pressed tight together.

"Don't rush back on my account. Max and I can put things on pause. It's more important for me that you take care of your health. I'm sorry for putting you in this position, having to read all these headlines." I'm trying not to cry, but for some reason the waterworks have opened a spigot and are free flowing today.

That's it. That's what I'll do. Later tonight I'll tell Max that we need to cool off for a while, at least until Papa returns. I'm sure Max will be okay with that since he's been so gentle and caring. We can figure out our future later—we've got the rest of our lives for that.

"That's probably the best plan, Lily. Focus on work now. And listen to Tanya about what to say to the press. She knows best. It's why I hired her, because she's ruthless. If she tells you to do something, do it." He tilts his chin downward and frowns.

I press my hand to my forehead. "Will do. I'll get through this. We'll get through this. I promise, I won't mess this up."

"I know you won't, kamari mou."

When we say our I love yous and our good-byes, then hang up, I should feel relieved that Papa isn't pissed. Somehow, though, his anger would've been preferable to the disappointment written all over his face.

EVIE

"How does it feel?"

Jack's Australian accent comes through loud and clear through the in-helmet headset. We're well into this practice session, and I'm slaying every lap.

"Fantastic. Is absolutely fantastic. None of the previous issues," I respond. "Even in this drizzle, it's performing a hundred and ten percent."

I've still got several curves to go, and the car feels so incredible, primed for speed, that I glance down at my multifunctional steering wheel and decide to kick it up a notch.

"Good deal. Box now, mate."

"Will do." That's the team radio phrase for "return to the pits." Box is short for *Boxenstopp*, a German word that means pit stop. Every team has its own lingo, but some terms, like *box*, are used across the sport.

I crest the straight, brake hard, and clip the apex of turn five, the tightest corner on the track.

The car feels good, and I realize I can keep this up for a little longer.

"I'm going to push to pass, Jack. One more lap."

"How's the engine performing?"

"I'll let you know when I get back." But the new power component seems to be working better than the last one.

Push to pass was a feature introduced to the cars some years ago. It awards drivers an extra thirty horsepower for five seconds to use when overtaking a competitor. At the moment, there are no competitors and I'm only running some free practice laps. Still, I like to test these things before quali.

On the approach to turn six I hit the power again, feel the rear end begin to slide, but the car grabs and sticks. I crest the small hill, brake for seven, and slam it into the long straight.

I'm grinning. In the cockpit, my body is held by a soft, adjustable carbon fiber seat. The belts will keep me secure in the event of a crash. My helmet stretches over my head and locks neatly into place. Through the clear visor, I watch the scenery whiz by as though I'm in a wild movie.

If I concentrate, I can feel the tires gripping the road, feel my heart lifting off the ground and flying through the sky. I need to sometime describe this to Lily.

The asphalt is smooth and constant. The snarl of the engine changes pitch slightly as I hit a slight bump, like a guitar chord moving from a low sound to a higher one.

"Max, what did you hit?" Jack's concerned tone comes through my headset right as I lose control for a fraction of a second. But a fraction is all it takes with such a powerful car, and now I'm swearing and swerving into the grass.

"Control it, Max, control it! You've lost part of your front wing."

I don't have time to respond to Jack because my front is now airborne, the car screaming on its back wheels.

In the blink of an eye, my right front tire hits a concrete barrier. The entire car tilts precariously to the left, and out of my peripheral vision I see the track whizzing past. Then I hit the concrete wall again, almost full-on. Somehow I'm still gripping the steering wheel like it's a life preserver, and maybe it is.

There's no stopping now, no way to correct. All I can do is try to survive.

The entire right side of my car is sheared away, breaking into thousands of pieces of fiberglass and rubber. A searing, intense pain grips my right shoulder. The force of the impact rips two wheels off and now the entire car's skidding along the asphalt, on the driver's side, inches from my head.

I don't have it in me to be scared, no time to scream. The last thing

I see is the mostly empty grandstand, and the gray, drizzly sky. I think I'm upside down. Or dreaming. Did I hit my head? Maybe I'm dead. I don't know what's happening. I'm losing feeling in my arms, and then my chest, lower back, and legs.

Everything goes black, then as suddenly as I lose consciousness, it's back.

I feel myself being yanked sideways, lifted out of the cockpit, and set onto a grassy patch adjacent to the track.

Jack's on the team radio, yelling. "Get the ambulance out there, now!"

I hear a frantic voice in an accent I can't identify. Someone else is screaming but I'm not understanding the words. I don't know if it's from the team radio or from the world around me, but either way, I don't seem to be able to answer.

I'm staring at the tattered remains of my car, and wondering when, or if, I'll see my parents. Or Lucas. Or if I'll ever hold Lily in my arms again.

CHAPTER FORTY-TWO

LILY

Because I've managed to make it an hour without checking the tabloid websites, I feel I deserve a medal.

Or at least a cookie. It's three o'clock, and I've finished okaying a round of expenditures for the New York race coming up. That's the way it is for team owners, always planning for the next race, barely able to concentrate on what's at hand.

This kind of work I can handle, though. I stretch, and feel a little sleepy, probably because all the adrenaline from earlier has ebbed from my body. Time for a coffee and that cookie. Probably I can go down the hall to the lobby of our headquarters and grab something from the espresso bar.

As I grab my purse, several things happen at once. My cell rings, the desk phone rings, and someone shouts my name. The door flings open, and it's Tanya.

"You need to come, now," she shouts. The sounds of other people yelling echo through the flimsy offices.

My immediate thought is that there's an attack of some sort, a person with a gun, a bomb, a knife. But, no, this is Canada, not America.

"What's going on?" I ask Tanya, whose face is pale. Her eyes are wide and wild, and even her normally sleek bob is disheveled.

"It's Max. He crashed during practice. It's bad."

There are moments in life when you'll always remember where you were. You remember the internal tingles, the sudden coldness that hits your core, the disorientation that something has suddenly rocked your world, and not in a good way.

Unfortunately, those are usually the worst times, the ones you'd rather forget. A couple of weeks ago, it was news of my father's heart attack.

Today, it's this. Max.

My hand flies to my throat. "How bad?"

"The medics are taking him off the track now. On a stretcher." She wrings her hands. "Come with me to the control room."

I tighten my grip on my purse strap. "Let's go."

We march in silence, past people who are murmuring in clusters in the coffee lounge. Outside, there are a handful of press people, and they jump on us the minute we push open the door. It's raining again, really pouring now. Was that why Max crashed? The thought cuts through the haze in my brain.

"Lily, Lily, over here," one reporter shouts. "Is Max Becker in critical condition?

The questions come in rapid fire. *What happened to Max? Did you see the crash? Where's he going?*

Tanya plows through while bellowing "No comment," but I take a deep breath and stop.

"I'm going to find out more information now. We'll let you know about his condition as soon as we know. Thank you."

Tanya grabs my arm and pulls me through the scrum. While photographers click away, we dash through the rain to the garage. It's not easy because I'm wearing a long skirt and flats, and every time my legs brush against the fabric, they itch anew. But I don't care because Max is hurt and I need to find out what's going on.

My gorgeous, loving Max. Just when we found each other again.

By the time I get to the Team Onassis control center my glasses are streaked with raindrops, and I have to pause to wipe them off with the hem of my blouse. When I slide them back on my face, Jack's at Tanya's side.

"Practice has been stopped for all the teams," Jack says.

I don't care about all the teams, I care about Max. "How is he? Where is he?" I demand.

"He's been taken to the track ER. Come."

That's not good, not good at all. If it was merely a small crash, he'd climb out of the car and walk back to the pits for evaluation. The track emergency center is a temporary triage unit, staffed with more than a hundred healthcare workers. They can do everything from X-rays to IVs in there.

I follow Jack through the control center, which is thick with the heavy hush of tragedy. I know this silence, felt it once when I was a teen and hanging out with my father's team when one of his drivers crashed. I've never forgotten the driver's girlfriend, stunned and shell-shocked in her glamorous outfit.

Now it's my turn to look shell-shocked. These are the moments no one in racing publicly acknowledges. It's as if speaking aloud the potential danger will court it, somehow. It's easier to dwell on the technical, the competition, the winning.

We make our way over to a bank of monitors, and I gasp when I see that every one is tuned to an image of an ambulance, with flashing lights, near a mangled, wrecked Formula World car. Lucas is standing before the monitors, open mouthed and stunned.

"Max was in that?" I whisper in horror.

"Yeah," mutters Lucas. "Christ, it looks awful."

My heart feels like it's grown fifty sizes and is threatening to beat right out of my chest. While practice is supposed to be a time when the drivers get to know how their car performs on a track, it's not without danger—like everything else in Formula World. There have been drivers who have been seriously injured or died during practice like . . .

"He definitely has a concussion," Jack says. "Would you like to see the crash?"

"Not now," I cry. "I want to see him. I need to be with him."

Funny how I've dropped every pretense that we're not dating. Right now, I don't care who knows our relationship status. All I want is to know he's okay.

Jack rakes in a breath. "Okay. Calm down. Let me get the latest."

He slides on a headset. "What's the situation? We've got Lily Onassis here."

A pause.

"Oh shit. Okay. Okay. Right. We'll follow along."

I gape in horror as Jack stands. His mouth is in a hard, grim line, sending shockwaves of cold panic through my body.

"He's not good. They're going to airlift him to Montreal General. We're going to meet him there."

◊

I listen, mute with fear, as Jack describes the crash on our drive to the hospital. Lucas and Tanya are with us.

"He went into the hairpin, collided with the curb, lost his front wing, and then somehow the nose of his car went airborne. It all happened in a fucking instant, Lily, I swear. Then he flipped and crashed into the wall. When they took him out of the car he was asking for you."

A whimper starts in my throat but I swallow it down. "The concrete wall? How fast was he going?"

"About a hundred forty-two."

One hundred forty-two miles per hour. He hit the wall going that speed.

"Here. *Autoweek* has a clip on Facebook." Tanya hands us her phone.

I'm not sure I want to watch but I'm too stunned to protest. I watch the seven-second video, my jaw slack with shock. Seven seconds of pure torture. Max's sleek, black car with orange trim skids for several yards on its side, then comes to a stop in the gravel.

"I can try to pull up the in-car camera if you'd like," Jack says.

"No. Not now." Turning toward the window, away from Jack, Tanya, and that devastating video that's now trending on social media, I shut my eyes and try to think positive thoughts. But the horrifying crash video runs in a loop through my brain all the way to the hospital.

"They're going to meet us at a side entrance," Tanya says to Jack.

I turn to Lucas, who is sitting next to me. "How terrible is this? It seems terrible."

He shakes his head. "I don't know, Lily. I wish . . ."

"What?" I stare at him. Lucas is a handsome guy, all bronze skin, green eyes, and dark hair.

"I wish he'd kept his mind on racing and not on you."

My eyes shut. Exactly what I need. More guilt.

Once there, we jump out and are ushered into a private waiting room. It's clearly meant for children and families because there's a rainbow painted on one wall and a kid-sized table and chairs in a corner, along with toys. The three of us wait for what seems like hours—but it's only twenty minutes, according to my phone. During that time I call my father and update him, then stare at the children's toys.

Finally, three doctors walk in. I leap from my seat. "How is he?"

They recognize that I'm practically breathless with worry, and tell me to sit.

"Calm down," one doctor, a man with a smooth bald head and a French accent, says.

That is never the thing to say to me when I'm worried, anxious, or upset. I fold my arms but don't take a chair.

"Max is relatively unscathed," another doctor, a woman, says. "Hi, I'm Dr. Sharon Cohen."

"Oh, thank god," Lucas says, slumping against a wall.

"What does that mean, relatively unscathed?" I can't help but raise my voice.

"He's now talking almost normally."

"Almost?" Now I'm yelling. "What does that mean? Sentences? Words? Grunts? Does he know his name?"

"He broke his shoulder in three places. It's quite bad, and he'll need to go into surgery in the next day, but for now we're stabilizing that part of his body. He doesn't have any other internal injuries in his torso. But he does have a concussion. We're still evaluating how bad that is and will need to keep him here for a while. He knows his name but is a little fuzzy on other details."

The whimper that's been living in my throat finally escapes, and I sink onto a bench. That's his bad shoulder.

"You're Lily Onassis, right?" Dr. Cohen asks.

I nod weakly. It feels like an invisible force has my chest in a vice grip, and I can only breathe using the top third of my lungs.

"He's been asking for you. I told him he could see you after his brain CT scan."

CHAPTER FORTY-THREE

LILY

Two interminable, excruciating hours later, Dr. Cohen walks me to the room where Max is recovering. His CT scan showed a mild concussion, but as she explains, any time the brain is injured they like to monitor the situation for a few days to make sure brain bleeds don't erupt.

"It all sounds so scary." I sniffle.

"I guess this comes with his profession. Max is extremely physically fit, but he's quite lucky that he wasn't more severely injured. His neck strength and his safety gear saved his life. But don't be alarmed, he might have some temporary gaps in his memory. That's normal."

We're at the door to his room now, and I steel myself for what I'm about to see. The doctor turns the knob and allows me to walk in first.

"Hey, beautiful." Max is sitting up, a huge smile lighting up his face. He's wearing a mint-green hospital gown and is only hooked to one IV. His right arm is in a sling-like contraption, and there's a bruise on his forehead.

Other than that, he looks incredible. Handsome. Healthy. Like the man I love.

I rush to him and collapse on his bed, on top of his legs. I'm ugly crying, snorting, and honking everywhere.

"Hey, hey, babe, I'm okay. Now that you're here, I'm all better."

He strokes my hair with his good hand, and I look up through tear-stained lashes.

"How do you feel? Are you sure you're okay? They told me about your shoulder and your concussion."

He reaches for his shoulder, but I stop him when I see the IV is about to tangle with the blanket. "That's probably not a good idea."

"Yeah, the shoulder hurts like hell. Well, not so much anymore because of the painkillers. What did your dad say? I'll bet he freaked out while watching in the pits."

"Uh, Max? Papa's in Miami." That's when it hits me that because of his concussion he's probably forgotten about the heart attack. This is also the third time I've been in a hospital this month, and my god, I hope it's the last. I'm becoming way too familiar with the sights and smells of emergency rooms.

"He is? Oh. Okay. The doctors said I might have some issues because of the concussion. I'm so glad you're here with me, Lily. So glad. Where's Lucas?"

"He's out in the waiting area. Do you want to see him?"

Max nods. "In a minute. I want a little time with you."

I trace his chin with my thumb. "I was so scared when I saw the video of the crash. I thought I'd lost you."

"I don't know what happened. I don't have any memory of it."

"It's okay. You don't need to." My sweet man, he's blocked out the terror of the crash. That's probably for the best.

"I'm not going to be able to drive this weekend, am I?"

I shake my head. "And maybe not next week. We'll have to see. You're going to be here for a while. Lucas will be here with you. I'll be here too."

Depending on his shoulder, he might not be able to finish the season. But that's not important. He's alive, and that's the only true thing I need right now. Jack will have to take over the team. There's simply no way I can handle that.

"You will? You'll stay?" Max frowns, like he's confused.

"Yes, the doctors said they'll bring in a bed for me. I'm not going anywhere."

"Hmph." He strokes my arm. "The last thing I remember is us, swimming. Did we go swimming at some point recently? And kiss in the water?"

I'm crying again, fresh tears. "Yes, we did. We stayed in a cabin in the mountains of Quebec and we went swimming. It was wonderful."

"I told you I love you after we ate apple pancake. I haven't forgotten that." He beams and looks at me with a loving gaze.

I laugh, and cry, all at the same time, then brush my lips softly over his, making sure to avoid his injured shoulder.

"And I love you, Max. So much." I bury my head against his arm and weep.

CHAPTER FORTY-FOUR

LILY

It's still dark when I slip out of our warm, cozy bed at six in the morning. Even though it's Miami, it's still a little chilly because it's February, so I go to the walk-in closet and throw on a pair of fuzzy socks, along with my favorite pink sweatshirt and a pair of pink-and-white flannel shorts.

As I'm padding out of the bedroom, Max's voice hits my ears.

"Babe? Why are you getting out of bed so early?"

I return to the bed, leaning down to kiss his neck. His smooth skin smells faintly of his cologne and warm, sleepy man.

"I'm making something special for today."

He reaches for me, trying to pull me back on the mattress. "What's today?"

For a second I think he's serious, and I'm about to reprimand him, but when he laughs softly, I realize he's merely joking.

"You know what day it is," I tease, nibbling on his neck. "Now let me go cook. Go back to sleep."

He lands a playful swat on my butt as I climb out of bed and head into the living room. The morning sun is about to break over the horizon of the Atlantic Ocean, and a soothing, dusky, blue hue illuminates the sky. Its warm glow reflects off the other skyscrapers nearby, the light bouncing off the cold steel and glass.

My first order of business is the most important: making a pot of coffee.

Then, as I check on my plants, I repeat my mantra. It's a new one, different from what I used to say each morning in my old job and during those crazy weeks when I ran my father's Formula World team.

First I say a little prayer silently to the universe, then to the people I love, and finally, to myself. The worry beads live in my home office, near my desk. These days I only touch them when I'm bored on a phone call. The morning mantra works fine, now that my life is in balance.

May I be happy, may I be healthy, may I be safe, may I live with ease.

I take a spray bottle off the shelf and squirt a fine mist onto the giant green leaves of my *Monstera* plant. It survived—barely—my mum and papa's stay here last summer.

I rescued it from a certain death when I came home that August, a few weeks after Max's terrible crash. When his shoulder was finally stable he flew here, too, and, along with the plants, I dedicated myself to nursing him back to health.

First we found Miami's best sports injury clinic and got him into physical therapy. I won't lie: those initial couple of months were difficult. Although he recovered from his concussion quickly and without any lingering memory issues, his shoulder was another problem altogether.

Max was in a ton of pain, and we both worried he'd never regain use of his right arm again.

But because of Max's fierce determination, he persevered with his therapy. Now he has almost full range of motion in the arm, although sometimes he still is in some pain if he overtrains. He made the decision to retire from the sport, and insists that he has no regrets about the timing of his exit. Lucas also left, and remains Max's full-time employee and trusted confidant.

Max and I also learned what it would be like to live together after years of him being on the road as a driver. He annoys me when he doesn't put the toilet seat down, and I annoy him when I leave mail stacked on the kitchen counter.

But other than minor issues like those, we're like peanut butter and chocolate: meant to be together. During the weekdays we're busy with our respective projects. He and Lucas are working on launching the new electric race-car circuit that's going to have a season opener next year in Miami.

I thought he'd miss driving more, but surprisingly, he doesn't. When he wants a fix, he takes his Porsche to a local track and drives like a bat out of hell for an hour. That seems to satisfy him. I also expect that we'll fly to see a few races this coming season and hang out with my father's team. As Max told the media during his official retirement press conference:

"My entire identity since I was a teenager has been as a race-car driver. It's time for me to step into a new identity. Several, even. A partner to my beautiful Lily. Perhaps, if she agrees, an identity as a father. Eventually."

He'd looked at me when he spoke those words, and I was so surprised—and charmed—that all I could do was press my hands to my heart. We're a ways away from children, because we're enjoying our life right now.

I'm also doing something racing related. Not long after Max's crash, a publisher contacted me and asked if I'd like to work with a top racing photographer on a coffee table book, writing profiles about pioneering women in motorsport. I've interviewed everyone from drivers to pit crew team members to my friend Savannah Jenkins, who owns a team. It's been inspiring listening to such incredible women, and it's making me wonder if I should truly be more involved in the Onassis team.

Papa and Max are giving me the space to work that out on my own. I'll reach a decision sometime this year, but for now, I'm ecstatic with the life Max and I have built in Miami. We're talking about adopting a dog, and we've found a circle of friends, people with ties to the racing world.

Anh is getting married to her longtime boyfriend, the motocross racer. I'm going to be her maid of honor. Thankfully, she's bought a beach condo in Miami and we're seeing each other more than ever, and spend a lot of time planning her wedding.

Another couple getting along is my parents. Although they're still their weird, bickering selves, they've been under the same roof since my father's heart attack. They even invited Max and me up to their home for Christmas. A few days after we flew to Germany to be with his family for New Year's. Papa's let go of the team, a little, and this upcoming race season, Jack will be more in charge.

Once I'm finished with the plants, I go into the kitchen. It's Valentine's Day, and I've been planning to make Max's favorite: *Apfelpfannkuchen*.

His mum taught me her recipe when we visited Germany, and I thought today would be an excellent day to surprise him with his favorite dish. We have reservations for dinner tonight on the beach, but romance can't start too early, can it?

I assemble my ingredients and am almost finished arranging the apple slices when Max comes out of the bedroom. He looks yummier than breakfast, wearing a black hoodie and gray sweatpants. Now that we're living together, I can be a little more open in my ogling of his body in those sweatpants, something he's always teasing me about.

He gives me a little grin as I pour him a cup of coffee, then asks if I need any help with cooking.

"Nope. You relax."

It takes me a little while to fry several pancakes, and while I'm doing that, Max streams some jazz music on the wireless speaker. The soothing strains of a bass and a piano waft through the morning silence, giving the atmosphere a perfect lazy Sunday vibe. This is exactly what I've wanted my entire adult life.

We eat at the kitchen island, talking about where we're going to adopt the dog, then we shift to the sofa. This is our weekend routine, snuggling and reading on our phones, sipping coffee, taking it easy in ways we weren't able to in our previous lives.

Max is still fitter than many athletes—old habits die hard—and now that his shoulder is better, he's training for a half-marathon. He wanted to run a whole, but his doctor and I convinced him to scale it back.

"You going for a run today?" I ask.

"Mmm, I think I'll take the day off. I'd like to go back to bed." He slides a glance at me and grins while waggling his eyebrows, and my face heats into a blush. His obvious lust for me still thrills me to my core.

The sun is almost entirely over the water now, a sherbet-colored ball that makes the blue water shimmer. I'm reading my emails on my iPad and Max is staring out at the ocean. We're sitting close enough on the sofa that I can feel the heat of his body on mine.

"I don't think I've ever seen a more beautiful sunrise," he says.

I set my iPad down and look out the window, straightening my glasses. It really is a gorgeous sunrise, and I smile and rest my head on his shoulder.

Max takes a sip of his coffee and sets it on an end table. He kisses my temple and shifts off the sofa. "I'll be right back."

His absence means the cool air hits my bare legs, and I pull a warm, pale-green throw over my lap. I love Sunday mornings like this, quiet and peaceful. Romantic in the best way to describe these moments, and they're everything I'd hoped for when we decided to live together.

I zone out for a few minutes, watching the ocean waves ebb and flow while sipping my coffee. Max has been gone a little while, and I'm wondering what he's doing. Finally, the slap of his bare feet against the wood floor echoes in the hallway, and he comes into view.

He shifts the coffee table a little to the left and stands over me while clearing his throat. I look up, confused.

"Did you want to rearrange the furniture today? Maybe go look at some new stuff? We probably should replace this fluffy rug if we're going to get a dog." We'd also talked about getting new living room decor recently.

"No."

I frown and untuck my feet from the blanket, placing them on the floor. Why is he standing there, all awkward, shifting from one foot to the next? Then he kneels at my feet and my heart rate kicks up so fast that I'm suddenly dizzy.

"I was going to do this tonight at dinner, but I think it's better I ask you here, in our home. I didn't want to wait because patience isn't in my DNA." He reaches into his sweatpants pocket and brings out a small, black velvet box.

I gasp so loudly that he fumbles and drops the box, which rolls a few inches toward my foot.

"Oops. Sorry. I'm really nervous." He's trembling as he reaches for the box, then opens it.

Inside there's a glittering diamond solitaire ring, and I gulp in a breath. The ring is set in platinum, the stone large, but not massive. Simple and elegant. Exactly what I would've picked for myself. I can't tear my eyes from it because it looks like it's dipped in fairy dust, something from my girlhood dreams.

"Lily, will you marry me?" His voice cracks as he asks the question. "I love you."

I nod, still unable to speak or breathe.

He exhales. I exhale.

"Oh, thank god." He's still shaking as he takes the ring out of the box. "Um, I need your hand."

"Yes. My hand. Yes. I'll marry you." A little nervous laugh slips out of my mouth.

He pushes the ring on my finger and all I can do is slide down to the fluffy white rug on the floor, onto his lap. I wrap my arms around him and we tumble back, onto the floor, kissing.

I sit up while straddling him. "You thought I wouldn't say yes?"

"I don't know what I thought. I was so nervous the second I woke up. Couldn't wait until tonight. And I figured you wouldn't want a big, showy proposal in public."

He knows me so well. I extend my hand in the direction of the window, and the diamond shimmers like the morning ocean. Then I reach for Max's face and cradle it in my hands. His hair is the color of spun gold, and his blue eyes no longer look icy and cool. Instead, they're warm and familiar.

Like home.

"I love you," I whisper, leaning down to press my lips to his as the morning sun bathes us in its light.

ABOUT THE AUTHOR

Tamara Lush is a Romance Writers of America Rita award finalist, an Amtrak writing fellow, and a *USA TODAY* bestselling author. She's a former reporter who writes contemporary romance set in tropical locations, and she writes mysteries under the name Tara Lush. A fan of vintage pulp-fiction book covers, Sinatra-era jazz, and 1980s fashion, she lives with her husband and two dogs on the Gulf Coast.